John Francome has been Champion Jockey seven times and is regarded as the greatest National Hunt jockey ever known; he is now a frequent broadcaster on racing for Channel 4.

John Francome has gained terrific acclaim for his previous bestselling novel, *Stone Cold*:

'Francome writes an odds-on racing cert'
Daily Express

'Romps home at a galloping pace to challenge *Blood Stock* in a photo finish. Move over, Dick Francis – here's competition'
Me magazine

And, together with co-author James MacGregor, for *Blood Stock* and *Declared Dead*:

'Gets off to a galloping start . . . with a surprise twist in the final straight'
Evening Standard

'A thoroughly convincing and entertaining tale'
Daily Mail

Stud Poker

John Francome

First published in 1991 by
HEADLINE BOOK PUBLISHING PLC

First published in paperback in 1992 by
HEADLINE BOOK PUBLISHING PLC

20 19 18 17 16 15 14 13 12

ISBN 0–7472–3754–9

Phototypeset by Intype, London SW19 8DR

Printed and bound in Great Britain by
Clays Ltd, St Ives plc

HEADLINE BOOK PUBLISHING
A division of Hodder Headline PLC
338 Euston Road
London NW1 3BH

ACKNOWLEDGEMENTS

The author is grateful to Terence Blacker for his help in the preparation of this manuscript.

Inspiration and information for the poker scenes in *Stud Poker* came from Anthony Holden's superb *Big Deal*, (Bantam Books, 1991).

Chapter 1

Like most jockeys' valets, Jim Wilson could read race-course rumour like a professional gambler could read a racecard. He knew what was true and what was bullshit. He knew the young jockeys who would still be in the weighing-room in ten years' time and those who would fade into obscurity after a season or two – or, as in most cases, a ride or two. He knew who was drinking, who was fighting a losing battle with the scales, who was in the pocket of the bookmakers. And, of course, he knew whose nerve had gone. There was something in the eyes of a jockey in those moments after he had weighed out for a novice chase and was waiting to be called to the paddock.

So when Jim Wilson, on a cold wet November morning, trudged through the car park at Plumpton racecourse carrying a suitcase full of breeches and saw Alex Drew sitting alone in his Audi Convertible with what appeared to be a fur coat on his lap, staring palely into space, he added the information to his vast storehouse of unofficial racing knowledge.

'Morning, Lex,' he called out, but Alex had seemed not to hear.

Jim glanced at his watch. Eleven-thirty. He was surprised to see Alex at the racecourse so early. His first ride was not until the fourth race and, until recently, he'd been one of the cool ones, turning up as late as possible in his flash car, exuding all the confidence of the young and talented.

Until recently. Wilson looked back at the Audi, parked in the far corner of the jockeys' car park. This season, something had happened to Alex. Two years ago, he had been no more than just another claiming jockey, an amateur with ambition. Last year, he had turned professional and a combination of luck – Ron Charlesworth's stable jockey had broken his leg in the first month of the season – and talent had marked him out as a possible future champion jockey. He had ridden over fifty winners, including a breathtaking success in the Champion Two Mile Chase at the National Hunt Festival on a horse of reckless brilliance called Spurgloss. Few, if any, of the top jockeys would have won on him.

But now something was wrong in the life of Alex Drew. Muttering to himself, the valet walked on to the racecourse, dismissing thoughts of Alex from his mind. Jockeys came, jockeys went. Promise turned to failure. It was life.

'He's gone.' Alex pulled back the mink coat and touched the blonde head that was resting on his lap.

'I was just beginning to enjoy it down there,' said Zena Wentworth, sitting up and checking her hair in the rear view mirror.

'Sorry.' Alex smiled palely. 'Jim's a bit of an old gossip. It's best to be careful.'

'Don't tell me jockeys aren't meant to be seen with girls before a race.' Zena put a well-manicured hand on Alex's thigh.

'Don't be daft.' Alex allowed a hint of irritation to enter his voice. Girls. That was a laugh. Zena Wentworth had stopped being a girl some time ago. In fact, even when she was a girl, to judge by some of the stories she had told him, she was doing wild, womanly things. 'It's just that talking to an owner's wife in the corner of the car park – people might misunderstand.'

'Spare rides?'

'Something like that.' A car drove by and parked some way in front of them. Two jockeys emerged, took their bags from the boot and walked briskly towards the racecourse entrance. 'Perhaps you had better tell me the message you've been asked to give me.'

'That won't take long,' she said. 'Just make sure that Dig For Glory doesn't win the handicap hurdle.'

'They've told me that already.'

'Something about keeping him on the inner, would that be it?'

Alex nodded. 'No problem. Paul always stays glued to the rails and I'll be on his outside making sure he can't squeeze his way through.'

'Make certain he comes unstuck.'

'Easy,' Alex said sarcastically. Of all the people in the world, Paul Raven was the one he wanted least to cut up on the rails – he was Alex's best friend. 'Piece of cake.'

Zena ran a hand up his thigh. 'It's only one race,' she said softly. 'No need to look so miserable.'

'I've been wasting,' Alex said. 'I have to do ten two in the last.'

'Ten to what?' said Zena, a coquettish smile playing on her lips as her hand came to rest. She raised a well-plucked eyebrow. 'You seem to be a bit over-weight there, Alex,' she said, slipping down in the seat and pulling her mink coat over her head.

'Not . . . now.' But what he had intended as a protest came out as a sigh. Life had been saying 'Not now' to Zena for several years but, even at the age of forty-three, with the evidence of too many good times written clearly on her face, she had refused to listen. She wanted it now, she had never been good at waiting. While other women faced middle age with careers or children, Zena extended her competence exclusively in the area that she understood. Pleasure, taken and given. That – Alex looked down as the fur coat undulated like an animal stirring after a long sleep – yes, that she understood all too well.

A mere twelve months ago, he would have laughed at the idea of a secret assignation with an owner's wife in a car park at Plumpton. The idea of submitting to the eager caresses of Zena Wentworth would have been absurd, but not as crazy as the notion that he would stop Paul winning a race. Closing his eyes and gasping, Alex tried to forget his lost innocence, to think of this afternoon's last race, which he would win. The fur came to rest.

'That should help your weight problem,' said Zena, sitting up, daintily dabbing at the corners of her mouth with a long finger.

'I'd better go.'

'Fine.'

She checked her face in the mirror, saying, 'Do I look like a woman who's just had sex in the car park?'

Alex glanced at her. Zena Wentworth always looked like a woman who had just had sex in the car park. 'You look the perfect owner's wife,' he said.

'Thank you, jockey.' Zena opened the door and got out. 'I'll see you in the paddock.'

'Old Lex is here a bit early today, isn't he?'

Jim Wilson, limping slightly from the back injury that, twenty years ago, had ended an unpromising career as a jockey, laid out breeches, boots and colours in the weighing-room.

'Lex?' Paul Raven smiled. He was glad that he had Jim for a valet. Not only was he reliable, but he was a purveyor of the latest, twenty-two carat gossip – rarely malicious, but often useful. His only irritating habit, that of using the one nickname you didn't like, Paul found almost endearing.

'Yeah, Sexy Lexy. Sitting in his motor in the car park like he's in a fucking trance. Bit early, isn't he?'

Paul shrugged, recognizing the gentle probe of a professional gossip. 'Maybe he's got a spare ride in the first.' He sipped at the half-cup of sweet tea which, however light he had to ride that day, he would drink about an hour before his first race. He was worried about Alex – normally they travelled to the races together but today he had made some excuse and driven from Lambourn alone – but he was not about to discuss it all with Jim.

He looked up at the weighing-room clock. It was time to change. Unlike Alex, who took a cavalier attitude to routine, Paul liked order in his life, particularly on race days. He would arrive well on time, walk onto the course to check the going, have his cup of tea and stay in the weighing-room until it was time to weigh out for his first ride. It wasn't that he felt superior to the drifters and hangers-on who liked to pass the time with jockeys, simply that he preferred to concentrate on the job ahead.

He was riding Tidy Item in the second race, a novice hurdle. The horse had a chance if it remembered that it wasn't running on the flat any more and that there were eight hurdles to negotiate. He'd ride Dig For Glory in the handicap hurdle, a dream ride but a little lacking in speed. The guv'nor, Ron Charlesworth, was confident, in that gloomy, monosyllabic way of his, although Alex's mount, Freeze Frame, was also in with a chance. Then, in the last, all being well, he was due to ride a novice chaser trained by a permit holder who, after it had fallen twice under its regular jockey, had decided to use Paul. The joker in the pack. Still, there was a touch of class about the horse and there was nothing else of note in the race. If he could get it round safely it ought to win. Maybe he'd ride a treble.

That perhaps was Paul's secret. Every time he received a leg-up on to a horse in the paddock, whatever its form, whatever the competition, he believed it would win. This steely confidence, which older, more battered jockeys would call crazy optimism, helped earn him a growing reputation among trainers, and thirty-three winners last season. While others would accept less promising rides – the dodgy jumper in the last, for example – thinking only of the fee and survival, Paul saw each as another potential winner.

A tall man entered the weighing-room, his expensive tweed suit, the bag he was carrying and his general air of unease marking him out as an amateur. You could always tell the guys who were doing it for fun. Big and soft-skinned, it was as if they belonged to different species from the wiry, weather-beaten, professionals. Their gear was new; they fussed about with their silks and made frequent trips to the lavatory.

At first, Paul had assumed Alex Drew would be like that – a privileged, public school wally with a foppish hairstyle that came straight out of *Brideshead Revisited*. Paul remembered the first time he had seen him. It had been an early season meeting at Fontwell and Alex, who was riding in an amateur race, had behaved as if he had been walking in and out of weighing-rooms for years, joking with the valets, chatting with the older jockeys with an easy, disrespectful charm. Paul had taken an instant dislike to him, had even permitted himself a smile when Alex's horse turned over at the last when challenging for the lead. Alex walked away, cursing, but back in the weighing-room, bruised and mud-spattered, he was soon back on song, as if he couldn't wait for his next ride.

There was something else that had been different about Alex Drew; the way he rode. He was better than any amateur Paul had ever seen. On form, his horse – Paul couldn't remember the name – had no chance, and the cocky little bastard had taken him along easily at the back of the field, keeping the more fancied horses in his sights, unflustered by the ridiculous early pace, making his move with all the coolness of an experienced professional. At the last fence, he had been upsides but struggling, so he'd taken a gamble, asking his horse to stand off outside the wings and win rather than fiddle the fence and take second place. It hadn't paid off and Alex had taken a bone-crunching fall. But Paul was impressed. Judgement and nerve – it was rare to find those in a young amateur.

'Morning, Mr Wenty,' Jim Wilson called out to the tall man who had sat down and seemed uncertain what to do next. He smiled thinly at the valet. 'Clay, please, Jim,' he said.

'Right, Cleggy,' said Jim, bringing Paul his breeches and winking. 'How many rides have we got today?'

'Just the one. Skinflint in the fourth.'

Now Paul knew who he was. Mr Clay Wentworth, claiming seven pounds, successful property developer, unsuccessful amateur jockey, son of Sir Denis Wentworth who had bought Skinflint as a present for his son – a touching family gesture that had landed one of the best chasers in the country with one of the worst jockeys. It was a waste but, in racing as in life, money talked.

Paul drained his cup of tea. It was time to get changed. As he checked his weight on the weighing-room scales, he became aware that Clay Wentworth was watching him.

'Nice horse, that Dig For Glory.' To Paul, the son of a brickie in Wigan, Wentworth's voice jarred. Nasal and authoritative, it belonged in the paddock or the members' bar, not here among the professionals.

'He's not bad,' he said, returning to where his clothes were. To his annoyance, Clay Wentworth followed him. The last thing he needed before a race was small talk, particularly with a man he didn't know.

'Fancy your chances?'

It was the apparently innocent question which all jockeys are asked. He shrugged. 'We've got as much chance as anyone,' he said.

'Thought of buying him once.' Wentworth opened a silver cigarette case which he waved, with a seigneurial gesture, in Paul's direction. Paul shook his head. 'We weren't sure he stayed the trip.'

'Oh yeah?'

'Needs holding up, they say.'

'Do they?' Paul smiled coldly. 'Thanks for the advice.'

As a general rule, cocaine and Plumpton Racecourse do not go together. Champagne at the bar: of course. Benzedrine in the weighing-room: perhaps. But a line of pure white powder inhaled through a rolled-up fifty pound note in the ladies' lavatory: no, not at Plumpton.

It was unusual, but then the presence of a moneyed pleasure-seeker like Zena Wentworth at a damp and modest National Hunt racecourse was in itself unusual. Zena needed something to help get her through an afternoon spent out of doors in the company of rat-faced men, large women with too much make-up, and horses. She was, by nature and inclination, a high-flyer and sometimes she needed help to fly as high as she liked to be.

Brisk and bright-eyed, Zena re-entered the bar, where a group of her friends were drinking champagne.

'Better, darling?' Lol Calloway, a former pop star who, even now that he was bald and pot-bellied, was occasionally recognized on the street by an ageing fan, gave her a knowing leer. 'Powder your nose all right, did you?'

His wife, Suzie, giggled.

'I just felt a little bit woozy,' Zena explained to a woman in a sheepskin coat who was sitting uneasily with them. The woman smiled politely. Owners were the worst part of training, Ginnie Matthews had decided some time ago, but since Clay Wentworth had brought something of a fan club with him, it had seemed ungracious to refuse the offer of a glass of champagne before the first race.

'D'you get nervous when Clay is riding?' she asked Zena.

'Not on Skinflint. He's as safe as houses, isn't he?'

'Almost.' Ginnie smiled, thinking that Clay Wentworth was capable of wrestling any horse to the ground, however safe.

'Zena's just a bit highly strung, aren't you?' A woman in her thirties with dark, cascading hair smiled at Zena. 'She has a lot on her mind, don't you, darling?' Alice Markwick smiled discreetly. She liked Zena, her sense of fun, the sparkle she brought even to a grey afternoon at a God-forsaken racetrack; the way, when she was in a really good mood, she let Alice sleep with her. Yes, she was fun.

'Look,' Zena trilled, pointing out of the window as the runners for the first race filed out of the paddock. 'Horses!'

'Did you have to get wired?' Clay Wentworth muttered as, a dark blue coat over his silks, he sat down with the group. 'Couldn't you stay straight for one afternoon?'

'I was nervous. There's so much riding on this.'

'Did you see Drew?'

'Yup.' Zena smiled at her husband, her eyes sparkling. 'He knows exactly what he has to do.'

'A winner for me, a loser for Paul Raven.' Wentworth lit a cigarette and inhaled deeply. 'Just what the doctor ordered.'

Racing journalists had taken to describing Paul Raven as 'cool', 'dispassionate', and 'machine-like' and it was true that, beside the sport's more extrovert characters, he might have seemed taciturn, possibly even dull. If you dressed him up in a suit and put him on the 8.20 from Surbiton to Waterloo, he would pass for a young, good-looking articled clerk on his way to work in the City.

Paul didn't care. To him, riding horses was a job, a way to escape the harsh poverty of his family background. As the other lads at Ron Charlesworth's yard could testify, he had a quiet, wry sense of humour and, unlike other jockeys on the brink of success, he was prepared to help the newer lads in the yard, giving them advice, intervening on their behalf when they were on the receiving end of Ron Charlesworth's icy disapproval.

He knew what it was like to be an outsider, to be starting on the lowest rung of the ladder in one of the harshest sports in the world. Like any large stable yard, Ron Charlesworth's had its hierarchy, its harsh traditions. Charlesworth himself, a tall, trim man with the cold, blue eyes of an executioner, was pitilessly ambitious – his horses and the men he paid to ride them were no more than part of a career plan.

His head lad, Jimmy Summers, a wiry Scotsman with a legendary temper, understood his boss as well as anyone. In racing, there was no gain without pain and Jimmy was an expert at ensuring that the lads under his care – particularly the teenagers stupid enough to think that shovelling horse-shit and riding out in sub-zero temperatures was the road to stardom – understood all about pain.

Watched by a handful of racegoers including the Wentworth party in the Members' Bar, Paul rode Tidy Item onto the racecourse.

'He's in great form; you could win this, you know, Paul.' Bill, one of the older lads, chattered away as he led the horse out. 'Just need to give him a view of the hurdles, hold him up, he's got the speed and . . .'

Paul turned out, as Bill told him yet again what he already knew. Tidy Item, a lightly-framed bay four-year-old, already had a great future behind him. In his first season as a two-year-old, he had won a decent race at Goodwood. The following year, his Timeform rating had plummeted and, by the end of the season, he had won only a moderate handicap over a mile and a half at Nottingham. As if aware that appearing in a novice hurdle at Plumpton, a gelding, was hardly what was expected of a horse of his breeding, Tidy Item had a listless look about him, his coat was stary and dull. For the first time today, he was wearing blinkers.

'Cheers, Bill.' As the lad released him Paul turned and cantered down to the start.

Tidy Item had a long, rangy stride which made him an easy ride on the flat. It was the hurdles which bothered him. The first couple of times Paul had schooled him at home, he hadn't had a clue what to do, hurling himself at them in panic. These days, he took the marginally safer course of galloping straight through them, often losing lengths in a race, shattering the hurdles as he went. Getting in close and fiddling a hurdle was something Tidy Item knew nothing of.

But he could win. 'Try jumping them this time, fella,' Paul muttered as he showed the horse the first flight, patting him on the neck. His seven years riding racehorses had convinced him that the best way of getting winners was the quiet way: settle them, relax, let the other jockeys scream and swear. Riding Tidy Item over hurdles might be like surviving eight earthquakes but, when he wasn't kicking bits of timber into the air, he was a good ride. Yes, he would win. Paul was confident.

The race followed the pattern Paul had anticipated. A couple of horses set a smart pace which had several runners, bred less aristocratically than Tidy Item, off the bit from the start.

Paul allowed Tidy Item to dawdle near the back of the field tight on the inside rail, a position which gave him little view of the hurdles but since even if the horse had the entire racetrack to himself he would crash through every flight, taking him the shortest way made sense.

Despite destroying six flights of hurdles, Tidy Item entered the straight at the back of the leading group still on the bridle. Paul let the leaders run off the bend and then let him run through smartly on the inner. He was going so easily it was almost embarrassing. As if sensing that the unpleasant experience of smashing timber at speed was soon to be over, Tidy Item lengthened his stride approaching the last hurdle and, by his standards, jumped the last well, diving through it a foot above the turf, and actually made ground doing it. Paul didn't even have to ride him out, as he won pulling the proverbial cart.

'Cocky bastard,' Dave Cartwright, who had ridden the second horse, called out as they trotted back having pulled up. No one, even at Plumpton, likes another jockey to get up their inside. 'You could have won that by ten lengths.'

'Somebody's got to ride them.' Paul trotted on. He didn't care what other jockeys, or journalists, or lads or even Ron Charlesworth said to him.

He had won it; and that was what mattered.

The bastard was cool. Clay Wentworth sipped the one bucks fizz he allowed himself on days when he was riding and watched a TV screen on which, in silent slow motion, Tidy Item was once again being gathered up after his mistake at the last hurdle.

'So *cheeky*.' Zena's voice, like a distant mocking soundtrack, penetrated Clay's thoughts. 'Why don't you try and win like that, darling?'

He smiled wanly without taking his eyes from the screen. For a moment, he had managed to forget that, in a little over an hour, he would be riding Skinflint. 'Maybe I will,' he said.

Where did it come from, the coolness, the poise, that converted the will to win into the ability to win? Nobody wanted to win races more than Clay Wentworth did but his determination was panicky and ineffective. Whereas jockeys like Paul Raven looked in a finish as if they were part of the horse, its powerhouse, he flapped about like a duck landing on ice with a broken wing. Occasionally his horse won a race but it was always in spite of his efforts, not because of them.

'Clay's psyching himself up,' Lol Calloway was saying to Zena and to Alice Markwick. 'It's like a big gig at Madison Square Garden. I'd get the band together and say "Guys, we're gonna fuckin' blow them away tonight, right?" They'd go, like punch the air, and say "Yeah, right, Lol!" Then, after I'd done a line and fucked a groupie, we'd go on like well psyched.'

At a nearby table, a local doctor and his wife, who liked an afternoon at the races, muttered poisonously to one another before draining their drinks and moving away.

He hated it, that was the truth. Clay Wentworth, never one for deep self-analysis, knew this at least. He hated the weighing-room where suddenly he was no longer the boss but some sort of junior. He hated the walk out to the paddock, the cold, the wet, the pervasive smell of horse shit and cigar smoke. He hated the moment he was given a leg-up, when he was left all by himself with the horse to canter down to the start. He hated circling round at the start, hearing the starters' roll-call – 'Mr Wentworth,' 'Sir.' He hated, Christ he hated, the moment when the field jumped off and there was no escape and the first fence, getting bigger and bigger, loomed up before him, the kick, the lurch, the shouts and curses all around him. After the first, it got better, particularly if he were riding Skinflint, but he never liked it, not until he was back among the racegoers, preferably in the winners' enclosure. There was nothing like the feel of the ground beneath his feet when he dismounted.

Clay took another sip of his drink. No, he sighed quietly to himself, he was not a natural.

That was what made Alex Drew the perfect patsy. The moment he had joined the Circle, playing poker like he rode horses – with style and bravado – Clay had known what had to be done. They needed someone who rode as a professional, competent enough to stop another horse, straight enough to keep himself out of the stewards' room, weak enough to bend under pressure.

Alex discovered that poker is not like racing, but he discovered too late. Nerve and skill are not enough. You have to know how to bluff, how to cheat, your every move must be informed by rat-like cunning and deception. That cheerful openness, which served him so well on the racecourse, had betrayed him at the table.

Zena had worried. What if someone got hurt? What if Alex's career was destroyed? Clay had frowned as if considering the moral options. There was no reason for things to go wrong. The risks were as low as the stakes were high.

He smiled. It was a lie, of course – as big a bluff as he had ever played at the table. If someone's career hit the rocks, he was certain it would be Alex's. If someone's body paid the price of Clay's ambition, there was no better body than Alex's.

'Everything all right, Clay?' As usual, it was Alice who understood better than anyone what was going through his head. Her dark, smoky voice carried concern but Clay was aware that there was nothing personal there. Alice's concern was always financial.

'He's thinking about his race, ain't you, Clay?' said Lol Calloway. 'Trying to decide whether to sneak up on the rails like the last winner or to take it easy and win by ten lengths.'

'Of course,' said Alice. 'It's a big day, isn't it?'

Clay Wentworth nodded. 'Yes, it's a big day.'

* * *

Paul Raven had never known Alex like this. In the early days, he had distrusted Alex's high spirits, his ability to make a joke even when things were going badly. Alex was an amateur when they had first met and it was as if the years of money and privilege had come bubbling to the surface in an excess of optimism and good humour.

Three years later, he knew better. Joking had been Alex's way of dealing with stress. Once he was in the saddle and the flag went down, he was a different person. It seemed odd now that it was Paul who was doing the talking before the fourth race, as Alex sat, pale and distracted, like a man facing a death sentence.

'That Tidy Item's going to bury me one day,' Paul said. 'When they send him chasing, the ride is yours.'

Alex didn't reply. He wanted it to be over, or at least to explain to Paul before it was too late and explanations were superfluous.

It was unusual for them both to be riding for Ron Charlesworth in the same race. Ron was good at placing his horses and, unless he was giving one of them an easy ride, or a fancied runner needed a pacemaker, he avoided sending out two runners to compete for one prize. This two-and-a-half-mile handicap hurdle had been intended for Freeze Frame, Alex's ride. It was only when the weights had been announced, allotting Dig For Glory an absurdly generous ten stone three, that Dig For Glory had been included. He needed the race to be fully fit but his owner Lady Faircroft had been anxious to see him run. Reluctantly, Ron had agreed.

The two jockeys sat together, having weighed out, the brickie's son and the former amateur, one dark and wiry, the other with the cherubic, long-haired look of an overgrown schoolboy. They were an unlikely couple.

'What's the problem then, Alex?' Paul asked. 'Anybody would think you were nervous or something.'

'You must be joking.' Alex tried a smile, but it was an unconvincing effort. 'I'm fine.'

With anyone else, Paul might have suspected normal jockey problems – money, weight, an unhealthily close association with bookmakers – but he knew Alex, for all his wild talk, was too sensible for that.

'Just tell me if I can help, that's all.'

Alex looked at him oddly. 'Thanks, Paul,' he said.

The bell sounded for jockeys out.

'Paddock, jockeys.' A bowler-hatted official stood at the door and the riders for the fourth race at Plumpton filed out to make their way to the paddock.

'Good luck, boys,' said Jim Wilson.

'Cheers, Jim,' said Paul.

Alex said nothing.

Chapter 2

Peter Zametsky had thought he was getting used to the English way of doing things. He had sat in pubs where Londoners gathered to complain about life. He had travelled by underground where they stared ahead of them, not acknowledging the existence of other human beings despite being pressed up against them in a position of forced intimacy. He had been to a football match where they stood up and swore at one another. He had visited a church on Christmas morning where they had seemed ill at ease except when booming out tuneless versions of the carols.

But nothing had prepared him for a betting shop.

There was a reverence here which had not been evident in the church. Through the pall of cigarette smoke, under the bright strip lighting, men – and just a few women – were staring, staring upwards as if praying for a miracle. Some held slips of paper in their hands; others were seated in front of newspapers. Around the room were television screens which were showing some sort of dog race. The murmur of a commentary could be heard, but Peter understood little of what was being said, although certain numbers seemed to be repeated like a mantra.

'Go, on, number three.' A tall West Indian, standing in front of Peter, was muttering. 'Go on, my son.'

'Excuse me, sir.' Peter was unsure of the procedure on these occasions, but his three years in England had taught him that no one helped you unless you asked first. 'To place a bet?'

The man seemed to be suffering from some kind of attack. 'Yes,' he said, occasionally looking away from the television screen as if the mystery unfolding there was too much for him to take. 'Yes, my son. *Here* he comes.'

As Peter waited patiently for an answer, the man gave a sort of moan and then, with intense loathing, balled the piece of paper he had been holding and threw it onto the floor in a gesture of terminal despair. 'Bastard,' he said.

'Where to place a bet, please?'

As if coming out of a trance, the man turned his bloodshot, tear-stained eyes in Peter's direction and burped. Peter, a small bespectacled man in his thirties, with thinning hair and a dreary suit, moved through the crowd of punters.

'To bet?' he asked an elderly woman who was staring into space. She nodded over her shoulder. 'Over there,' she said.

Peter made his way to a counter at the back of the shop.

'In the two-thirty at Plumpton,' he said nervously to a plump girl behind the counter. 'I'm wanting...'

'Slip,' said the girl. As Peter frowned helplessly, she pushed a piece of paper across the counter. 'Fill it in,' she said loudly. 'Comprende?'

Peter found an empty corner in the betting-shop and sat down on a stool. There was a small, slightly chewed biro on the ledge in front of him which he looked at, as if it were a specimen in the lab, before picking it up. 'How is it, Peter,' his wife used to say, 'that in some things you are so brilliant, in others so completely foolish with your frown and so innocent eyes?' Klima was right: at work, Peter was almost masterful, as he sat at his bench, crouched over a microscope or tapping easily at his computer. It was real life that caused him problems.

He looked up at a screen. Four to one. He was not by nature a gambler but he had confidence in his work. Carefully, he wrote on the betting slip. 'FREEZE FRAME – £100 (win), Plumpton, 2.30', adding as an afterthought, 'Ridden by A. Drew'.

Once you're in the saddle, it's just another job of work. From his earliest days as an amateur, Alex had learnt to exclude the personal from his race-riding. Cheerful and outgoing before the race, the chat and the jokes were put on hold as soon as he was in the paddock. As for the other jockeys, they were no longer friends or enemies but simply part of the job. It was the two-ride-a-week merchants that were the trouble. Most of them were all over the place in a race, just like weekend drivers. It was beyond some of them to ride in a straight line, which when you're doing fifty miles an hour towards a fence doesn't make life easy, especially when the horse you're riding doesn't jump very well. As for the bends, well, if you were foolish enough to be on the girth of one of them there, then you deserved whatever happened.

Those were relevant considerations; character – friendship, in particular – needed to be forgotten until after the race.

And yet. Cantering down to the start, Alex watched the orange and black colours of Lady Faircraft, worn by Paul on Dig For Glory some five lengths in front of him. And other images of Paul flashed before his eyes – the quiet lad at Charlesworth's yard taken for granted by everyone, the workaholic, the jockey glancing across at him as they raced knee to knee on the Lambourn downs, helping him to polish up his riding, the friend who was always the first to say well done when he rode a winner and most important, the one who always came to make sure he was all right after a fall. On paper, there was little to separate Freeze Frame and Dig For Glory although, given the choice, Alex would have chosen Paul's horse, a big five-year-old whose inconsistent form last season due to weakness had ensured that he was well down in the weights. Dig For Glory had developed over the summer months and, even though the ground had been firmer than he liked, he had run promisingly in a two-mile handicap hurdle at Leicester. The soft ground and the extra half-mile at Plumpton would suit him. Under normal circumstances, Alex would have fancied Paul's chances.

They pulled up at the start and Paul glanced across at Freeze Frame, who was sweating up slightly. 'He looks well,' he said quietly.

Alex smiled, patting Freeze Frame. The horse was small and a brilliant jumper but he lacked finishing speed. Ron Charlesworth's instructions had been to lie up with the leaders and make the best of his way home from three flights out but – Alex felt a wave of nausea as he remembered the task before him – today he had other priorities.

'Where are you going?' he asked.

Paul looked at him, surprised. If there was anyone in the world who knew that he always rode his races from the inside, hugging the rails, it was Alex.

'Guess,' he said.

'There are some bad jumpers in the field.' Alex tried to sound casual. 'I'd keep him out of trouble on the outside.'

Paul grinned. 'Nice try, Alex,' he said. It was at that moment, as the jockeys circled around the starter, that Paul realized that, for some reason, this race was not like all the others. He couldn't put his finger on it, but something wasn't right. Everything seemed the same as normal – the other jockeys chatting, the sound in the distance of the racecourse loudspeaker, but something was different.

'Smith.' The starter's voice was briskly military.

'Sir.'

'Drew.'

'Sir.'

It was Alex, that's what was different. He had sensed it on the gallops, in the yard – that look of a man haunted by something stronger than ambition or friendship, but it had never happened on a racecourse before.

'Raven.'

Keep him out of trouble. What had Alex meant, what was he trying to say?

'*Raven*.'

'Sir.'

'Wake up, we haven't got all day.'

The starter, still grumbling, mounted the steps and brought them under orders. Paul took up a position directly behind Happy Fella, who usually made the running. As the tape rose and one or two of the jockeys slapped their horses down the shoulder, helping them into their stride, Paul banished all thoughts of Alex from his mind and concentrated on the race before him.

The race was a good one, considering the state of the ground, and, by the time the field streamed past the stands with two circuits to go there were one or two struggling to lay up. Dig For Glory was going easily in sixth place, some eight lengths behind the leaders. Paul looked at the horses ahead of him and noticed with some surprise that Freeze Frame was not among them. As they turned away from the stands, Alex loomed up beside him, on a tight rein.

Paul looked over. 'They're not hanging about. I hope I'm going this well next time around.'

'So do I.'

By the time they'd completed another circuit, the pace had slowed considerably, Paul had Dig For Glory precisely where he wanted him, in fifth place on the rails with the leaders, including Freeze Frame, well within striking distance and that was where he stayed as they raced down the hill on the far side for the last time. A good jump at the third last took Dig For Glory even closer. All four jockeys in front of him were now pushing hard for home, and Paul began to niggle at Dig For Glory. The ground and the pace were taking their toll and Paul wasn't certain Dig For Glory's stamina would see him home. As they rounded the bend and turned towards the finish, Alex and Freeze Frame looked beaten and Paul called to his stable companion to lay over and leave him the inner. Alex immediately pulled Freeze Frame to his right as Paul urged Dig For Glory through the gap. They were within two strides of taking off for the second last when Alex suddenly shut the door. Dig For Glory, whose heart was bigger than himself, was suddenly faced with a large, solid wood wing and instead of slamming on the brakes made a vain attempt to jump it. There was a sickening sound of splintering wood as horse and jockey went crashing through to the ground, where both now lay motionless.

'Dig For Glory, a faller at the second last.' The commentary from Plumpton to betting-shops throughout the land laconically recorded the facts without dwelling on the human drama behind them. 'Over the last it's Happy Fella and Sweet Charity with Freeze Frame getting into it. It's going to be close, they're all tired, but it looks like Freeze Frame's going to do it there at the line. Freeze Frame the winner. Happy Fella second. Sweet Charity third.'

Peter Zametsky stared at the slip of paper in his hand. It had worked. The one gamble in his life had paid off. He would buy Klima new shoes, perhaps a fridge, clothes for the baby. Yes, it had worked. Peter felt sick.

In a trance, he walked to the counter and passed the betting-slip to the teller.

'Not weighed in yet,' she said.

Peter frowned. 'Weighed in?'

The woman sighed. 'You wait five minutes. Then we give money and you go and don't come back, okay.' She turned to the young man sitting beside her at the counter. ''E's won £500 and doesn't even know what weighed in is.'

'Please,' Peter ignored the man standing behind him who was muttering impatiently. 'What happened to the jockey?'

'*Jockey*?' The woman leaned forward as if talking to a child. 'I expect he's very happy now. Celebrating, you know.'

'No, not him. Can we see the television again?' Peter pointed to a nearby screen on which, once again, greyhounds were racing. 'The other jockey. The one who fell. Is he all right?'

'What's he talking about?' the woman asked her colleague. 'Only races here, mate. Just winners and losers and odds, d'you understand?' She looked over his shoulder to the man behind him. 'Next.'

Only the ignorant or those greedy to collect their winnings hurried away from the grandstand after the two-thirty at Plumpton. The binoculars of most regular racegoers were trained on the second last flight where Dig For Glory and his jockey Paul Raven still lay motionless.

Alex was not the praying type. At a Christmas carol service, he might pray for a hat-trick on Boxing Day; the next day, perhaps he might pray that his modest turkey dinner wouldn't show up as overweight when he sat on the scales, but these were light-hearted, insurance prayers intended for any Superior Being who happened to be tuned in to him.

But he prayed now. 'Let him be all right,' he whispered as he trotted Freeze Frame past the stands, standing in his stirrups in an attempt to see what was happening down the course. 'Just let him be okay.'

An older jockey, Dermot O'Brien, who had finished way down the field, cantered up to him.

'Nice one, Alex,' he said, pulling down his goggles.

'Cheers, Dermot.' Alex smiled thinly. O'Brien was one of the old school, a tough Irishman who had broken every bone in his body and had little time for small talk or sentiment.

'Sure, I couldn't have done him better myself,' he added with a trace of admiration in his voice.

There was a subdued welcome at the winners' enclosure where, to Alex's surprise, he was met by Liz Charlesworth, the plump and apologetic wife of his trainer.

'Where's the guv'nor?' Alex asked, dismounting.

'On the course.' Even by her standards, Liz seemed distracted and unhappy. 'It doesn't look good.'

Bad news reaches the weighing-room fast. By the time Alex had weighed in and returned with his saddle, the word was out. An uneasy silence greeted him as he walked in.

Jim Wilson took his saddle, unusually avoiding his eyes.

'How's Paul?' asked Alex nervously.

The valet looked up at him accusingly. 'If he hasn't broken anything it'll be a miracle.'

'It was an accident,' Alex said quietly. 'He went for a gap that wasn't there.'

Dave Smart, whose horse Sweet Charity had finished third, stood in front of Alex. 'The gap was there. I was a couple of lengths behind him. You did him.'

Alex shook his head in weary denial.

'Some fucking friend,' Smart muttered, wiping the mud from his face with a towel.

Five long minutes later, one of the jockeys told Alex that his trainer needed to see him outside the weighing-room.

Ron Charlesworth was not an emotional man – love, regret, sadness and humour played an insignificant part in his life – but on the rare occasions when he was angry, it was plain for all to see. Although his voice remained as dry and precise as that of a solicitor reading out the details of a particularly unfavourable will, two vivid blotches of colour appeared high on his cheekbones, remaining there until the rage had subsided.

So, although he smiled at Alex as, with an arm around his shoulder, he led him to a corner away from the scales and the ever-alert ears of racing's gossipmongers, Alex knew that he was in deep trouble.

'I should give you the fucking sack,' Charlesworth said quietly. 'You don't deserve a job in racing.'

'I've just ridden you a winner.'

'You've just killed one of my best horses.'

Alex looked at Charlesworth, expecting news of Paul from him.

'What were you playing at? Did you two have some sort of lovers' tiff? What the fuck's going on?'

Running a hand through his thick hair, Alex closed his eyes. 'How's Paul?' he asked.

'You're damned lucky they've got lenient stewards here. They're having an enquiry and it isn't going to look good and I ought to let you take what you deserve for this.' The trainer made no attempt to conceal the disapproval in his voice. He paused for a moment. 'Trouble is I'll lose the race if I tell them what I think, so I'll just say that the horse has a tendency to duck to his left and we'll stick to that.'

'It was an accident,' pleaded Alex, trying to convince himself more than Ron.

Charlesworth looked at him coldly. The normal pallor was slowly returning to his cheeks. 'I hope so – for your sake.'

'How's Paul?'

'Hospital.' Charlesworth shrugged as if another injured jockey was the least of his problems. 'You'd better get ready for the fourth. You're lucky I'm not jocking you off.'

Lucky. Alex felt the unluckiest man alive. As he returned to the weighing-room, the jockeys for the amateur race were being called out to the paddock.

The tall figure of Clay Wentworth loomed up before him. 'Well-ridden, Alex.' Although the voice was neutral, there was mockery in his expression.

Alex looked away, apparently muttering to himself. Only Clay Wentworth was close enough to hear the words, 'Debt repaid.'

Alex was just pulling on a new set of colours when he was called to the enquiry. As he watched the head-on of what he'd done to his best friend he felt sick.

A jury could have found him guilty of attempted murder. The stewards took no action.

It was cold. It was wet. Something rather disgusting seemed to have become attached to the sole of her Gucci shoe. The noise in the Members' Bar was like feeding time at the zoo. The company at her table was neither intelligent nor attractive enough to be remotely interesting. She hated horses.

All in all, Alice Markwick had decided, National Hunt racing was not for her. She glanced at her watch. One more race – Clay's big moment – and she would be off. There was work to do back home. Then, later tonight, she would slip down to Heaven, her favourite club, to pick up someone soft and understanding. God knows, she deserved it.

Beside her, Zena was conducting a coke-fuelled monologue that had already covered a variety of topics including the excitement of the last race, except for what happened to that poor jockey who fell off, how she loved to go racing when Clay was riding, why she needed to buy some more clothes, a woozy reference to a night she had once spent with Alice, a discussion of how cocaine and champagne worked together, a scurrilous commentary on a group of men standing at the bar, her husband's obsession with work, a brief attack on that cold, sinister bastard her father-in-law, and some rather sordid story involving a jockey in the car park before the races.

Alice smiled at Zena, her thoughts miles away.

The great advantage of substance abuse was that it required no effort from the other person. A woman on coke was her own best company, entirely self-sufficient. In her thirty-five years, Alice had learned that to make love to someone so wired that she was on another planet was a ghastly, monotonous, exhausting experience but, when it came to conversation, the stuff had its uses. Red-eyed, her chin working overtime, Zena would dribble on like a running tap until it wore off and she returned to the civilized world.

'There he goes,' Zena trilled, pointing to the racecourse where her husband was cantering down to the start on Skinflint. 'He's in the lead, Alice!'

'I don't think they've started yet.' Alice sighed. She was no expert but even she realized that, with one horse walking and another trotting, these were mere preliminaries.

'Haven't they?' Zena laughed girlishly, then covered her mouth. 'Where's Lol gone?'

Alice sighed. Even the short-term memory was going now. 'They've gone to watch the race from the course,' she said. 'Remember?'

'Aha, yup, right. *God...*' Zena looked wildly around the bar. 'They're so serious in here, why aren't they excited? *I'm* excited, and sort of nervous at the same time –'

It was a long way from Prague, Alice thought to herself, as Zena resumed her monologue. Yet even this, a grey afternoon at Plumpton, represented a new start. Alice was not nostalgic – she rarely looked back to the days when, as simple Alzbeta Flaishman, she had arrived from Czechoslovakia to make her life in London. After all, there were a few good memories, apart from the day when, by some act of an ever-merciful God, her husband had suffered a heart attack and died, leaving her a legacy that only now, over fifteen years later, was coming to fruition.

Alice thought of the humiliations that she had suffered to reach this point, of the freedom and riches that lay ahead of her. What a strange place this was for your life to change. She must have drifted off into a distant world of moneyed fantasy for it seemed only seconds later that she became aware of Zena gripping her hand and bouncing up and down in her seat. And there, down on the racecourse, she saw men on horses galloping past the finishing post. Ahead of them, by some ten lengths, also bouncing up and down, was Clay Wentworth. Even to Alice's untutored eye, Clay looked absurd, more like a drunk trying to direct traffic than a jockey riding a finish.

'He won!' Zena's eyes sparkled. 'He *won* the race, Alice.'

'Isn't that just great?' Alice smiled. 'Today, everyone's a winner.'

More than once, as Alex sat in the reception area of Lewes Hospital, he was asked if he needed Casualty. He had the look of a patient – deadly white and apparently in shock.

'No,' he shook his head. 'I'm waiting for a friend.'

It was early evening and he had been at the hospital for over an hour. On his way out to ride an undistinguished young horse in the novice 'chase, the second last race of the day, a reporter had walked beside him and asked him for his version of the incident involving Dig For Glory and Paul Raven.

Alex had walked on, declining to comment.

'They say he's pretty smashed up,' the journalist had said, adding quickly, 'there's been a press release. No limbs broken but badly shaken.'

Alex looked at the reporter. He might have been making it up but that phrase 'badly shaken' had the ring of truth to it. If some of the racecourse officials had been 'badly shaken' in the way that jockeys had been, in that phrase they used so easily, they would be on the way to the mortuary.

'D'you know anything more?' Alex asked.

'One of the press boys claims that he was still unconscious when they took him off to hospital.'

Alex closed his eyes for a moment. Then, remembering he had a race to ride, he walked towards the paddock, wondering whether Ron or Liz Charlesworth knew anything more. Knowing the guv'nor, he would be driving home by now. Alex touched the peak of his cap as Eddie Marwood, a small West Country trainer whose horses he sometimes rode, gave him his instructions.

Within moments of finishing well down the field in the novice 'chase, he was back in the weighing-room, giving Jim Wilson his mud-spattered gear before changing and hurrying out to the car park.

'He's not going to be able to see you tonight.' A young nurse stood before Alex.

'I'll wait,' he said.

'He's really not very well.' The girl was slim, with her short blonde hair tied back severely. She seemed too young to endure the daily sadness of a hospital. At any other time and in any other place, Alex would have been thinking of ways to get her telephone number.

'Is he conscious?'

'Yes,' she said quietly. 'He's conscious, but we're keeping him in intensive care for the time being.'

Alex rubbed his eyes wearily. To his surprise, the nurse sat down beside him.

'What about you?' she asked. 'You don't look so good yourself.'

'I'm all right.'

'You're a friend of his?'

Alex nodded, reflecting with a wry smile on the kind of friend he had been that afternoon.

'Go home,' the nurse said. 'Perhaps you could call his family to reassure them. Ring in tomorrow morning. He might be able to see you then.'

'No,' said Alex. 'I'll wait here.'

Dr Michael Evans had had a bad day. He estimated that he had worked a daily twelve hours for the past six days and he was on a late shift again tonight. He had had enough sick people to last him a lifetime.

And now even the healthy were giving him grief. When Nurse O'Keefe had asked him to speak to some idiot jockey in reception, he could hardly believe it. If Dr Evans had his way, little men with bandy legs who cluttered up the hospital every time there was racing at Plumpton would be sent to a special clinic for racing fools.

'There's absolutely no point in your staying here,' Dr Evans said loudly as he walked into reception.

Alex looked up at the man with tired eyes and a white, unbuttoned coat.

'I'd just like to see him,' he said.

'Impossible. Even if you were his long-lost brother, we couldn't let you in.'

'But he's conscious now, is he?'

Dr Evans sighed. 'Yes of course he's conscious. He just had a bang on the head.'

'So, if he hasn't broken anything and he hasn't serious head injuries, he might be out of here soon?'

'He won't be out of anywhere soon,' said the doctor impatiently. 'At least, not under his own steam. It looks like he's broken his back.'

Chapter 3

Life had been hard on Ginnie Matthews. Born some forty-seven years ago into a racing family, she had never known her mother who, when Ginnie was three years old, had run off with a travelling salesman to live in Scotland. From the age of five, it seemed to her now, she had looked after her father whose unpromising career as a trainer near Malton in Yorkshire had been seriously impeded by an ever-increasing dependence on whisky. Ginnie remembered him as a kind, weak man, awash with whisky and self-pity.

By the age of sixteen, she had learned the art of lying to owners, a talent that would stand her in good stead later in life. Daddy was a bit tied up at present. Daddy was out at the stables. Daddy was seeing another owner. Her best efforts were finally in vain. When she went racing, people smiled at her politely but their eyes said it all: Daddy was a loser, a piss-artist heading hell-for-leather for the gutter. Daddy was finished.

Owners deserted him. Horses were taken away. Lads sought other employment. Eventually, Ginnie left, too. At the age of seventeen, she came south and worked in a yard near Lambourn.

She was slim in those days and had a certain chirpy competence that men – particularly weak, mother-fixated men – found attractive. Four years after she had left home, she married Harry Matthews, who was assistant to the legendary Arthur Williamson, by general consent the most successful trainer of his day.

It was early morning, two days after Skinflint had won at Plumpton. Ginnie stood by her Range Rover, watching the string making its way through the early morning mist towards her and thinking about the only man she had ever slept with.

On the face of it, Harry Matthews had been quite a catch. A charming, good-humoured man, whose ten years in the army had left him with an easy manner with employees and a faintly ludicrous moustache which suited his healthy, high-coloured face. Harry was a card, a character; he was good company, always popular on the dinner-party circuit. Despite their age difference – he was forty when they married – she fell for his charms, ignoring the rumours that he had something of a weakness for fun and fast ladies.

'Charm,' Ginnie muttered as she stepped forward, standing in the centre of a circle formed by her horses like a ringmaster at a circus. 'Down with charm.'

She ran an expert eye over the horses, noting which were carrying too much weight, which needed building up. Ginnie prided herself on turning out horses that not only won races but that looked well too.

'How is he?' she called to the lad riding Skinflint.

Pete, a quiet lad who had worked for Ginnie five years now, smoothed Skinflint's coat behind the saddle. 'I don't think he knew he was in a race.'

Ginnie smiled. 'I'm not sure he was,' she said.

It was Wednesday, the day when most of the string were given half-speed work over a mile. Today Rock Steady, a four-year-old hurdler belonging to Clay Wentworth, was being schooled over hurdles. Mr Wentworth was not an amateur jockey who was prepared to tack his horse up and ride him out with the rest of the lads. He liked all that to be done for him so that he could drive to the gallops, work his horse, then return to London. Today, as usual, he was late.

As the horses cantered away from her to the end of the gallops, Ginnie found herself wondering why, at this of all times, she had been ambushed by reminiscences of the past. Under normal circumstances, she rarely looked back – the past, as far as she was concerned, was not just another country, but an alien, distant land hardly worth considering.

It was the thought of a visit from Clay Wentworth that had done it. He was the sort of owner her former husband had cultivated for social as well as financial reasons. Beefy, empty-faced officers, flabby City men, the occasional farmer made good – they had flocked to Harry Matthews when he established his own yard in Lambourn. He had loved it, spending night after night with these idiot amateur jockeys, flirting, getting drunk, frequently returning the following day, leaving Ginnie to look after first and second lots. He called it a sales drive and, for a while, she had believed him.

But Harry's amateur friends let him down. The officers were late paying their bills. Every time the economy dipped, the City men sold their horses – almost always out of the yard.

In the distance, Ginnie saw Clay Wentworth's Mercedes making its way up the lane by the gallops. Harry would have liked Clay. Doubtless he would have joined the famous Wentworth poker circle, if he were still in charge of the yard, if his charm hadn't let him down in the end.

After ten years of marriage, Ginnie had concluded that, perhaps through some odd psychological need, she had managed to find a husband who, in his way, was as big a loser as her father had been. The other women she could just about understand – her infertility was the excuse he used for his philandering; the booze she could live with. It was the lying and incompetent dishonesty that she hated.

Harry lost owners. Like many other trainers, he tried to escape financial ruin by setting up gambling coups. Even that, he screwed up. Horses that were meant to lose, won; good things turned out to be bad things. The Jockey Club took an increasingly close interest in his affairs and, after a particularly transparent act of fraud, took away his licence for two years.

At that moment, Ginnie had decided she was through with charm. She filed for divorce, borrowed enough money to buy him out of the yard, and began to rebuild.

Now, seventeen years later, she was one of the most successful trainers in the country, and her only use for men was as employees. She had learned the hard way.

'Ginnie, the top of the morning to you.' Clay Wentworth emerged languidly from his car. To Ginnie's surprise, he was wearing a pin-striped suit.

'Are you schooling like that?' she asked.

'Bit stiff after Plumpton.' Clay arched his back, wincing slightly. 'Thought I'd let one of the lads have a go.'

Ginnie nodded. She had often wondered why Clay put himself through this. His nerve was bad and he lacked any natural ability or understanding of horses. There was something apologetic about his tall, slightly stooped figure, particularly when his father was present. She glanced in the direction of the Mercedes and there, sure enough, was Sir Denis, sitting stonily immobile in the passenger seat.

'Morning, Sir Denis,' she called out.

The old man nodded curtly.

'My father was wondering why you were working

Skinflint.' Clay smiled weakly. 'I mean, hasn't he done enough this week?'

Ginnie looked away towards the string as it came up the gallops. She couldn't stand owners who thought they knew better than she did. 'He thrives on work,' she said eventually. 'A half-speed will relax him.'

'That's what I told Dad,' said Clay.

'I've entered him in a couple of decent handicap 'chases in the New Year,' she said. 'If he's well in at the weights, we might consider giving him a crack at the big guns.'

'Excellent,' said Clay, adding as an afterthought, 'We don't want too light a weight, of course.'

She said nothing.

'I'm a bit strapped to do anything under twelve stone, to tell the truth.'

As she watched the horses trot back towards them, having pulled up at the end of the gallops, Ginnie swore silently. An owner for whom money and the pleasure of having a top-class horse in his name were enough, would have understood what she was saying. There comes a time when the owner should step down and make way for a professional jockey. Skinflint had the ability to beat the best in the country over three miles but, under the dead, uneven weight of Clay Wentworth, he was nothing special.

Unfortunately Clay and his ill-tempered old father were not interested in prizes or the pleasure of owner-ship; they wanted to see a Wentworth riding into the winners' enclosure, whatever the cost in money and wasted opportunity.

Clay patted Skinflint, who was hardly blowing after his exertions. 'Good boy,' he said. 'We're going to win lots more races together, aren't we?'

'Pete, can you get on Rock Steady and pop him over a couple of hurdles with old Home Boy?'

While the lads exchanged mounts, Clay muttered, 'You do understand why I want to ride him, don't you?'

'He could be a Gold Cup horse.'

Clay smiled. 'Maybe next year. This year it's the Kim Muir. A big amateur race at Cheltenham – it's not bad, is it?'

'No.' Ginnie smiled wearily. 'It's not bad.'

Some horses are lucky with owners – the great Arkle was owned by the Duchess of Westminster throughout his racing career. Others are less fortunate. As a four-year-old hurdler, Skinflint had been sold out of a yard in Newmarket to a Colonel Gilbert, an old enthusiast who kept a few horses with Ginnie.

By the time the Colonel died two years later, Skinflint was a top novice 'chaser with the temperament, toughness and turn of foot to become a Cheltenham Gold Cup prospect. When Mrs Gilbert, who had always resented her husband's interest in racing, put all his horses on the market, Ginnie had worked hard to find a new owner who would keep him in training with her. Clay Wentworth, who had just sent her a young hurdler called Rock Steady, had seemed ideal.

But Ginnie had underestimated Clay's – or rather, his father's – ambition.

'Will Sir Denis want to come over to the schooling ground?' she asked.

'He'll watch from here,' said Clay. 'He just likes to feel involved.'

Together, they walked to the schooling ground, an area of about twenty-five acres with lines of hurdles and fences of varying heights. They watched Rock Steady canter down to the far end of the gallop with Home Boy. Both horses were shown the first flight of hurdles.

'Do we know who are going to be our two main rivals in the Kim Muir?' Clay asked.

'Not officially, but I could take a pretty good guess.'

'You couldn't be terribly kind and jot them down for me, could you?'

'Jot them down?' Ginnie looked at Clay with some surprise. 'Can't I just tell you?'

'No, put them down – with owners and trainers. On a piece of paper. Know your enemy and all that. Besides, with my memory I'd forget them.'

She shrugged, as the two horses turned towards the first hurdle and set off at smart gallop.

'Here they come,' she said.

The more they talked of miracles around Paul's bed at Lewes Hospital, the more depressed he became about the future. It had been a miracle, Dr Evans had told him, that the impact of a racehorse falling at racing speed on top of him had not been fatal. It was a miracle that he had recovered consciousness so quickly. It was a miracle the way his body was responding to treatment so that now, five days after his fall, he was out of intensive care and back in a ward.

Then, subtly, the emphasis began to change. It would be a miracle if he were out of hospital within six months, and – the one that went through his mind a thousand times a day – it would be a miracle if he ever walked again. Three days after he had been brought into hospital, Paul had asked Dr Evans when he would recover the movement in his legs. 'Tell me what's going to happen,' he asked. 'Without the miracles.'

And the doctor, normally so direct, had been evasive, explaining with the help of X-rays he extracted from the folder he was carrying that the problem was a series of crushed vertebrae at the base of the spine. 'If the damage had been two inches lower,' he said, 'the risk of fundamental damage would have been less. As it is, we have to wait for your body to recover from the shock of the fall and for the swelling to subside, before we can conduct an exploratory operation. Only then will we know what the future holds for you.'

'Fundamental damage.' Through a haze of morphine Paul sensed the reason for Dr Evans' uneasiness. 'Does that mean I'm out for the season – or for ever?'

47

Dr Evans gestured to Nurse O'Keefe, who was standing at the foot of the bed. The nurse drew the curtains around the bed.

'Listen, let's take one step at a time.'

'What about walking?'

'I honestly don't know, only time will tell.' The doctor paused.

Paul had closed his eyes as the doctor had explained, as dispassionately as a science master, the medical advances in the field of spine damage.

'We find that attitude's important.' Dr Evans tried a smile but there was something chilling about his bedside manner, as if somehow Paul had brought this on himself.

Attitude. Paul understood that. After Dr Evans had left to continue on his rounds, he stared ahead of him at the plastic curtains which the nurse had left closed, thinking of the path which had led him to this hospital bed.

His family had laughed when he had told them his ambition. They had been having tea as usual, after his father had returned from work at the building site and the mood had been jovial, it being the end of the week and times in the building trade being good. His two older brothers, both in their teens, had been unenthusiastic about the idea of work but had grumpily given the impression that, like their father, they would work in construction. Mary, Paul's sister, wanted to be a nurse.

'I'm going to be a jockey,' Paul had said. He was five at the time.

But, to the Raven family's amazement, Paul's obsession with horses had grown stronger as he grew up. He watched racing on the television, discussing form with his father from the age of seven. There was a riding-school on the outskirts of Wigan and, ignoring the taunts of his schoolfriends, he worked there during the school holidays. He was even allowed to compete in the local shows and, although the ponies he rode were less well-fed and schooled than those ridden by the sons and daughters of local farmers, he won his fair share of show-jumping classes.

It took attitude to overcome the opposition of his father, who wanted him to serve an apprenticeship on the site like his brothers, and his teachers, who claimed he was too bright to leave school at the age of sixteen, and to come south, looking for a job in racing.

He had rung three trainers for work and luckily it was the fourth, Ron Charlesworth, who had agreed to take him on. Surly and mean, Charlesworth believed in bringing on his own lads, and that had been the making of Paul Raven.

Maybe he should have stayed in Wigan, he thought. His father and his two brothers were on the dole now; his sister was married with two children; but at least none of them faced a future in a wheelchair.

'How are you feeling?'

Nurse O'Keefe stood at the foot of his bed. Paul was grateful that she wasn't wearing the hospital smile, an expression of phoney sympathy that he found increasingly irritating.

'Numb,' he said. 'I can't take it in. I keep thinking that the drugs have got to me and I'll snap out of it.'

The nurse walked around to the side of the bed. As she was tucking in his sheet, she said quietly, 'If you need someone to talk to, just say the word.' She smiled at Paul in a way that verged on the unprofessional. Then, as if the sister had just walked into the ward, she said more loudly, 'That's what we're here for.'

'Thank you, nurse.'

'Angie.'

'Thank you, Angie.' Paul watched the slim, pale figure as she made her way down the ward to see another patient. 'Angie,' he said, and for the first time for five days, he smiled.

That night, Angie O'Keefe had agreed to go out for a meal with some of the other girls but, when they knocked on her door in the nurses' hostel, she told them she was tired, she had a headache. Eventually, she agreed to meet them later at the restaurant. Now she sat on her neatly-made bed, thinking of the quiet, dark jockey who, Dr Evans said, could be paralysed for life.

Angie's small room was a credit to the convent in Berkshire where she had been educated: neat, well-dusted and decorated only with photographs of her parents and two younger sisters. Unlike many of her contemporaries, she had never reacted against the discipline of her education by running wild in her late teens. Now twenty-one, she had avoided drinking to excess, swore only occasionally and she was a virgin. Not that sexual purity was something to boast about – Angie felt almost jealous when she heard tales of heart-thumping promiscuity from the other girls – she simply preferred to wait for the right man.

She saw the dark, even features of Paul Raven in her mind's eye and shook her head firmly. On every count, he was Mr Wrong. First of all, he was a patient and it was a golden rule among the nurses not to make a difficult job worse by falling in love, or even flirting, with one of the customers.

Then he was a jockey. Angie smiled as she remembered the scandal of one of the old girls who was said to be dating a bookmaker. Fast men who made a questionable living out of fast horses: nothing could be more dangerous for the purity of a girl's soul.

His connections hardly inspired confidence. Two days after Paul had been admitted, his mother, a short angry woman who seemed ill at ease away from the north, had appeared in the ward. Mrs Raven had not exactly told Paul to pull himself together and stop moping about like a big girl's blouse, but she was hardly sympathetic, implying to her son – and, indeed, to the rest of the ward – that, if he were daft enough to ride horses for a living, what else did he expect but to end up in hospital? Like the majority of people, she had no perception of the word paralysed.

The same day a Mrs Charlesworth, the wife of Paul's trainer, had shuffled in. Ron was away racing, she said. Ron needed him back as soon as possible. Ron had been in a filthy mood ever since the race at Plumpton. Without enquiring into Paul's state of health, she had eaten the grapes she had brought, then scurried out of the ward, leaving it smelling faintly of the stables.

Slowly, Angie unbuttoned her nurse's uniform. She walked across the small room to a basin in the corner above which there was a mirror. Angie had never been vain – she had never understood why men looked at her the way they did – but now she stood before the mirror, taking in the pale skin, the athletic figure, the shadows of tiredness under her eyes, the practical, no-nonsense haircut. She ran her hands over her hips as if smoothing down an invisible skirt.

Above all, there was the third reason why Paul Raven should be erased from her thoughts as soon as possible. Angie was a good nurse, but she was no Florence Nightingale. When she gave herself to a man – and she hoped it would be soon – she was old-fashioned enough to hope that he would sweep her off her feet, take control. There was little chance of Paul being able to do that. Caring and convalescence belonged at work, not at home.

Yesterday the other jockey, Alex – the one several of the nurses were talking about in the staff room –

had visited Paul once again. There was something wild and distracted about the man; his conversation was too loud and cheerful to be entirely natural. While they were talking, Angie had called by to check that Paul's drip was still working and, as she walked away, she had sensed that they were discussing her. Paul said something quietly, and she had heard the clipped tones of Alex Drew, saying, 'You know what they say, Paul. There are only two certainties in life – death and nurses.'

She had been unable to resist glancing back. To her relief, Paul wasn't laughing.

That evening, after Alex had left, the customary calm had descended on the ward as the patients watched early-evening soaps on the television. For the nurses, this was about the only time during the day when they could relax, confident that, for a few minutes, the sun-drenched domestic dramas of Australian suburban life would distract the patients' minds from their own troubles.

Angie noticed that Paul never bothered with these programmes. Tonight he seemed quiet, more distant than usual, as if the visit from his friend had unsettled him. Most of the lights in the ward had been switched off, the curtains drawn, so that, briefly, it was lit only by the light from the television.

'So you're not an addict.' Angie smiled, sitting on the chair which Alex had left beside the bed.

'Can't follow the plot.'

She laughed softly. 'How are you feeling?'

'Alex is taking this badly. He keeps going over the race, talking about it. He knows I can't remember anything about the fall but it's as if he wants me to blame him. I've seen the video of the race and there's no doubt he stopped me deliberately. What happened was a chance in a million, but it's eating him up. He looks terrible.'

Angie remembered his remark about nurses, the confident tone of the young middle-class male. 'He seemed all right to me,' she said.

'You don't know him.'

Paul was staring sightlessly in the direction of the television. In the gloom, he reminded Angie of some wounded hero of an old black-and-white film, his dark troubled features against the white of the pillow, his eyes catching the light and seeming to sparkle feverishly. A dying member of the French Resistance, perhaps, even a consumptive poet. Raven – he was well named.

'Tell me something, Angie,' he said. 'Not as a nurse but as a friend. Assuming the worst – that I'll never walk again – ' He paused then plunged on. 'Does that mean that I'm finished as a man too?'

'No. It doesn't.'

He had turned to look at her, surprised by the confidence of her reply.

'You understand what I'm asking?'

'You're all right,' she said. 'If you had no feeling in your legs, there would be a problem. As it is, your – ' Angie hesitated. 'The rest of it will be unimpaired.'

'You're sure about that?'

'I'm sure.' In the semi-darkness, she lay a hand softly on his. 'I asked the doctor myself.'

Back in her room, as the warm water filled the basin before her, Angie remembered the conversation with Paul. She rubbed her hands on the soap, then carefully washed her face. Once she had prided herself on being in control of her life. Too many of her friends had fallen in love with the wrong men at the wrong time and in the wrong way. Not her, she had always vowed. Now she wasn't so sure.

She rinsed her face. Perhaps, after all, she would join her friends at the restaurant. She felt like company.

'Fifty to come in.'

Clay Wentworth pushed a small pile of plastic chips into the middle of the table and allowed his large, fleshy features to assume the expression of relaxed inscrutability he felt was appropriate for these occasions. He stared at the suit – king and five – he held in his hands, as four of the other players – Lol Calloway, Alice Markwick, Digby Welcome and Harry Biddulph – came in.

Clay felt lucky. They were playing his favourite form of poker, Texas Hold 'Em, and already he was seven hundred quid up on the night, thanks to a combination of good hands and cool play. The dealer for the game, Perry Smythe, rolled two more kings and another five and laid them in the middle of the table. Yes, it was his night. When Clay bet £250, the maximum allowed on Thursday Poker Night, Alice, Digby and Biddulph folded. With his usual confident smile, Lol raised it to five hundred.

Lol couldn't handle poker politics. Never had and never would. Clay glanced across and for a moment he was fixed by Calloway's hooded eyes. There was something impressively sinister about him, his bald pate and long, lank hair giving him the look of a bank robber rather than a former rock star, but he was no card-player.

It was time for a spot of Wentworth bluff. Clay glanced down at his hand, frowning as if his best plan was going horribly wrong. He chewed his bottom lip for a moment like a man whose every instinct told him to cut his losses and fold.

Lol Calloway had never been able to read a bluff. Clay looked to him for a 'tell', some small tic that would betray the strength of weakness of Lol's hand, and found it. When the God of poker was smiling on him, Lol would purse his lips, draw the cards together, then re-open them. This, Clay had learned over the two years in which he had been doing poker nights with Lol, was a sure sign that he held a good hand. Despite appearing in cameo roles in the occasional TV detective series, the man was no actor.

He drew his cards together, shook his head, and looked at them again.

A certain etiquette had evolved on Thursday Poker Nights. A player who had folded, or who was sitting out the game, was not meant to comment on proceedings, however light-heartedly. Now Alice, Digby Welcome and Harry Biddulph sat at the table, silent and straight-faced, as Clay called Lol's five hundred and re-raised him another six hundred.

Two cards remained to be shown. Clay judged that Lol must hold the last king and possibly an ace. To match Clay's full house, he needed an ace from one of the next two communal cards. Smythe the dealer dealt the top card, laying it aside face down – an entirely unnecessary touch of melodrama since no one, on Thursday Poker Nights, had been known to cheat – then rolled the top card. It was a four. Lol closed his eyes briefly then nodded. Smythe dealt again. A jack.

'Fuck.' Lol threw down his cards, revealing a king and a nine, and with a passable show of nonchalance wandered over to an open fire on the far side of the room near which there was a drinks trolley. He poured himself a large whisky. 'A whole day's fucking PR receipts. You are one lucky bastard.'

Clay smiled as he raked in his chips, estimating over a grand of clear profit on the game. Sure, he was lucky – not so much with the cards he was dealt but with his poker partners. Over the past two years, a small but significant percentage of Lol's massive earnings had found its way into his pocket and those of the other Thursday regulars. It was as if Lol were punishing himself for making so much money so effortlessly. Three good years as a guitar hero in the early seventies, some clever management of his diminishing assets and the new obsession of advertisers for revising old tunes had yielded a salary that hit the half million mark – on a bad year.

'It's called skill,' Clay said amiably, leaving the game and placing his chips on a side table. That was the great thing about the Thursday game. From Lol Calloway, for whom losing fifteen thousand pounds in ten minutes was mildly irritating but soon forgotten, to Digby Welcome, for whom an equivalent crash-out would be three hundred or a week's drinking money, the regulars knew how far to take it. Maybe that was why they were regulars – the guys who lost it, who went 'on tilt' as they say in gambling circles, desperately throwing good money after bad, tended not to last long.

'We need new blood in the school,' Lol muttered, as if reading Clay's thoughts. 'Another fuckin' Alex Drew. Otherwise it's always going to be me that's turned over.' Clay sat in the armchair opposite Lol and crossed his long legs.

'Couldn't you tell I was looking at a full house? You were crazy to follow me up.'

Lol stared gloomily into the fire. 'You looked so fuckin' depressed,' he said. 'I was thinking, it's got to be bullshit. No way has Clay got a king in the hole and a five. No one can get that lucky. Oh well – ' he slurped noisily at his drink. 'Can't win 'em all.'

'No, you can't.'

'Heard from Alex, have you?'

'Had a couple of calls.' Clay noticed that, even though Digby, Harry Biddulph, Alice and a couple of the newer members of the group had begun another game, the focus of attention in the room had shifted from the poker table to the conversation. 'He's not a happy boy. In fact, he's rather upset about what happened.'

'Too right,' said Lol. 'A broken back's a fuckin' bummer in any language.'

'As I understand it,' said Digby Welcome, without taking his eyes off the two cards in his hand, 'the boy Raven has crushed vertebrae. Not what I'd call a broken back.'

A silence descended on the room. It was odd, Clay thought, that Digby, the one Thursday night regular who claimed to understand racing, to have it in the blood, was the person least concerned by what had happened. Even Alice, in her glacial way, had noted that there had been what she called 'an unscheduled casualty'.

He didn't like Welcome, but then few people did. For a moment Clay watched the stout figure, whose comical little legs hardly reached the floor, as he played his normal tight, careful game of poker. If it was true that in every fat man a thin man was trying to get out, the inner Digby was a sour, ungenerous bastard strangely at odds with the roly-poly exterior and the flushed round cheeks.

'I fold.' As was his custom, Digby decided that discretion was the better part of valour and left the game at an early stage. The man was a dull poker player, meanly backing good hands while taking few chances. Every Thursday, he gained between £100 and £200 – but then again he probably wasn't there for the money.

No one knew the truth about Digby Welcome. He claimed to be an old Etonian but this, like so much of his personal history, might have been a fraud. By guile and cultivating the right contacts, he had, it was said, established himself as a National Hunt trainer and had a fairly successful yard in Sussex during the 1960s. More surprising still, he had married the reasonably attractive daughter of one of his owners.

It went wrong, but not in the usual way of racing failures – Digby's was not a gambling yard. His innate meanness found him out. The horses were underfed, the lads underpaid. As the winners dried up, owners deserted him and so, amid rumours of unseemly marital demands in the Welcome bedroom, did his wife. Digby gave up his habit of paying bills late, opting instead for not paying them at all. The withdrawal of his trainer's licence was followed, within a month, by bankruptcy.

These days, Digby Welcome represented a small

and somewhat shady manufacturer of horse tonics, travelling in his Volvo Estate from stable to stable. He still went racing, but had more enemies than friends and was frequently to be seen drinking alone at the members' bar.

Having left the game, he placed himself in front of the fire, his short, tubby figure shielding Clay and Lol from the warmth.

'That's racing,' he said, almost sitting in the fire in an attempt to warm his over-generous behind. 'I always used to warn my jockeys about coming up on the inner. Raven's been around long enough to know the dangers.'

'Do me a fuckin' favour, Digby.' This was too much, even for Lol Calloway. 'We all know there was more to it than that.'

Clay darted a warning glance in the direction of the table where the two new members of the Thursday Night school were still playing with rapt concentration. 'Not all of us know that,' he said quietly.

'Well, I feel bad about it,' Lol muttered.

Briefly Clay looked troubled. 'There's nothing we can do now,' he said.

They were on their last game for the night when the call came through. It was almost four o'clock, and Clay was back at the table, taking some money – off Perry Smythe and one of the stockbrokers who had recently joined the school. Alice was just about breaking even and Digby had made his almost statutory two hundred pounds. Only Lol was by the fire, moodily nursing a large glass of whisky.

He looked at his watch without any particular surprise as the telephone continued to ring.

'Must be the fuckin' Coast,' he murmured as he made his way unsteadily across the room. In Lol's world, the only time it was inconsiderate to call was during daytime working hours when he was normally asleep.

''Ullo.' He swayed backwards and forwards like a sailor in a storm. 'Who the fuck is this?' he asked. The answer appeared to take some time. 'Oh, it's you. Why didn't you fuckin' say so? He's in the middle of a game right now.' Lol winced and held the telephone away from his ear. 'All right, all right, keep yer 'air on.' He turned towards the table where the game was taking its course. 'It's for you, Clay. Alex. Says it's important.'

Clay frowned, laid down his cards and walked over to the telephone.

'Alex,' he said silkily. 'Where are you? We were expecting you.'

The call took ten minutes and when he put down the receiver, Clay's good humour had faded. He returned to the table, looking pale and weary.

'Alex Drew wants to talk,' he said.

Digby looked up from his cards. 'He should have come round this evening. A touch of poker therapy would have done him the power of good.'

'To the authorities, I mean.' Clay sat down slowly, still deep in thought. 'I think I dissuaded him.'

'There's not much to talk about.' Alice looked only mildly concerned. 'Nothing can be proved.'

For a moment, there was silence in the room, and from outside the first early twitterings of birdsong could be heard.

'Fuckin' dawn chorus,' muttered Lol.

Clay threw his cards into the middle of the table. 'I'm out,' he said.

From his chair by the fireside, Lol gave a little, drunken laugh. 'Alex was well gone. That little bastard was feeling no pain.'

Clay stared into the dying embers of the fire. 'If only that were true,' he said.

Alex Drew sat on the side of his bed, pressing the mobile telephone to his forehead as if it were a poultice. He didn't cry – he was past all that – but he muttered to himself, again and again. 'No going back. No going back now.'

In his twenty-three years, Alex had experienced his share of good times. He had been to all-night parties. He had lived hard and wildly, drinking and making love. He was no stranger to the more fashionable of recreational drugs – cocaine, amphetamines, even, on a couple of occasions, heroin had assailed his senses. It was life – at least, it was life if you were young, good-looking and from a family where money was never going to be a problem.

And yet he had retained the smooth-faced innocent look of a grown-up choirboy. One day maybe his body would protest, fast-lane wrinkles would appear on his face. Then again, maybe not.

Carefully, Alex switched off the telephone and laid it on the bed. Anguish and guilt had marked his face in a way that too many parties never had. There were rings under his eyes, the once-smooth cheeks were unshaven, the hair, which he wore longer than most other jockeys, was lank and dull.

Like a man preparing for an execution, he stood up, took off his jeans and slipped into his riding-out clothes – jodhpurs, boots, a dark polo-neck sweater. He took a trim jacket from the wardrobe, picked up his car keys from the dressing-table and left.

It was light now. Within an hour the lads would be arriving at Charlesworth's yard to prepare for first lot. Alex unlocked his Audi and, driving with a care that was unusual for him, set off towards Lambourn.

A horse-box was already in the yard, and Alex cursed softly. Having told the guv'nor that he was ill, he hadn't ridden out for three days. Presumably one or two of the horses were running at a distant race-meeting today and needed to set off early.

'Och aye, he's back at last.' Jimmy Summers, the head lad, was putting a couple of hay-nets in the horse-box. 'Better, are you?'

Alex kept walking. 'Much better,' he said.

'You look fuckin' terrible,' said Jimmy cheerfully.

Behind the stables were some farm buildings. He needed to get there and back to the car without arousing Jimmy's suspicions.

'Who's running today then?' he asked.

'Och, it's the big time,' Jimmy smiled. 'We're taking Smile Please and Pretty Marie up to Fakenham. Fuckin' waste of petrol if you ask me.'

The head lad disappeared into the horse box and Alex continued on his way across the yard.

'No going back now,' he said, as memories, unwelcome memories, flashed through his mind.

Someone, somewhere had said to him, as if revealing one of life's eternal verities, that those who play must pay. It had stuck in Alex's mind as being as stupid a cliché as he had ever heard.

The girl – yes, it was a friend of his older sister who, during her brief and otherwise forgettable affair with Alex had allowed herself to get pregnant – had really believed it. She had actually held out her hand and, for a moment, he had failed to understand the precise nature of the payment she was looking for. She was more specific. The cost of the abortion was down to him. He had given her £300 in cash, which was the cost of the operation plus £50 for her trouble – an uncharacteristically spiteful touch, but then he had only been eighteen at the time.

If that was how those who played paid – with a trip to the bank – Alex was unconcerned. Life had given him a blank cheque. The world was his plaything.

By the time he had first met Paul Raven, Alex had decided that there was only one activity about which he would be wholly serious. When he rode horses, the nonsense, the laughter ended. He had ridden his first winner under rules, an amateur hurdle at Devon and Exeter, when he was eighteen. The following year, he was champion amateur and, to the dismay of his father, a wealthy and shrewd Scottish landowner, he had decided on a career in racing.

The idea of becoming a professional jockey – of riding for money – had come later. Until he was twenty, Alex had assumed that he would work among the ranks of racing's tweed-suited elite – an assistant trainer perhaps or something in bloodstock. His father, a generous man who believed that youth should have its fling, paid for Alex's year at Ron Charlesworth's yard, confident that, by the time he reached his twenty-first birthday, his son would be ready to embark on a serious career.

It had been Paul who changed all that. At Alex's request, he was treated like a normal stable lad at the Charlesworth yard, living in the chilly hostel and spending long, harsh hours mucking out stables and cleaning tack. It was a far tougher baptism than Alex had expected, for his accent, his clothes and, above all, his sports car set him apart from the other lads and made him an obvious target for persecution. Only Paul, the quiet northerner who had already ridden several winners for Charlesworth and other trainers, recognised that behind the soft-skinned facade of a privileged amateur, beyond the playboy image, there was a steely determination.

They should have been enemies. Their backgrounds, their characters, the growing competition for spare rides from the stable seemed sure to set them on a collision course. But, as they rode work together, discussed the horses in the yard, the qualities of the top jockeys they both admired, a mutual respect developed between them.

'Leave him be,' Paul would say with quiet authority. 'Just 'cause he doesn't talk like you, it doesn't mean he can't do the job.'

Gradually the jibes subsided, Alex established his position at the yard and the professional regard between him and Paul developed into friendship.

'How come that leery bastard runs for you when he won't do a tap for me?' Paul had asked half-jokingly after they had worked a couple of three-year-olds over a mile and a half.

'I talk to him nicely.'

'Typical.' Paul had smiled. 'Even the horses are snobs round here.'

Thanks to Paul, Alex had the confidence to join the ranks of professional jockeys and, thanks to him, he had the strength to withstand the storm of disapproval that broke over his head when he told his parents. In a way, he owed Paul everything.

Larks were singing in the pale morning sunlight over the downs as the Audi made its way up the lane beside the gallops. It stopped at a point where there was a hedge beside the track, on the far side of which was Ron Charlesworth's schooling ground.

Moving more deliberately than was his habit, Alex got out and lowered the roof of the convertible. He reached on to the back seat, picking up the rope that he had picked up in Charlesworth's farm building. He glanced up the gallops to ensure that no early morning joggers or dogwalkers were watching and briefly he heard the thunder of hooves as the string made its way up the slight slope towards where he stood. Then, shaking his head as if to rid himself of memories, he took the rope and adeptly formed a loop at one end, smiling to think how the knowledge of knots he had acquired when sailing as a boy was being put to belated use. Laying the coiled rope on the back seat of the car, he took its other end and attached it to the trunk of a stout oak that formed part of the hedgerow. He tugged at it twice then walked slowly back to the car and sat in the driver's seat.

For a moment, it was as if he had drifted off into a trance. Then he reached behind him, took the end of the rope and, as carefully as a woman trying on a hat in a shop, he placed the noose around his neck, tightening it so that the knot rested against the back of his neck.

He glanced at the coils lying on the back seat, then fastened his safety belt. Twenty yards, and in a car with powerful acceleration. It would do.

Alex switched on the engine, gunned the car, priming it as if it were a sprinter in the stalls. He slipped it into first gear, saying quietly, 'Those who play must pay.' This, at least, was true payment.

Taking the handbrake off, he closed his eyes and pressed the accelerator to the floor, drowning out the singing of larks for ever.

Chapter 4

'The VART man?'

There were times when the deep and husky voice of Alice Markwick became aristocratic in its disdain, when a stranger might be forgiven for assuming that she was the daughter of a White Russian countess rather than of a factory worker in Prague.

'The VAT man, yes.' Norman Little, her secretary, stood in the door to her office. A neat, unambitious man in his late twenties, Norman was used to Mrs Markwick's ever-changing moods and had learned to ignore them. 'He claims he has an appointment.'

Alice looked at the leather diary on her desk. 'He is wrong. Tell him to come back next week. Say it's a bad moment.'

Norman touched his temple with thumb and forefinger, like a man sensing the first twinge of a migraine. 'I think that would be unwise, Mrs Markwick. They can make life very awkward, these VAT people.'

'V.A.T. spelt G.O.D. This country's bureaucracy gets more Eastern European every day. Ask Simon to show him the books. He wants the finance director, not me.'

'He insisted that he should see you.'

'Hell and damnation. Get me the books and the last company accounts. And show him into my office – after a quarter of an hour or so.' Alice grimaced as her secretary shook his head disapprovingly. 'All right, five minutes.'

'Yes, Mrs Markwick.'

'And give him a cup of tea – or whatever VART men drink.'

Norman smiled. 'Already done,' he said, retiring from the office like a well-trained butler.

'Bloody VAT.' Alone in her office, Alice closed the desk diary and lit a cigarette. She had nothing to hide from any government money snoop and, if there was one thing you learned from being brought up in Czechoslovakia, it was how to deal with bureaucrats. All the same – Alice stood up and walked to the window – it was bad timing. She felt uneasy, as if some small part of her carefully laid plans had gone wrong, but she didn't know how.

Perhaps it was the jockey. Just over three weeks ago, Alex Drew had committed suicide. There had been an absurd amount of fuss – Alice had never understood the seriousness with which violent death was taken in this country – and the press had pored over his last days in a way which briefly had unnerved her.

'Another casualty,' the fool Wentworth had said when he had rung her with the news. Barely keeping hysteria at bay, he had described how a torso had been found in Alex's car by the lads riding out for Charlesworth. His head had later been discovered in a hedgerow, near a noose.

'How frightfully macabre.' She had tried unsuccessfully for a lightness of tone. 'There were no notes or anything, I hope.'

'I don't think so.'

And there hadn't been. Alex may have been as flashy in death as he had been in life but at least he had been discreet. His death changed nothing, in Alice's view. He had served his purpose.

'You know how your saying goes,' she had said to Clay. 'The one about making omelettes, breaking eggs.'

'Yes.' Clay seemed to be pulling himself together now.

'You're right, of course.'

'Remember. It's some omelette we've got cooking.'

Alice looked down at the laboratory, across a yard from her office. It was a modest set-up, a complex of ill-designed modern buildings, entirely in keeping with the other small businesses run, mostly by Asians, in this particular part of Willesden. Only the discreet but highly sophisticated security system suggested that Markwick Instruments plc was anything out of the ordinary.

The door opened behind her.

'Mr Birtwhistle,' said Norman. 'From the local VAT office.'

'Ah, good.' Alice turned, smiling, even shaking her dark curls with a hint of coquettishness. This, after all, was an occasion for charm. 'So sorry to have kept you waiting, Mr Birtwhistle.'

After two decades in England, Alice could still be surprised. The young man standing before her eyes was not at all her idea of a Mr Birtwhistle from the VAT office. With thick dark hair slicked straight back, a raffish moustache, and smooth, even features, he looked a successful City man, a broker or commodity man with a mobile phone, a Porsche and a string of girlfriends. Even his dark, pin-striped suit seemed rather too well-tailored for a VAT inspector in Willesden.

'The apologies are mine,' he said, a suggestion of a south London twang in his soft voice. 'I was thirty minutes late myself. I had a bit of bother with the address.'

'It's a warren round here.' Alice sat behind her desk, gesturing in the direction of the guest chair nearby. 'People can get lost for days.'

Birtwhistle sat down, laying his shiny black briefcase on his knees. 'I'm still a bit of a stranger to the area,' he said.

'When did you arrange the appointment, exactly?'

'Must have been last Monday.' The VAT man had opened his briefcase and had taken out a form. 'The lady I spoke to assured me this morning was clear for you. Now I needn't detain you long. My department is involved in a background briefing exercise involving businesses in the area whose turnover exceeds half a million pounds and which . . .'

Alice nodded politely as the young man recited his well-rehearsed lines. He was sounding more as she had expected now. Perhaps his manner and style of dressing were merely a sign of the times – these days, even VAT inspectors were upwardly mobile.

He had been talking for about a minute when Norman entered the office, bearing a number of files which, with an apologetic smile, he hid on the desk with a muttered 'The books, Mrs Markwick.'

Birtwhistle paused until Norman had left. 'Sorry,' he said mildly. 'I should have explained. I don't need the figures today – just a few details from you.'

'Details?'

'As I've explained – it's for our local firm profile operation.'

'Ah, yes.' Alice glanced at her watch. 'Well, my late husband set up the firm in 1964. He was a physicist, specialising in optics, in particular early research into lasers. By the time he died we were selling optical instruments to a number of medical establishments and engineering firms throughout the United Kingdom.'

Birtwhistle looked up from the form on which he

was making notes. 'He died when, precisely?'

'1972. Heart attack.'

'And you were . . .'

'We had married in 1969. I had been his secretary.'

'It must have been a great shock.'

'Yes.' Alice quickly closed down that line of questioning which had nothing to do with anybody but her. 'He was only forty-three. But – ' she smiled bravely ' – he left the firm in good shape, with some excellent researchers.'

'Local people, I imagine?'

'They came from all over. Some from England, some from my native country. If they knew about lasers, I didn't care where they were born.'

'And you continued to run the firm.'

'I have a good team. Our turnover topped five million last year.'

'D'you take on defence work?' Birtwhistle asked casually. 'Lasers can be used as a weapon, as I understand.'

Alice smiled. 'Not our type of lasers. We work to make people better, not to kill them.'

'I see.' Birtwhistle took some time to note it down. 'Perhaps you could show me round – when we've finished.' His smile was boyish, almost mischievous.

'Of course,' Alice said. 'I have a meeting in fifteen minutes. Until then – ' she returned his smile with a hint of professional flirtatiousness ' – I'm all yours.'

'One more step.'

Angie O'Keefe stood behind Paul, a hand on each of his hips, ready to catch him should he fall backwards from the walking frame on which he was leaning.

'Jesus.' Paul gritted his teeth as, with effort which seemed to wrack his whole body, he willed his right foot forward. 'Whoever said nursing was one of the caring professions?'

Angie laughed. 'Cruel to be kind,' she said. 'Go on, Paul. One more – for me.'

It wasn't really a step. It was a desperate, unsteady, old man's shuffle which covered barely six inches of the shiny floor in the Physiotherapy Room – but for Paul it felt more important than his first winner. As time had passed and the swelling reduced, relieving the pressure on his spinal cord, so the feeling in his legs had gradually returned. There was no paralysis, but the injury to the bone was quite extensive.

'Enough,' he gasped, as Angie placed his wheelchair behind him. He swayed as she took away the walking frame and stood in front of him. He placed his arms around her neck, saying with a weary smile, 'We can't go on meeting like this.'

She lowered him gently onto the wheelchair.

'I'm exhausted just looking at you,' she said.

Paul smiled. Love and rage were a potent combination, motivating him to push himself faster than ever the doctors wanted.

Thanks to a contribution from the Injured Jockeys' Fund, he had been transferred to the Croydon

Rehabilitation Centre where he devoted his every waking hour to walking once again.

Angie had taken to visiting him on her days off work, talking through his despair, helping him to look to the future, always encouraging him.

'Thanks, nurse,' he said. 'I don't know what I'd do without you.'

Angie stood in front of the wheelchair smiling, her arms crossed. 'All part of the service,' she said.

Paul looked away. 'Don't feel you have to visit me,' he said. 'You should be going out – this must be just like work for you.'

'I'm not a health visitor,' she said leaning forward and touching his cheek briefly with her hand. Then, as if she had suddenly made some rather important decision, she kissed him – at first tentatively, then with a firm, deep insistence.

When she stood up, there was colour in her normally pale cheeks.

Paul smiled. 'What do I get after walking six steps then?' he asked.

'I've never kissed a man like that before,' Angie said distantly. 'I mean – it's not like me to make the first move.'

Paul looked into her clear blue eyes, so close to him as she stood, one hand on each arm of the chair. Her face, framed by the short blonde hair, seemed younger, more vulnerable than when he had first seen her in the hospital. 'If you hadn't, we might have had a long wait on our hands,' he said.

Slowly, she pushed the wheelchair down the corridor and back to his small room. Only when she had closed the door behind them did Paul finally speak.

'I need your help,' he said hesitantly. 'I've no right to ask you and I'll understand if you refuse.'

'Don't be . . . '

Paul held up a hand. 'I'm not talking about . . . all this.' He paused. 'I've got to know what happened to Alex.'

Angie turned away to a desk on which there lay some newspaper cuttings. A headline – 'JOCKEY IN SHOCK SUICIDE MYSTERY' – caught her eye. Paul had reacted with incredulity to news of Alex's death but, in time, grief had turned to anger. Although he had been unable to speak of his friend until now, she had noticed the look of quiet determination, almost of anger, that crossed his face when the memories returned.

'What can we do?' She laid a hand on Paul's shoulder. 'Alex is dead. You saw how he was after your fall. He was obsessed with guilt about what had happened.'

'I'm not saying he didn't kill himself. Just that – he was involved in something before the race at Plumpton. I think – I know – that if my fall was just an accident, he would never have killed himself. He was too strong for that. He was a survivor.'

'How long had you been friends?'

'Three years. When he first came to work for Charlesworth, I couldn't stand him – he was so jaunty, so confident. The lads took against him – the way he talked, his good looks, his car. And of course he was an amateur.'

'That matters?'

'It matters. A few years ago, trainers used to put amateurs up on their horses to save the cost of a jockey's fee. These days, they have to pay the Jockey Club so that amateurs and professionals are competing on level terms but the idea that somehow they're taking bread out of the mouths of lads who have worked their way up the hard way lives on.'

'I can understand that. If it weren't for his father's money, Alex would never have made it as an amateur. Compared to someone like you, he had it easy.'

'Didn't matter to me. It wasn't his fault that his parents were rich. But it was never his background that made him different from the lads – it was the fact that he rode better than them. I knew he'd turn professional that first time I rode work with him. It was the only thing he really wanted to do – ride horses and win races.'

'You encouraged him.'

'Of course. We were a bit guarded, at first, but soon we got on well.

'Although we were different, in many ways we were in the same situation – more than lads, once we started getting rides, yet not fully-fledged jockeys. That brought us together. And we trusted one another – in racing, that counts for something.'

Angie sat down at the desk and picked up one of

80

the cuttings. For the week following his death, there had been lurid speculation about why a young jockey, on the brink of a successful career, should commit suicide. There were rumours of gambling debts, problems with a girlfriend, a rift with his father and mother. A couple of reporters had even tried to talk to Paul but he had refused to comment.

'A few days after Plumpton,' Paul said, 'a reporter from the *Guardian* wrote to me in hospital. It was before it had been announced how badly I was hurt. He had seen a video of the race. He knew nothing about horses, he said, but he was surprised that there was no investigation.'

'Why?'

'He seemed to think Alex put me through the wing deliberately. He wanted my view.'

'What did you say to him?'

'I said he stopped me getting up his innèr, which he is entitled to do, and that there was no way he could have known Dig For Glory would take on the wing. Anyway the article he was writing didn't interest me at the time – he was an anti. Believed racing should be banned. He seemed to be more interested in poor old Dig For Glory than he was in me.'

For a moment, there was silence in the room. Outside, a number of patients in wheelchairs were making slow progress down the drive. It was like a procession of war veterans.

'I read the piece,' Angie said eventually. 'It

mentioned your race. I thought – ' she hesitated ' –
I thought he had a point. Over two hundred horses
were killed last year – it seems a lot for a sport.'

Paul glanced at her, surprised. 'Don't tell me you're
an anti too.'

'I have an open mind.' Briefly, she had the look of
a sixth former asked to defend her position in front
of the class. 'Perhaps now's not the best time to discuss this.'

'I kept the article.' Paul wheeled himself to the
desk and leafed through the cuttings until he found
it. 'I was wondering if this man – ' he glanced at the
byline ' – Gavin Holmes – knew anything. If he's
right – and Alex wanted to stop me in that race for
some other reason – it would explain a lot. Why he
was so distracted that day. Why he was so concerned
about how I was going to ride the race.'

'Why he killed himself.'

'Could be.'

Angie took the cutting and, folding it carefully, put
it in the back pocket of her jeans. 'As your nurse,'
she said, 'my advice would be to look to the future,
not the past.'

'But you're not my nurse any more.'

'No.' She smiled and kissed Paul lightly on the lips.
'I'm not your nurse any more.'

One day, Clay Wentworth thought, he would live in
Ireland. He liked the pace of life, the sense that
nothing – not jobs, not politics nor your home life –

was quite as important as horse-racing. One day, when his father died – if his father died, he was tempted to say – he would sell up, buy some land in County Limerick, and breed horses for the rest of his life.

Leaning on the rails at Leopardstown racecourse, Clay felt at ease with the world. He was more of a countryman than his father had ever been. On the rare occasions Sir Denis Wentworth gazed at a green field, his only thoughts would be of the number of houses it could accommodate and what percentage profit the development would earn.

'Silly old fool,' Clay muttered, as the runners for the Dunraven Handicap Chase cantered past him on their way to the start. Clay was never happier than when a stretch of deep blue seawater stood between him and his father.

He respected Sir Denis, of course. He was immensely grateful for what he would give him one day. The son of a Luton warehouseman, his father had trained as an accountant, then during the 1950s he had become interested in buying and selling property. Thirteen years later, thanks to energy, enterprise and a winning way with corruptible local councillors, he had become a millionaire, one of a new generation of tough industrialists. A knighthood followed and soon, all talk of corruption and ruthlessness forgotten, Sir Denis Wentworth was a pillar of the establishment. Leaning languidly on the rails at Leopardstown, his only son could hardly resent that

– nor the considerable fortune to which he was heir.

Clay made his way from the rails to the grandstand. This was the race he had come to see and he had no intention of being jostled by over-excited Irishmen during its closing stages.

Ballina Lady was the last to go down and, taking his position, Clay followed her progress with binoculars. The publicity surrounding the mare had not been exaggerated – she was impressive-looking, a good seventeen hands and powerful with it. Although she was only six and this was her first season over fences after a successful career as a hurdler, there was an intelligence, an authority to her which suggested real class. There was a stir of interest from the crowd as she cantered down, ridden by the top Irish amateur, Tim Heaney.

It was occasions like these that made Clay aware that he was happier in a warm tweed suit, standing in the grandstand, than out on the course, the reins in his hands and half a ton of horseflesh beneath him.

Clay had been unable to resist a small bet of a hundred pounds on the second favourite. Although he knew little of its form, the prohibitive price on Ballina Lady – three to one on at the bookmaker Clay had used – had pushed out the odds of the other eight runners. On paper, the mare would have little trouble recording her fifth successive win of the season – her jumping was impeccable, the going was as she liked it and, even with a penalty from her last win, she was well handicapped.

There was a buzz of anticipation as the racecourse commentator announced that the field for the Dunraven Handicap 'chase was under orders. As the starter let them go, Clay felt the same clammy-handed expectancy that he had experienced before the race at Plumpton – only now he could enjoy it in the knowledge that today he wasn't riding in a later race.

It was clear why Ballina Lady demanded such a following from racegoers. Ears pricked, she made the running, taking lengths off the other runners at every fence. As the field passed the stand, led by some five lengths by the favourite, one or two racegoers were unable to resist applauding her as she went.

She jumped from fence to fence and seemed to take one stride for everyone else's two. At the end of the back straight for the last time, with three quarters of a mile to run, the race had become a procession, with Tim Heaney hunting the mare along easily, now some fifteen lengths to the good of her nearest contender who was fading.

As Ballina Lady rounded the final bend, with two fences to go, Clay raised the binoculars to his eyes.

Later, they said the roar of the crowd had distracted her. Others claimed that, in the split second before she took the fence, the mare had suffered a massive heart attack. She had met the fence right, Heaney riding her as strongly and confidently as ever. But then she seemed to falter, to lose her way at the last crucial moment. Instead of taking off for the fence, she crashed through it, cartwheeling before landing awkwardly on her neck on the far side. Heaney, thrown clear by the fall, lay still as the rest of the field galloped past him, then sat up on the damp ground.

Ten yards from him, the best horse he had ever ridden was not so lucky. It took one look to see that the mare would never race again. Ballina Lady had broken her neck.

Clay Wentworth lowered his binoculars. The horse he had backed had jumped the last fence well clear but Clay had forgotten about the race. He reached into the inside pocket of his jacket and took out a handwritten list. Carefully, with his gold-plated biro, he crossed out one of the names on it.

'Fucking horses.' Gavin Holmes sat slumped in front of his screen on the vast open-plan floor at the *Guardian*'s Farringdon Road office. He was tired, he needed a drink and the editor had wanted yet another update on his racing story. Yesterday, at some poxy racecourse in Ireland, another nag – apparently a good one too – had gone belly-up. There were rumours that a member of the RSPCA Executive was about to launch a campaign to ban steeplechasing. One of his stringers was trying to find out how many horses were killed in training every year.

Gavin looked at his watch. It was six o'clock and his piece was complete and on-screen. In the unlikely event of his date for the night coming up with something tasty, he could always phone it in.

Gavin, who was thirty-five but had the muscle tone and liver of a man ten years older, stood up, hitched his jeans over the beginnings of a paunch and slipped on the leather jacket that had been draped over the back of the chair. His reputation as a ladies' man surprised some of the younger journalists – he had the jowly, pallid look of a man allergic to any kind of healthy living, he dressed like a slob and he was distinctly light on romantic charm, 'Are we going to do it or what?' being one of his more subtle approaches.

He made his way to a corner office in which his news editor sat, checking copy, a cigarette dangling from his mouth.

'Checking out a lead, Harry,' he said, standing at the door. 'I'll ring in any changes to the racing piece.'

'Hope she's worth it,' said the news editor without looking up.

Gavin took the lift to the ground floor. Once upon a time, he'd enjoyed his reputation for wildness but now he was discovering that today's tearaway is tomorrow's randy old drunk. Once he had been discussed as a future foreign correspondent; of all his contemporaries, Gavin Holmes was thought most likely to land his own column – witty, informed, knowing. Instead he was still on home news and his only claim to fame was that he had bedded a healthy percentage of his young female colleagues. 'Better than nothing,' he muttered, stumbling out of the lift.

Standing outside the *Guardian* building, the

journalist patted his pockets. He had his cigarettes, he had his tape machine and, the eternal optimist, he had in his wallet a packet of condoms. Gavin smiled as he hailed a taxi. Maybe it was true what they said about girls and horses. Maybe tonight, he would get lucky.

'I don't ride horses myself. I – my boyfriend does.'

Angie felt uneasy as she sat across from the over-weight, chain-smoking journalist at a corner table in a city bar. All around her, there was noise and laughter, punctuated by the occasional pop of a champagne cork. Somehow she had found herself backed against the wall, her knees unavoidably touching those of Gavin Holmes. If she tried to move them, she had no doubt that he would misread her body language as some kind of response and move in closer.

'Tell me about him. Your lover.'

Gavin filled the two glasses in front of them with champagne, drained his glass, and refilled it. In the ten minutes since they had met, he had smoked two cigarettes, made light work of a bottle of Möet et Chandon and casually dropped the names of several politicians and actors with whom he appeared to be on first-name terms.

'He comes from the north,' Angie said. 'He's a jockey. He's brave.' Angie was unhappy at the way the discussion was going.

'Will he ride again?'

'Probably not. He can't really walk yet.'

'Poor bastard.' Gavin waved at the barman and, ignoring Angie's protests, ordered another bottle of champagne. 'Where do I come into this?' he asked.

'In your article, you mentioned a video – taken head-on at Plumpton.'

'Right. I used a contact on the racecourse staff. He gave it to me.'

A waiter brought the second bottle of champagne to the table, filled Gavin's glass and poured a polite drop into Angie's which was already full.

'I thought your friend would have wanted to see it. What does he think?' Gavin asked. 'It looked deliberate to me.'

'He thinks – ' Angie checked herself, her head was aching now from the smoke and champagne. 'He thinks there's more to it than just one jockey stopping another.'

Gavin looked at Angie with his best knowing smile. This girl was cute – very cute. Young of course, and a bit shy, but he liked that.

'So it's a favour he's asking,' he said.

'A small favour.'

Angie closed her eyes, as the journalist moved his knee up and down against hers. She decided, for Paul, to give it one more try, then to leave.

'There may be a story in this,' she said. 'A big story. Paul would give you first shot at it.'

Suppressing a belch, Gavin muttered, 'Stories – who needs fucking stories? I've got stories up to where my hair used to be. They're the last thing I need – particularly if they're anything to do with sodding horses.'

'Fine.' Angie picked her bag off the floor. 'It was just a thought.'

'On the other hand,' Gavin said quickly. 'You never know. Why don't we talk about this over dinner? Maybe we could – ' the hint of a leer entered his voice ' – work something out.'

'I have a train to catch.'

The journalist muttered, 'How about a quickie then?' Misunderstanding, Angie smiled politely. 'No, I've drunk too much already. I really ought to go.'

'I'll get you a taxi later. The paper'll pay.'

Angie tried to stand up but found her way barred.

'I think I might be able to help you with that favour,' Gavin was saying. 'Maybe two favours.'

Angie pushed back the table and, trying to ignore the hand that touched her thigh as she passed, paused briefly. 'Two favours?'

The journalist smiled. 'He can't walk, you say, your lover. Disabled. It must be tough on you. No nooky.'

Ignoring Angie's angry look, Gavin added quietly, 'I'll get you back in the morning. You and me, eh?'

She turned and walked quickly out of the bar.

The photographer sat in his BMW, some thirty yards away from the entrance to Markwick Instruments plc. He was a heavy man but the watchful look in his eyes and the slightly tanned face suggested that, should he ever be required to, he could defend himself in a tight corner. He had risen early that morning and now, at ten thirty in the evening, he looked unshaven and tired.

Peter Zametsky emerged from the front door of the office building, looked quickly left, then right, and walked towards the car. As he approached, the photographer got out, handed him the keys. The two men spoke briefly and quickly in their own language. Then the photographer crossed the road, unlocked an old Jaguar and drove off at no particular speed.

Peter sat in the BMW and spoke into the car telephone. When he had finished he drove the car towards the office building. As he approached, the metal gates that led to the office yard opened, allowing the car through.

After they had closed, a man watching from the darkness of a nearby alley walked away quickly down the gloomy side street towards the lights of Willesden.

Chapter 5

Racing likes its heroes dead and dignified, or alive and winning. It has no place for the halt and the lame. If Paul had been killed by Dig For Glory's fall at Plumpton, his tragically brief career would have been commemorated by an annual race at the course – the Paul Raven Memorial Hurdle or something similar. If he had walked away unharmed, the calls from trainers would have continued to come in. As it was, he was no more than a distant memory. In the harsh, enclosed world of racing, there's no place for fellow travellers.

It was a month after his discharge from the Home in Croydon and, on the face of it, he had much for which to be thankful. With the help of two walking sticks and occasional pain-killers, he could walk, albeit slowly and uncertainly. The doctors, whose experience had taught them to be pessimistic about back injuries, had found themselves revising their prognoses as, step by painful step, Paul proved them wrong. Those who once confidently predicted that he would never be free of his wheelchair admitted that a few, shuffled paces a day would be a possibility. When Paul walked twenty, then thirty, then fifty yards, they admitted they may have over-estimated the damage to his vertebrae. On the day he discharged himself from the Home, they warned him of the consequences but, among themselves, they were pleased to see him go. He was a difficult patient. Bloody-minded. He had never done what he had been told.

Yes, he was thankful to be away from the men in white coats, thankful to be walking slowly, still with two walking-sticks but more confidently now, down Lambourn High Street. He was home and, although he could do nothing to help in the yard, he had been allowed to stay in the small flat rented by Ron Charlesworth for his more favoured staff. This, by Charlesworth's standards, was an act of almost unprecedented generosity.

It was too early to say what he would do with his life. Angie, who visited him on her days off, believed he should get out of racing altogether, but Paul knew he couldn't. Not yet at least.

He turned into a newsagent where an elderly man handed him a *Sporting Life* with a cheery 'What do you know, Paul?'

'Not much, Bill.' Paul smiled. Like several of his friends in Lambourn, Bill Preston overcame the embarrassment of his disability by refusing to admit it existed. Every day, he was as eager for tips from Paul as if he were on his way to the races, at the centre of things, as he had been in the old days.

He took the paper and glanced at the headlines, the tips and whispers about the day's runners. No, Angie was wrong – racing was in his blood. Until he knew what had happened to Alex, it would stay there.

Paul was greeted by a couple of stable lads from Charlesworth's yard but resisted the temptation to ask them of any news. Although the trainer was making use of freelances, it could only be a matter of time before he signed up a new stable jockey. For their part, the lads seemed uneasy, hurrying on after exchanging a few pleasantries with Paul, as if his bad luck could be catching.

A dirty yellow Rolls Royce cruised down the High Street. It passed Paul, then stopped some twenty yards ahead of him. The driver had made no attempt to park, leaving the car some two feet from the kerb. A woman, blonde and in her late thirties or early forties, emerged and half walked, half ran, a fur coat billowing behind her, tripping on high heels towards where Paul stood. To his surprise, she held out an elegant hand.

'Mr Raven?'

'That's right.'

The woman smiled, perfect capped teeth gleaming behind the lipstick.

'Zena Wentworth. We haven't met.'

Guardedly, Paul hooked the walking-stick over his

arm and shook her hand. The woman's breezy confidence and cut-glass tones were not endearing. 'How can I help you?' he asked.

'It's about Alex Drew,' she said. 'I was a friend of his.' Behind her, several drivers, held up by the badly parked Rolls, were sounding their horns. 'Dickheads,' she said conversationally.

'How did you know Alex?' Paul asked.

Zena flashed another smile and glanced over her shoulder. 'The natives appear to be getting restless,' she said. 'Let me give you lunch.'

Paul thought for a moment, then nodded. 'All right,' he said. 'Let's go to a pub.'

Zena Wentworth wasn't used to pubs. Three had been rejected on the grounds of being too smoky, too common and too full of darts players before they found a hotel on the outskirts of Wantage which she found acceptable. A fast driver, she had kept up a monologue, rarely interrupted by Paul.

Half listening, while gripping the side of his seat, Paul had discovered that Zena was married to Clay Wentworth, that she had not the slightest interest in racing and that she appeared to be on first name terms with most of the well-bred wallies whose faces Paul had seen in gossip columns and glossy magazines.

It was only when they were sitting in the dining-room of the Bell Tavern, Wantage that Zena mentioned Alex Drew. Already, she had made it clear that the quiet, unpretentious atmosphere was not what she was used to, bewildering the young waitress by asking for a tequila before settling sulkily for a large vodka and tonic. When the waitress brought them the menu in a plastic folder, she had opened it, placed a hand over the typed contents and said, 'Let me guess. Steak and chips. Gammon and chips. Plaice and chips.' And she was right, of course.

After the waitress had taken their order, she lit a cigarette. 'God, I hate the countryside,' she said cheerfully. 'This is the sort of place Alex used to take me to.'

Paul watched her as the cigarette smoke caught the winter sun shining into the half empty dining-room. There was something odd about Zena Wentworth, a tension which suggested that her sophistication and worldliness were a disguise, a cover.

'How did you know Alex?' he asked again, quietly.

'Met him at a party in London,' she said vaguely. 'Usual thing. Boy meets girl. We – ' she gave him a knowing smile ' – clicked.'

'Are you telling me – ' Realising that his incredulity might be taken for rudeness, Paul hesitated. 'But he had a girlfriend.'

'Everybody has a girlfriend. And everybody cheats.'

The waitress brought the drinks. Zena raised her glass before drinking deeply. Paul sipped at his tomato juice, thinking about Alex. That his friend had been unfaithful to Joanna was hardly a surprise. But Zena Wentworth? She could have been his mother.

'What's this got to do with me?' he asked.

Zena seemed more relaxed now that she had a glass in her hand. 'I heard – a little birdy told me – that you wanted to know more about Alex's death.'

Paul nodded. For all her apparent lack of interest in racing, Zena Wentworth seemed well-informed. Over the past month, he had been ringing around his contacts, people who knew or had worked with Alex. The story had always been the same. Until the beginning of this season, Alex had been fine. Since then, as Paul had noticed himself, he had become less reliable, turning up late for work, struggling to make weights that last season would have been easy. Like Paul, no one seemed to know what his problem was. But there was something outside racing that had been distracting him. Paul had spoken to Joanna but she had seemed embarrassed by the call, as if Paul's interest was no more than a morbid obsession with the past.

'I want to know why he killed himself,' he said. 'I haven't been able to do much – I only started driving last week – but I'm convinced he was involved in something.'

'There's a little man I know who's become rather interested in Alex's story. A somewhat unsavoury journalist called Gavin Holmes. I believe you know him.'

'I know the name,' Paul said carefully. 'I wouldn't have thought he was on your circuit.'

Zena gave a contemptuous little laugh. 'He isn't, thank God. A couple of years ago he developed an interest in the scandalous use of drugs in society. Some little prig gave him my name. We developed what you might call a working relationship.' She paused, as if expecting a question. 'Like most journalists, the man's infinitely corruptible. I hadn't heard from him for a while until he called the other day. It appears that he's taking an interest in Alex. He told me that a little friend of yours had seen him.'

'Yes. He wasn't helpful.'

'Tell me why you're so interested.'

'I need to be convinced that it was an accident.'

'Did you know Alex gambled?' Zena asked suddenly.

'He didn't gamble. I'd know if he was in the pocket of the bookmakers. Stewards may not be able to tell the triers from the non-triers, but one jockey can't fool another, and believe me, he always did his best.'

'Not bookmakers. Cards. He fancied himself at stud poker, poor boy.'

'I know. He used to play with the other jockeys in the weighing room. He was quite good. How did you know he played cards?'

Picking unenthusiastically at her microwaved plaice and chips, Zena told him about the Thursday poker nights – how Alex, at first an occasional player, had over the months before his death become a regular. When Paul shook his head incredulously, she said, 'He wanted to be a grown-up, poor boy. He wanted to be one of the big guys.'

'Did he win?'

Zena shrugged. 'You should understand that, in my marriage, communication is limited to the practical. Clay would no more tell me about his poker nights than I would tell him about my... private business. I understood from Alex that he was in some difficulty. He didn't like talking about it.'

'What sort of people go to these poker nights?'

'They're either rich and bored, or on the make. The only regulars that I know of are Lol Calloway, the clapped-out rock star, and a man called Digby Welcome. I can try to get more names, if you want.' She smiled, lighting up another cigarette although Paul was still eating. 'Maybe we could work together on this.'

'The names would be useful, although I still don't see the connection between Alex's gambling and what happened at Plumpton.'

'Nor me.' Zena picked up the leather bag that she had laid beside her chair. 'I must be going. I'll see if I can find out any more for you.'

'How?'

Zena Wentworth gave a histrionic little shudder. 'I don't even want to *think* about it,' she said.

Later, driving back to London, Zena thought about Paul Raven. She had, of course, told him only part of what she knew, but the information would revive his faltering attempts to discover what had happened to Alex Drew.

She was coming down, the couple of pills she had

taken that morning to get her through the day had been nullified by the vodka. Zena accelerated, pushing the Rolls up to a hundred and ten as she fumbled in her bag. Expertly, she removed another pill from a small bottle and tossed it back into her mouth.

She smiled at the thought of Paul Raven's expression when she had left. For a man who rode horses, he was no fool. He realised what she meant. He was so young, so innocent. For him, the most simple of sexual transactions had a deep significance. Zena tried to remember what that purity had been like, but failed. It was all so long ago.

She thought of Alex, of how she and Clay, in different ways, had corrupted him and felt a fleeting pang of guilt. Yes, what she was doing was right. Paul Raven was a bonus. On the racecourse at Plumpton, he had seemed just another scrawny jockey but weeks of inaction had filled out his face. Pain and anger had made it interesting.

'Just once,' she said. 'Once is all I want.'

In America, Alice Markwick had always thought, they organized things better. If her first stop from Prague had been New York rather than London, she wouldn't have found herself dealing with bungling, weak amateurs, with the astonishing complexities of Britain's subtle class system, with the obstacles placed in her way by interfering government bureaucrats.

Behind Alice's large desk, a cold winter dusk was settling sullenly on the streets of Willesden. The workers from the factory below were making their way home, doubtless cursing her name and dreaming of a time when their futures would not be bound up with that of Markwick Instruments plc.

She didn't give a damn. Dispensing human happiness had never figured among her priorities. Once, three or four years ago, she had employed a Personnel Officer but he had disagreed with her on a matter of basic policy – as to whether to treat personnel like human beings or expendable units – and she had fired him within the month. Her firm was no place for tenderhearts.

She pulled a small white telephone on her desk, her personal line, and stabbed out a number. It was time to put a call through to the man who made even her short-lived Personnel Officer seem like a tower of strength.

'Clay,' she said. 'Alice. I hear we're in business again.'

At the other end of the telephone, Clay laughed nervously. 'Went like a dream,' he said.

'No problems at all?'

'There are one or two comments in the racing press but everyone puts it down to bad luck.'

'It's a funny old game,' said Alice flatly.

'D'you have the *Sporting Life*?'

'I'm not a regular reader, I'm afraid, Clay.'

'Let me read you their report.' There was the sound of rustling paper and Alice imagined Clay in his large office, the huge photograph behind him showing Mr

C Wentworth as he jumped the water at Kempton on Skinflint. She sighed. A captain of industry. God help England.

'Here we are,' he said finally. ' "JINX HITS CHELTENHAM HOPE . . . . The extraordinary run of bad luck that has befallen the season's contenders for the top amateur prizes continued yesterday at Huntingdon when the highly fancied Brut Force failed to finish after a bizarre accident in the Valentine Hunter Chase. The experienced nine-year-old, who started at eleven to four on, appeared to be making light work of the field of six when, after jumping superbly throughout, he entered the final turn with a ten-length lead only to fail to negotiate the bend, crashing through the stand side rails in a horrific fall. His young amateur rider Jamie Saunders, who was miraculously uninjured, was mystified by the normally reliable Brut Force's lapse. 'Until then, he hadn't put a foot wrong,' Saunders told me. 'But, as we came out of the bend, he seemed to panic and I couldn't steer him.'

' "Trainer Charlie Dixon had been mystified as to what went wrong and added that the horse appeared to have injured his back and had lacerations to his hindquarters.

' " ' Brut Force won't run again this season,' he said, 'but we hope to patch him up for next year.'

' "Brut Force is the latest of a series of horses fancied for one of the major amateur races at the

National Hunt Festival which have been forced to withdraw, after the tragic deaths over the last month of the Irish mare Ballina Lady and the crack northern 'chaser Whataparty." '

'Accidents will happen,' said Alice. 'Perhaps we should leave it there. We don't want to stretch coincidence too far.'

'One more,' Clay said briskly. 'Thursday, Wincanton. As we agreed.'

Alice sighed. 'At least there's no danger of a post mortem this time,' she said.

'Right,' said Clay. 'Are you coming to play poker this week?'

'I hope so.'

After she had hung up, Alice sat at her desk, deep in thought. True, Clay was a bungling amateur, but he was a useful bungling amateur, and expendable. After all – she glanced at the photograph of a frail-looking man that was given pride of place in the office – bungling amateurs had served her well.

Not that the late Dr Eric Markwick was an amateur in every way. As a scientist, he had been years ahead of his time. It was real life that caused him problems.

As Alice's ambitions had begun to seem realizable at last, she found herself thinking more and more of Eric. Doubtless he would have thought her plans dangerous, immoral even. His risks and gambles rarely extended beyond the theoretical and scientific; his weakness was not for money or power, but simply for Alzbeta Flaishman, an innocent little Czechoslovak girl trying to find her way in a wicked western metropolis.

Alice smiled. She must have been innocent once, when she was Alzbeta, but she really couldn't remember when. Prague during the 'fifties and 'sixties was no place for childish illusion. Her father worked in a munitions factory, spending what little he earned on vodka, occasionally venting his rage against a grey, unjust world on Alzbeta, her older brother Tomas and, above all, on her mother. Partly to earn extra money and partly to escape from the bellows and the flailing of her husband, Alzbeta's mother Irina had taken a job, cleaning government offices in the evening and late into the night.

She was beautiful. No misery could extinguish the sparkle of those dark eyes, the long dark curls, the frail but womanly body.

Their life changed. Mr Flaishman was given promotion and an honorary post in the local party. The family was able to move to a larger flat in a better part of town. Maybe, when she was seven or eight, Alzbeta might have believed that this was the way life was – you worked, you were rewarded – but there was something in her mother's eyes that told her differently, that spoke of corruption and compromise.

There was one moment that changed it all. One night – Alzbeta was just ten – word came from the local bar that old Flaishman had hurt himself, having become involved in a brawl. A neighbour had seen the fight and ran to tell Alzbeta and her brother that their father had been taken unconscious to the local hospital. Tomas had gone to the hospital while Alzbeta went through the dark streets of Prague to the Central Party offices where her mother was working.

It was ten-thirty when she arrived in the vast building. Frantically she had asked a couple of crones sweeping a downstairs corridor where she could find Mrs Flaishman. Her question had caused much hilarity, but eventually they had directed her to the top floor.

The building was five floors high, there was no lift and by the time she reached the top, she was breathless and tearful. She tried office after office, nervously opening each door in the brightly-lit warren of corridors. It seemed a lifetime but it must have been five minutes at the most when she pushed open the large door to a corner office.

The man was large and wearing the grey uniform of a senior officer in the army. His face was red and transfixed by an ugly smile, or perhaps a grimace. His fat hand, like that of a priest conferring a blessing on a communicant, lay on her mother's head as, kneeling – crouched under the pendulous bulk of the man's paunch – she worked on him, nodding like a doll with a broken neck. As Alzbeta stood there, the man tightened his grip on her mother's head, not allowing her to turn towards the door. 'Welcome, little one,' he said thickly. 'Have you come to join the party?'

She stood there for twenty seconds, perhaps thirty. Then, without a word, she had turned, rushing blindly down the corridor, almost falling down the stairs and into the icy cold night where she had run, tears streaming down her face, back to the flat.

Because everyday existence in Prague was full of such humiliations and sleazy compromises, nothing much changed among the Flaishmans after that night. Alzbeta's father recovered but, whenever the mood was upon him, would blame Irina for not visiting him in hospital that night. But then little Alzbeta had failed to find her. While old man Flaishman grumbled and Tomas mocked Alzbeta for her ineffectiveness, the two women of the family had caught one another's eye and each had looked away quickly, unwilling to acknowledge the guilty secret they shared.

When she grew up, she came to think of her mother as a heroine, abasing herself night after night, an unofficial whore, so that her family could survive. But then, with the clear, unforgiving eyes of childhood, she felt nothing but a deep sense of betrayal – of her father, of the family, above all, of her. A coldness entered the home as little Alzbeta extinguished the warmth and laughter she had once brought to it.

Seeing her mother kneeling before the soldier changed Alzbeta's life for ever. She knew, even at ten years old, that she had to get away from the family, possibly even from the country. Never political, she spent her teens begging her parents to be sent to the west to study, professing a deep interest in the ways of capitalism. An exit visa, of course, was impossible; the Flaishman family had little enough money without the expense of sending a daughter abroad.

And here was the ultimate compromise. Alzbeta knew the way things worked in Czechoslovakia. She understood that her mother could win her escape only one way, yet she asked for it. While treating her mother with cold disapproval, she accepted the rewards of whatever Irina did at the government offices into the early hours of the morning. On her eighteenth birthday, Alzbeta was given an exit visa and one hundred pounds in English money. When she cried, her father and Tomas assumed it was out of gratitude. Only Irina knew the truth.

Something else changed that night when old Flaishman got drunk and was taken to hospital. As the girl became a woman, as beautiful as her mother, with the same dark curls and slender waist, Alzbeta knew with a deep certainty that, whatever else she did, she would never make love to a man. She would lose her virginity, of course, she would use her beauty, but in submitting to men, she would be the exploiter, not the exploited. She might smile, flirt, feign desire but it would be done with a clear-eyed coolness that had nothing to do with love. The idea of being penetrated was loathsome to her; it was a foul invasion, for which she would demand, and receive, the highest price.

The heating in the offices of Markwick Instruments had been turned off, and Alice shuddered. 'Poor Eric,' she said quietly, as she tidied the papers on her desk. Poor Eric had only discovered that too late.

Turning off the lights in her office, she made her way downstairs, across the yard to the laboratory. Zametsky would be there, of course. Despite the young wife and baby whom he worshipped, Peter usually worked late, so absorbed in his work that he would hardly have noticed that the sun had set, that his colleagues had gone home. Sometimes he worked until nine or ten at night, the light in his corner cubicle shining like the beacon of pure research into the grubby gloom of Willesden.

Pure research. Alice Markwick smiled as she entered the laboratory.

'What about that poor wife of yours, Peter?' she called out as she made her way down one side of the lab, switching off work-lamps.

There was a distracted grunt from the direction of Peter Zametsky's desk. Sometimes, when she had interrupted him as he worked on a problem, stabbing at the keyboard of his computer, making swift, feverish notes on a lined pad on the desk, he had seemed in a different world, had turned to her with a look of fierce concentration, the light in his eyes fading slowly as he turned back into the dull world of reality. He should have been at a university where such intensity was regarded as normal but there again no university could give Peter Zametsky what she could offer.

Alice was about to leave the genius in his laboratory, working for the good of human knowledge and Markwick Instruments – though not necessarily in that order – when she noticed through the frosted glass of his corner office, that he appeared not to be sitting on his chair. Then she saw a foot, trembling slightly, obtruding from the office.

He was lying on his back, his legs awry and his hands palm downwards on the floor, clawing at it. His shirt appeared to have burnt around the chest and neck but Peter's head was hidden behind the desk. As Alice stepped, his body shook epileptically. Then she saw his face – or, at least, what remained of his face under the bubbling, suppurating purple surface that had once been his flesh. The eyes were gone, the nose was no more than a white bone extending from a featureless mass. His hair, like the carpet beneath his head, had been burnt away, but the mouth – a lipless, gaping cavern – was open in a silent scream of pain.

Alice stepped back. She took a deep breath, swaying slightly. Then she walked quickly to a nearby telephone, stabbing three digits quickly. Her voice, when it came, had only the hint of a tremor.

'Ambulance,' she said.

Digby Welcome was asleep in his deep and comfortable single bed when the call came through. He had had a busy day – a full five hours work on the daytime job, followed by a late evening trawl among his Kensington contacts, and he was tired. As his head touched the pillow, he was off, enjoying the profound, untroubled sleep of a man with no conscience.

'Is it a bad moment?' The voice at the other end

of the telephone was Clay Wentworth's. He sounded more than usually rattled.

Digby looked at the leather-cased alarm clock by his bed. 'Two thirty in the morning is always a bad moment, dear boy.' He sat up in his bed and switched on the light. In his well-cut flannel pyjamas covering his globe-like stomach, he looked almost cuddly. 'But I'm not fucking anyone, if that's what you mean.'

'We have a problem. Alice's senior boffin appears to have been attacked. She's spitting – thinks there's been some sort of security leak.'

'Bloody fool. Why does she think that has anything to do with us?'

'It appears she's had her suspicions for some time. She rang me a few days ago about some taxman snooping around. She had managed to convince herself that he was part of the opposition. Just turned up out of the blue, claiming to have made an appointment through a female secretary.'

'I thought she only employed male secretaries.'

'Precisely. Then this chap Zametsky had told her that he thought the offices were being watched – cars parked across the road and so on. Next thing she knows the guy's had some sort of acid splashed over him.'

'Oh shit.' It was an utterance of vague annoyance, like that of a man finding he hasn't a clean shirt in the morning.

'She's managed to keep the police out of it. Luckily the acid came from the Markwick stores so she managed to persuade the doctors that it was an accident. Anyway, I promised her I'd ring round. You haven't been talking have you, Digby?'

'Don't be absurd. I may not be good for much but my discretion's phenomenal. Have you tried Lol?'

'He said the same thing.'

'Zena? No one could be less discreet than your wife when she's on the stuff.'

Clay Wentworth gave a humourless laugh. 'She knows nothing about this.'

'Well then.' Digby yawned, running a hand over his large stomach. 'No problem. Probably Alice getting the jitters. You know how she is. What about her chap – the one with the acid? Has he said anything?'

'He's in intensive care. Alice seems to think that he won't make it.'

'Poor bastard,' said Digby cheerily, promising to see Clay at Wincanton.

'Yes, poor bastard,' he muttered after Clay had hung up, but he was thinking of himself now. He was awake, his fat frame full of an unmistakeable restlessness for which there was only one known cure. He reached into a drawer in the bedside table, taking out a small black book. He found a number and dialled.

Chapter 6

It was a long, painful walk from the car park at Wincanton to the weighing-room. Even now that he had graduated from two walking-sticks to one, Paul could shuffle only slowly, and with many rests. Then there was the pain: in spite of Angie's protests, he had weaned himself off painkillers, determined, in an obscure, unmedical way, to fight his handicap on his own terms.

There was another kind of pain. It was Paul's first return to a racecourse after his fall at Plumpton and he had to endure the sympathy and covert, sideways looks of those who had known him when he was fit and on the way up. A few pretended not to notice him and hurried by, but most of them – particularly the trainers and jockeys – paused to talk to him, their voices unusually loud and hearty, their eyes betraying embarrassment, fear and, worst of all, pity.

Angie helped. She walked beside him slowly, with the easy amble of one who's happy to take her time.

She asked him questions about racing – innocent daft questions that, had they been asked by anyone else, Paul would have found irritating. It was the first time she had been racing and her clothes – a light girlish dress, a beret on her head, a bright green scarf wrapped around her neck – gave her away. Paul glanced at her and smiled. She looked sexy, fashionable, and desirable. On the whole, people who came racing at Wincanton in February were none of these things.

'You look good,' he said quietly, as they made their way onto the course.

'I'm not sure I approve of all this. I might stage an anti-racing demo in the paddock.'

Paul laughed. 'That would be the end of a beautiful friendship,' he said.

'Bloody hell, I thought you were crook, Raven.' The unmistakeable, booming tones of Ginnie Matthews interrupted their conversation.

Paul stopped, leaning briefly on his walking-stick, as the trainer sized him up, as if he were one of her charges after a spot of work. 'Not finished yet, Mrs Matthews.'

Ginnie glanced at Angie. 'So I see,' she said, introducing herself to Angie with a smile. 'Better go and see my fella at the stables. How about a drink later? Catch up on the news.'

'That would be good.' Paul smiled. For all her bluff heartiness, Ginnie Matthews was one of the few trainers who wouldn't make him feel uneasy. 'Just the one runner today?'

'Skinflint. We should win the amateur race.'

'Tanglewood's useful.' Ginnie dropped her voice to what she assumed was an undertone but still made nearby heads turn. 'Which is more than could be said for our jockey.'

'Who's the jockey?' Angie asked, after Ginnie had left.

'A man called Clay Wentworth,' said Paul. 'It was his wife who came to see me.'

'Small world.'

'Yes. Everybody knows everybody else's secrets.'

'Which should make it easier to find out what happened to Alex.'

'Let's hope so.'

Paul took Angie to the bar where he bought her a drink and found her a quiet table. 'I'm going to the weighing-room,' he said. 'I need to talk to someone. I'll be back in a few minutes.' Then, seeing the look of uneasiness that crossed Angie's face, he added, 'Don't worry. It's one of life's golden rules – no one gets picked up at Wincanton.'

Angie looked around the bar, where men and women were earnestly discussing the day's racing. Apart from the occasional, distracted glance in her direction she might have been invisible. 'Don't be long,' she said.

It was strange re-entering the weighing-room, leaning on a stick, a bystander to the day's action. Already, Paul felt an outsider. Although the official at the door, who was only supposed to admit jockeys riding that day, had nodded him through, there was a hint of sympathy to his smile; there was no mistaking the warmth of the greetings given to him by his fellow jockeys and by the valets but here, for the first time, in the smell of cigarette smoke, linament and saddle soap, he became aware of the void that would be left in his life now that he was unable to ride any more. Suddenly he was an outsider, a hanger-on, a has-been.

'You look better than ever, Pauly.' Jim Wilson sat down beside him during the brief lull that followed the jockeys for the first race trooping out of the weighing-room. 'If it weren't for that stick, I'd be laying out your gear as if nothing had happened.'

Paul smiled. 'And I'd be getting into it. I can't get used to this spectator lark.'

'When will you be back? End of the season?'

'They don't know.' Paul looked away. He wasn't in the mood to discuss his future. 'Tell me what the lads have been saying about Alex.'

'Lex.' The valet wiped his hands with the cloth he was carrying. It was an odd, uncharacteristic action and he suddenly seemed older and more fragile than his years. Alex, Paul remembered, had been one of Jim's favourite jockeys. 'Now there's a thing for you.'

'Someone must have an idea what made him do it.'

'He was in a bad way. We all knew that. Even before – ' Jim hesitated ' – even before Plumpton, he had been acting strange. But you know how he was, he'd keep on joking, never letting on what was really happening.'

'Bookies?'

'No. I asked around. He didn't bet – at least no more than any of the lads did. I have a feeling it was something to do with his life outside racing.'

'I saw the head-on of our race at Plumpton,' Paul said quietly. 'There's no doubt that he was up to something.'

'You mean he put you through the wing.'

'Let's just say he could have given me more room.'

'I can't understand it. He was your mate.'

'Nor can I. But if he did put me through the wing and then thought that I'd never walk again, it could explain why . . .' Ambushed by obscene imaginings of his best friend, Paul stared ahead in silence.

'I saw him alone in the car park that day. Then one of the lads said he was talking to Digby Welcome near the Members' Bar.'

'Welcome?' Paul was incredulous. 'That bastard offered me two grand to stop a horse at Lingfield once. What would Alex want with him?'

For a moment, the two men sat in silence, thinking of Alex Drew. Then Jim stood up. 'Is it a good idea, this?' he asked. 'Maybe you should be thinking about your own future, rather than digging around in the past.'

'I'll have plenty of time for that.'

'Better get on, Pauly.'

'Let us know if you hear anything, right?'

117

Jim nodded. 'I'll do some asking round,' he said.

Angie had always considered herself an easygoing, gregarious sort of person who could adapt to most social environments. A couple of years ago, her father had taken her to Henley where she had smiled her way through a tiresome afternoon of straw hats and champagne without too much difficulty. One of her first boyfriends had been obsessed by grand prix racing – hours at Silverstone spent jostled by men in sheepskin coats with their willowy girlfriends against a background of screaming engines had posed no problem. A passing-out parade at Sandhurst, a *thé dansant* at the Savoy, a fashion show in aid of Africa's starving millions, an acid house party in a disused hangar off the M25 – Angie had endured them all with the same sweet tolerance.

But National Hunt racing on a Thursday, particularly now that Paul had left her on her own while he visited old friends, was proving to be a trial. Wherever she went, she felt eyes following her, as if no one young and well-dressed had ever been seen here before.

In the bar, she had been ignored until two men in officer issue overcoats had, after a languid enquiry in her direction which she had failed to understand, sat down at her table to conduct a hearty conversation about breeding and bloodstock. Occasionally one of the men had glanced at her with undisguised suspicion so that eventually, feeling like a spy, she had left the table and stood at the bar to wait for Paul.

There was only one group of racegoers, Angie decided, that belonged to a world that she recognized or understood. Some ten yards away from her was a table already laden with champagne bottles. Two women – one dark and with her back to her, the other a jaded blonde who was doing most of the talking – sat across the table from a long-haired man, whose face seemed vaguely familiar to Angie, and a red-faced, pot-bellied character whose glittering little eyes darted around the bar-room as if looking for someone he recognized.

It occurred to Angie that, despite the ease with which they were working their way through the champagne, these people, like her, were outsiders.

'Hullo, darling. Come 'ere often, do you?'

Angie turned, her social defences at the ready, to see Paul, smiling.

'Thank God you're back,' she said, laughing uneasily.

'What happened to your table?'

'I was joined by two middle-aged men who started talking about sex.'

'Sex? At Wincanton?'

'Between horses.'

Paul laughed. 'That's all right then.' He told her about the conversation with Jim Wilson. 'I need to see one or two people. Then we'll have that drink with Ginnie Matthews and be off.'

Angie looked away. 'I don't like being the little

woman, Paul,' she said quietly but firmly. 'It's not my style.'

'Give me until after the second race. Why not get away from these idiots and go onto the racecourse. Stand by a fence. You can find out whether racing's as cruel as you think.'

Reluctantly, she agreed. Sometimes these days she wondered about Paul Raven. The icy, almost obsessive determination that had helped him out of the wheelchair onto his feet was praiseworthy enough, but he could be cold. Nothing would stand in the way of his need to find out what happened to Alex. The desire for revenge was there, at the centre of Paul's life; perhaps, Angie thought now, not for the first time, it excluded the potential for love.

'Talk of the devil.' Paul was looking across the room to the party of two men and two women that Angie had noticed.

'Which devil is that?' she asked quietly.

'A man called Digby Welcome. Sitting with Zena Wentworth, the blonde woman on his left.'

'Wasn't she the one who came to see you?'

'Aye.' Paul smiled as Zena looked in his direction but she pointedly ignored him. 'But it seems she's forgotten me already.'

So, with a reluctance that she hoped was obvious even to Paul, Angie agreed to watch a race by herself and made her way to join a small crowd of spectators and photographers standing in the centre of the course by the last fence. She looked at her racecard.

Twelve horses were running, including Skinflint, the horse Paul had discussed with the hearty woman trainer. Its owner-rider was Mr Clay Wentworth.

Angie shivered slightly in her light overcoat. At least she had an interest in one of the runners.

It's not easy to follow a man when you can hardly walk, and Digby Welcome, despite his bulk, moved with the sprightly gait of the school fat boy heading for the tuck shop. Briefly Paul had considered asking Angie to tail him but he knew that was impossible. Besides he had something to tell Welcome in person.

After he had seen Angie making her way onto the course, he returned to the bar, just in time to see Digby pushing back his chair. 'Time for a little punt,' he said, patting Zena Wentworth on the shoulder, and scuttling off.

Slowly, Paul followed in the direction that he had gone, watching the broad back as it was engulfed by the crowd of racegoers who were making their way to the Silver Ring to put on their bets before the second race. Although he couldn't stay with him, Paul noted the name of the bookmaker, Bert Lomax, at whose stand Digby placed a bet. Then he turned and made his way back to the bar.

Paul played his own small gamble. Digby had consumed a fair amount of champagne. Even that fat gut would need relief sometime. Pushing his way through a door marked 'Gents', Paul selected a cubicle and waited.

There was no mistaking the approach of Digby Welcome. He wheezed like a tired steam engine approaching a station. Paul heard the sound of a zip being undone and a heavy sigh, before silently drawing back the bolt.

It was perfect. There was no one else there but Digby, his little legs apart, humming to himself, enjoying the moment of relief.

Paul turned his walking stick upside down, swung it back in an easy golf swing, and brought the heavy curved handle up sharply between Digby's legs.

It wasn't a scream of pain, or a gasp – it was the surprised yelp of a brutalized puppy. Digby collapsed, his face sliding down the urinal before he lay on the ground clutching at himself, his normally flushed face drained of colour.

Recovering his balance Paul took the handle of his walking-stick, placed its point on the side of Digby's neck and leaned forward, pinning him to the ground.

'Not me,' Digby managed to say, his eyes squeezed shut with pain and fear.

'Get in the toilet,' Paul said with quiet urgency.

'Wha – ? Wha – ?'

'Get your fat arse off the ground and into the cubicle.'

'Can't . . . move.'

Paul jabbed the end of his stick and Digby gave another little yelp as he dragged himself towards the cubicle.

There was wetness down the front of his trousers.

122

'For fuck's sake, put yourself away,' Paul muttered following him. 'Sit on the seat.'

Digby opened his eyes now and shook his head as he scrambled miserably onto the seat of the lavatory. 'There's been some mistake,' he whispered.

Outside, there was the sound of voices approaching. Paul closed the door of the cubicle, holding up a warning finger to Digby. They heard voices outside, two men discussing the amateur race. By the time they had left, a mottled unhealthy colour had returned to Digby's cheeks and he was breathing more easily.

'Would you care to explain why you've assaulted me, Mr Raven?' he said with a feeble attempt to retain his dignity.

'No.' Paul held his stick to Digby's neck, pushing him back against a pipe behind him. 'Tell me what you know about Alex Drew.'

'Racing. I used to see him racing.'

Paul jabbed the walking-stick. 'Friends, were you?'

The normal look of evasive cunning had returned to Digby's eyes. He was no hero but, now that the throbbing pain in his groin was receding, he could see that a man with a walking-stick – a man who had difficulty walking – was hardly in a strong position.

'We met occasionally,' he said. 'And unless you let me out of here, I'll report you to the stewards.'

Paul laughed. 'Get me warned off, will you? Excessive use of the walking-stick?' He lowered his voice.

'I know things about you that would destroy you. I just need information.'

'Alex wasn't the saint you seem to think he was.'

'Go on.'

'He couldn't keep his hands off women. He was addicted to it.'

Paul shrugged. 'People don't kill themselves for getting too much sex. Was he stopping horses for you?'

'Not his own. He was too ambitious for that.' Digby took the point of the walking-stick and, with an ironic wince, pushed it slightly aside.

Slowly lowering the stick, Paul asked, 'So he gambled, right?'

Digby Welcome nodded, as he attempted fussily to adjust his clothing.

'I don't understand why having the occasional punt on a horse should have destroyed him.'

Checking in his top pocket, Digby took out a betting-slip as if to reassure himself it was still there, then returned it to the pocket. 'Punt?' he managed a pained smile. 'It wasn't horses. It was poker – stud poker.'

Paul reached into Digby's top pocket and examined the betting-slip. 'Got a good thing for the next race, have we?'

The fat man swallowed hard. 'Steal that,' he said quietly, 'and you won't have heard the last of it.'

'Mmm.' Paul examined the slip. 'Sounds like a very good thing – but I'll resist the temptation. Jockeys aren't allowed to bet.' He pulled back the bolt behind him and backed out of the cubicle. Holding the betting-slip before him, he tore it up, throwing the pieces into the next-door toilet and flushing it away.

Hearing the rushing water, Digby darted into the cubicle in a doomed attempt to retrieve the slip. His hands wet he turned red-faced to where Paul was standing. 'You don't know what you've started, Raven,' he said.

Paul smiled coldly. 'I'd tidy yourself up before you go back to the Members' Bar,' he said. 'You've got piss in your hair.'

The crowd was thinning as Paul made his way down to the Silver Ring. Glancing down the course, he could see the runners and riders, circling around the starter in the last moments before the 'off'.

Although unlike many jockeys, Paul had always considered betting too risky a way of supplementing his income to justify breaking the rules of racing, he had a nodding acquaintance with the bookmakers whose pitches were frequently on courses where he was riding.

Bert Lomax was one of the old school. A small hunched man with the lined, expressive face of a lugubrious music-hall comedian, he rarely smiled and, when he did, it was while the rest of the world was cursing. An odds-on favourite that broke its leg, a housewife's choice going arse over tit at the first fence in the Grand National – these were moments when there would be the faintest trace of facial movement around the fat cigar Bert invariably smoked. 'Lovely job,' he would say before his features settled back, into impassivity, like mud disturbed by a passing gumboot.

'Wounded hero, is it?' Bert Lomax glanced at Paul as he approached. 'When you going to start riding again, Paul? We need a few more beaten favourites.'

'Thanks, Bert,' Paul smiled. 'I knew I could count on you for a few encouraging words.'

Bert puffed at his cigar without removing it from his lips. 'Bloody shame it was,' he said. 'Bloody diabolical.'

Paul looked at the bookmaker's board. In the field of eight for The Gentleman Jim Handicap 'chase for Amateur Riders, two horses – Skinflint and Tanglewood – were joint favourites at six to four. Punters had seemed to give the other runners little chance, the next most fancied horse being Drago's Pet at six to one.

'Busy?' Paul asked.

'Not bad for a bumper,' Bert said. 'Lot of late money for Tanglewood.'

'Nice horse,' Paul said. 'I rode it once in a novice hurdle. I always thought it would make a chaser.'

There was a scurry of activity as the racecourse commentator announced that the field was under orders. As Bert had said, most of the money seemed to be going on Tanglewood. 'They're off.' Bert wiped the chalked prices off his board and stepped down from the small ladder on which he had been standing.

'Did Digby Welcome have a bet with you?'

'Yeah, the fat bastard.' All the bookmakers knew Digby and most disliked him. 'Had to lay it off too. He had three grand on that Skinflint and a couple of ton on Drago's Pet. He must be flush. Tight bastard usually. Fancy Tanglewood, do you?'

'Don't know about that.' Paul smiled at the bookmaker. 'They've all got a chance until the tapes go up.'

He made his way slowly back to the grandstand. If he had been a betting man, he would have ventured a few bob on Tanglewood, the big bay he saw bobbing along the outside of the field as they jumped the fence in front of the stand. Although he was held on form by Skinflint, he had two great advantages over him: a pull of eight pounds in the handicap, and the fact that he wasn't being ridden by Clay Wentworth.

With mild interest, Paul watched the runners as they wheeled right-handed into the country. Wentworth was easy to spot – he was the one standing up in the stirrups like a policeman directing children across the road. Even two hundred yards away the man exuded incompetence.

There were even more people at Wincanton than usual, local racegoers having been tempted by the bright, wintry weather and the prospect of seeing several fancied candidates for the big prizes at Cheltenham running for the last time before the National Hunt festival. Paul trained his binoculars on the second last fence where Angie stood in a small group of spectators, a splash of colour against the grey and brown.

Maybe she would learn to like racing, discover that there was more to it than small men lacerating horses with their whips, more than broken bones and heart-break. Paul smiled. She had been nervous about coming. She'd embarrass him, she had said – use the wrong terms, say the wrong things, she would be an outsider. As if that mattered.

The field was strung out on the far side of the course. As happened so often with amateurs, the early pace had been too fast, and already the horses or jockeys who needed the race were losing touch. With a mile to go, one of the outsiders, thirty lengths behind the field, tumbled wearily over a fence, unseating its jockey as if protesting against the whole absurd business. Tanglewood had moved closer to the leaders but was still a couple of lengths behind Skin-flint who, in spite of Wentworth's worst efforts, was gaining ground with every fence.

At least, Paul thought, the face that Angie saw at close quarters from the racecourse was unlikely to reveal the sport's harsher face. There was a gentility about the way amateurs rode: most of them lacked the killer instinct that caused crashing falls over the final fences, and excessive use of the whip was beyond their area of capability. Amateurs of the type Alex Drew had been were rare. Of those riding in this race, only Bill Scott, the young farmer's son who was on Tanglewood, had any hope of turning professional.

Of course, Jim Wilson was right. The obsession with Alex's death, with the past, could lead him nowhere. A sensible man would weigh his assets – youth, a passable brain, a loyal girlfriend – against his liabilities – the small matter of a broken body – and look to the future. Acting the avenging angel, he risked losing more than he had already lost.

Four horses were left in it with a chance. Snow Leopard, a big grey who had made all the running and whose lead had been narrowed to a couple of lengths, Drago's Pet who was being tracked by Tanglewood and Skinflint. Distracted by thoughts of Alex, Paul trained his binoculars on the leading group as they took the turn into the straight.

It was one of the favourites' race, that was for sure. Although Skinflint was going the easier, Clay Wentworth seemed intent on making the cardinal error of riding against one horse in particular. Glancing across at Bill Scott on Tanglewood, he pushed Skinflint half a length up so that he was challenging Drago's Pet. The grey was now falling back as if he had decided that two and three quarter miles was quite far enough to gallop at racing speed.

As they entered the straight, Paul found himself watching Clay Wentworth. Every few strides, he glanced back, taking Skinflint wider and wider of the bend, as if inviting Bill Scott to challenge him on the inner. Sensibly, Scott had followed Skinflint so that, as they approached the third last fence, the two favourites were on the stand side, leaving Drago's Pet to approach the fence on the inner. The crowd in the grandstand stirred in surprise and some amusement. There was no reason for jockeys to take the long way home – the going was good on both sides of the course – and for the leaders to be dividing, leaving ten yards of course between them, was inexplicable.

'Prats,' Paul muttered to himself as he watched Clay bump uneasily over the second last fence. There was no doubt in his mind that, barring accidents, Bill Scott had his race won – Tanglewood had a fair turn of foot while Skinflint's jockey would be nothing but a handicap in a tight finish. He was watching the two favourites so closely that at first when he heard the gasp from the stands, he thought something had happened to one of the backmarkers. Then he trained his binoculars down the fence. Drago's Pet lay motionless on the landing side; his jockey had rolled under the rails but at least he was conscious.

Paul lowered the binoculars. The spectators by the fence had backed away but he could see the slash of green that was Angie.

He had started shuffling towards the fence by the time Tanglewood and Skinflint passed the post. It had been a closer race than Paul had anticipated, Skinflint having put in a stupendous leap at the last, but on the run-in the wild efforts of Clay Wentworth, which defied all laws of rhythm and gravity, had pulled the horse back and Tanglewood, ridden coolly with hands and heels by Bill Scott, had stolen the race. Even pulling up, Clay conspired to look inept, looking over his shoulder as if to see how and where he had managed to lose the race he should have won.

Angie stood before him, having run across the course towards the grandstand. She looked pale and was breathing heavily. Paul wanted to say something, to explain that falls as heavy as that of Drago's Pet were unusual in racing but words seemed inadequate.

'Can we go?' she said quietly.

Peter was lost in a nightmare of pain and darkness.

He knew little beyond the fact that he was in hospital, that his skin was on fire and that he was afraid. The morphine they gave him induced wild, technicolour dreams but slowly the memory of how he came to be here became clearer, like a ship of death, looming through the fog.

Twice they had changed the bandages on his face and his hands, and the black before his eyes had changed to a dark and muddy yellow but, beyond that, he had no sense of time. At least, they had left gaps in the bandages so that he could hear the sound of the hospital – the muttered consultations of the doctors, the chatter of the nurses, the soothing tones who had visited him three times, the cries of fear of the baby which gave the only clue to how he looked.

No policemen. That surprised him.

Once he had tried to communicate with Klima to tell her what happened but his words come out as a rattle, behind an eerie monotone. He had moved his chin but felt only pain where his lips should have been.

'Another visitor, Peter,' the sing-song voice of one of the nurses interrupted his thoughts. 'You're popular today.'

He turned his head slowly in the direction of the voice. Klima had just left. The Markwick woman was unlikely to call. The police – it had to be the police at last.

'It's your brother,' said the nurse. 'Come to see how you're getting on.'

'Poor old Peter. You look like an Egyptian mummy.'

'Not too long,' warned the nurse. 'He's still very weak.'

Peter raised an arm feebly, as the nurse with a cheery 'I'll leave you lads together, then,' left the room. He heard the squeak of her rubber soles as they receded down the corridor.

'So how are we, Bruv?'

Breathing heavily, Peter let his head fall back against the pillow. He was beyond fear, yet his heart thumped painfully in his chest. Helpless, he listened to the voice of a stranger.

'As it happens, we didn't want this,' the man said. 'When I asked a friend of mine to lend me a spot of acid, I thought he'd give me the stuff they put in car batteries.'

The man paused, as if expecting Peter to interrupt.

'I had no idea that it would take your whole fucking face off.'

Peter struggled to remember where he had heard that voice before. It was villainous, plausible and would have suited a new-style City broker as easily as it would a bank robber.

'Still, look on the bright side, eh? At least this way we know where we stand. You've got what we want and you're going to tell us how to get it. We want to deal with you, not Alice. She can be so unreasonable.'

There was the slightest pull on the drip leading into his arm. The man, he was sure now, was trying to cut the supply of morphine which kept the waves of pain at bay.

'So you get well soon, eh? I'll be back as soon as you're talking.'

'Don't touch the drip, please.' The nurse's voice, as she returned, was brisk.

'I thought it wasn't working,' the stranger said. 'I can't bear to think of my brother in pain.'

The nurse dropped her voice. 'I think you'd better go,' she said. 'He gets very tired.'

'Right.' The man stood up. 'I'll be off, Bruv.' Then from the direction of the door. 'I'll give Klima your love. I plan to visit her soon. Family's got to stick together, hasn't it?'

After the man had gone, the nurse turned to the bed. Peter seem disturbed, upset. He kept making that odd, keening sound though his lipless mouth, almost as if he were trying to tell her something.

She checked his drip once more and straightened his sheets. Poor man. He would be unrecognizable when the bandages came off, but he would never be able to see that horror his featureless face would cause in others. Sad because, if he had been anything like his brother, he must have been a good-looking man before the accident.

Still, at least he had a family to look after him.

It had not been a successful day. Paul had hoped that Angie would be won over by the atmosphere and excitement of a Saturday's racing. Instead, her worst prejudices had been confirmed by a horse turning over at speed only yards from where she had been standing.

They drove back to Lambourn in silence. Angie was still distracted by what she had seen and Paul's back ached from the hours spent standing up. Doubtless the tussle with Digby Welcome had hardly helped.

He parked the car beside her Mini on the street outside his flat. Remembering that she was working on the early shift at the hospital, he asked, 'D'you want to go home?'

'Not yet.'

'I can offer you supper. Frozen chicken pie à la Raven.'

She smiled and he saw that she was sad, not angry. 'My favourite,' she said.

There was a tension between them that evening.

They talked little, like a married couple who had fought and were carefully choosing topics of conversation in which there was no risk of renewed hostilities.

After they had eaten in the kitchen, they sat on each side of the open fire, Paul nursing a whisky while Angie, who had seen too many road crash victims to risk a drink when she was driving later, sipped a cup of coffee.

'I spoke to Digby Welcome today,' Paul said eventually. 'A friend of mine had told me that Alex had some connection with him.'

'What's he? A jockey?'

Paul smiled. 'Hardly. He's the sort of character you find on the fringe of racing. Part fixer, part crook. A hanger-on.'

'Doesn't seem Alex's type.'

'Alex was a good jockey, but he was no angel. He wanted to be in the fast set – parties, girls, his face in the gossip columns. Whenever he had a spare moment, he would be into his car and up to London. He wanted me to come but I couldn't live like that.'

'And that's how he knew this Welcome man.'

'Everybody knows Digby Welcome. If you're sensible, you keep your distance. There's a corruption about him that's catching.'

Angie found herself thinking of Gavin Holmes, the journalist. 'I know that type,' she said.

'I asked him whether Alex was in trouble with the bookmakers. He said something strange – something

135

about stud poker. That Wentworth woman mentioned poker too. When I asked if he had stopped horses, he said, "Not his own." '

'Which would confirm your suspicions about your race. You think he had been told to stop you.'

Paul stared into the fire. 'I don't understand it. When a jockey's been got at, there's gambling involved. Yet at Plumpton, there was nothing unusual in the betting pattern; I checked with the Betting Officer – no late support for Freeze Frame, Alex's horse. More importantly, Dig For Glory's price never drifted. It seemed that everybody thought I'd win.'

For a moment, Angie watched as he poked at the fire, the glow lighting up his dark eyes. She wanted to go to him, to hold him and tell him that nothing could come of this obsession with his friend's death, but something held her back. 'You're really hooked now, aren't you?' she said.

Without a word, Paul stood up and, with some difficulty made his way to the telephone. He dialled a number.

'Mrs Matthews,' he said. 'Paul Raven. Sorry I couldn't make that drink. My... back was playing up a bit . . . Yes, some other time. Sorry about Skinflint. Thought you were a bit unlucky there.' He laughed quietly. 'He's no Lester Piggot in a finish that's for sure.' Angie heard the raised tones of Ginnie Matthews as she enlarged, with a string of obscenities, on the performance of Clay Wentworth as a jockey. 'Somebody told me he was a bit of a poker player,'

Paul added casually. 'They asked me if I wanted to join some sort of gambling party.' He listened for a minute or so before saying, 'Aye, perhaps you're right, Mrs Matthews. Bit out of my league.'

After he had hung up, Paul turned to Angie. 'Wentworth has a poker evening once a week. High stakes. You need to be invited.'

'What's that got to do with Alex?'

'A couple of times I've seen Welcome with Clay Wentworth. It would explain how Alex knew Zena. If I could get into the poker circle, maybe I could find out what was going on.'

'School. It's a poker school.'

Paul smiled. 'Don't tell me you're an expert.'

'I know a bit.' Angie gave a self-mocking woman-of-the-world smile. As she looked up at him, Paul noticed that the top button of her blue dress, so wrong for Wincanton and so right for now, had come undone revealing a pale throat, the shadow of a breast. 'It was about all I learned at school.'

'Will you teach me?'

'While you were making that telephone call in the middle of our conversation – ' smiling, she held up a hand to stop his interruption ' – I reached two decisions. The first was that I'm leaving the hospital. If you're serious about finding out what happened to Alex, you're going to need help. I'll do agency work – it's better paid and I can work the hours I want.'

Paul looked at her in amazement. 'Angie, that's crazy. You don't have to do that for me.'

'It's not for you, it's for me.'

'And the second decision?'

'Ah, that.' Angie looked away and Paul thought he could see a heightened colour in her cheeks. 'For the second decision I'll need a drink.'

'But you're driving. What about – ?'

'That's the second decision.' Angie turned to him solemnly, her lips slightly parted. 'Tonight I'm not driving anywhere.'

It wasn't how she had imagined it. In her fantasies, she had imagined a powerful man, his heavy weight on her. She had expected fear and pain with the pleasure.

Instead, when she came to Paul's bed, her athletic body caught by the lamplight from the street outside, his body dark and taut against the white sheets, she was the seducer, the conqueror.

'You realise you're going to have to do this,' Paul said quietly.

'That's what nurses are for,' she said, and she knew as she caressed his body with her hands and her lips that this, all along, was how she had wanted it. Her fears of doing the wrong thing, the last vestige of shyness, disappeared as she made love to him, gasping more with pleasure than pain, when she lowered herself onto him, sighing with relief, and gentle aching desire, her days of waiting for the right man, for Mr Right, over at last. The girls had never told her that at the end, she would cry with happiness.

Afterwards they lay together for several minutes.
'Where did you learn all that?' Paul asked at last.
   'I learned that at school too.'
   And, in the semi-darkness, they both laughed.

Chapter 7

There were some virtues left within the soul of Gavin Holmes; not honesty, or industry, or fidelity – which he had outgrown within his first year on Fleet Street – but he still had one quality in which he took a certain amount of pride. He never bore a grudge against a woman who had refused to sleep with him.

In this, he was unusual. Most of his male colleagues would express their frustration and guilt by spreading unpleasant rumours about the woman who failed to be attracted by them. Not Gavin – he almost admired someone who had the spirit to reject him. From that moment on, she moved out of the sexual arena to become something else – a friend, a rival, a person. Oddly enough, he had more difficulty with the ones he *had* slept with, who either wanted to do it again when he would rather forget the whole thing, or if he did happen to fancy a spot of auld lang syne, pretended nothing had ever happened. That was another point in his favour – he never forgot the face of someone he had taken to bed, however drunk he had been at the time, however messy and unfortunate the subsequent experience.

'In fact, I'm full of fucking virtues,' Gavin muttered to himself, sitting in the wine bar where his blundering attempt to seduce the O'Keefe girl had gone so wrong. Yet here he was, waiting for her again – only this time she was bringing her boyfriend.

A story, she had said. Gavin drank deeply at the glass of wine in front of him. They always had a story.

'Not more gee-gees, please,' he had said, when little Angie O'Keefe had rung him at the office.

'We think we have something which could interest you. About the death of a jockey. It's confused but we think Clay Wentworth's involved.'

He had asked a few more questions, the answers to which had faintly quickened his interest. Money seemed to be involved. Maybe even sex. The equestrian element had seemed to be mercifully small.

Angie had asked him about a man called Digby Welcome and, after an hour of punching up a selection of old stories from the information service database, he had become more confident. Yes, it was distinctly possible there was a story here.

'Gavin, this is Paul.'

The journalist looked up from his drink, and there was Angie, her hand resting gently on the arm of a dark, good-looking man carrying a walking-stick.

'Hi, Paul.' Gavin extended a hand, nodding curtly in the direction of his legs. 'How's it coming on?'

'Not bad,' Angie laughed as she drew up a chair for Paul.

'According to the doctors, he should still be in a wheelchair.'

She was hardly recognizable as the pale, edgy girl whom Gavin remembered. There was an openness about her, a warmth in the eyes that seemed entirely new. 'What's his secret cure?' he asked, a hint of irony in his voice. Nothing made Gavin more nervous than young love. It made him feel his years. Angie blushed, looking at Paul as if the question were absurd.

After a waitress had brought two more glasses, and Gavin had poured, he said 'Okay then, what's the story?'

Paul looked across the table with an unnervingly direct gaze.

'First,' he said, 'tell us what you know about Digby Welcome.'

It took a lot to rattle him. Over the years, after more tumbles and setbacks than most men were forced to endure in a lifetime, Digby had learned to roll with the punches.

Some five miles west of the bar where his chequered career was being discussed, he sat in a restaurant at his usual table, eating his usual meal and wondered how best to discourage Paul Raven. Contacts, of course – Digby had plenty of those. Violence, almost certainly. He shifted his bulk uncomfortably, wincing with pain as he did so. Yes, the jockey had certainly done enough to be damaged a little bit more than he was already.

A dark girl in the tight white tee-shirt that the waitresses were required to wear when working at the restaurant hurried by, pointedly not looking in Digby's direction. Languidly, he held up the empty wine bottle on his table, letting it swing between two fingers. On her return, the waitress hesitated nervously and took the bottle. Digby held onto the neck and looked up, his greedy little eyes taking their time to work their way up her body.

'Everything all right at home, is it, Diana?'

The girl took the bottle and said in a heavy East European accent 'Is good, Mr Welcome, thank you. Another bottle wine?'

Digby nodded slowly. These girls, he sighed. The trouble they caused him.

'It's as if he's had several incarnations.' Gavin was interested enough in the case of Digby Welcome to slow down his drinking for a while. 'I kept reading these Digby Welcome stories from the archives to find a different character popping up each time.'

'I would never have thought that he was that interesting,' Paul said.

'First of all, he was at Eton – his name keeps cropping up whenever some nobby businessman or cabinet minister is asked about his schooldays. Apparently he was something of a card – a practical joker, smart but lazy. They say he was good-looking then.'

'Bloody hell,' Paul muttered.

'He was expelled for some prank. Joined the army. Appeared to be something of a high-flyer until he left under a cloud when he was in his mid twenties.'

'More pranks?'

'No, the army can handle that. Something more serious – money or sex, I suspect.'

'Then he got into racing.'

'Yes. Again it all looked very promising. He got a yard on the Sussex Downs when he was quite young, trained a few winners, seemed to be going places. The next thing the cuttings reveal is that he was banned from all racecourses for two years. Something about not paying bills.'

'Right.' Paul nodded. 'That's the part I know about. He was a tight bastard – not unusual in racing, but he didn't pay wages, his cheques bounced. He underfed the horses. In the end, even his friends at the Jockey Club couldn't ignore it.'

'So there he was – fat, nearly forty and famous for all the wrong things. He had a marriage that had gone wrong – his wife divorced him for mental cruelty. He ended up in a part-time job selling horse tonic.'

'It doesn't make sense,' Paul said. 'Clay Wentworth only hangs out with people who are useful to him. And another thing. If Welcome was so chronically mean, what was he doing putting three grand on a horse in an amateur race?'

Gavin shrugged. 'Maybe he was doing it for

someone else. Clay, for example.'

'There's no rule against amateurs betting. Clay would have an account with a bookmaker.'

'Unless Digby has yet another incarnation.' Gavin filled his glass. 'Another source of income.'

'Something mucky, I imagine,' Paul said.

Gavin smiled. 'Could be very mucky. I asked one of my colleagues about Digby. He had heard some nasty rumours. Apparently our friend's popular on the coke and champagne circuit. They say he's an ace supplier.'

'Dope?' Angie laughed at the idea of the tubby buffoon in tweeds as dealer in narcotics to the fast set.

'Not drugs.' Gavin sipped at his wine, enjoying the drama of the moment. 'Girls. Wives.'

Zena Wentworth wandered from room to room like a restless and unhappy ghost in the large house in Harley Gardens. She felt empty and alone, trapped by a gloom so deep that not even a trip to the medicine cupboard where she kept all kinds of mood-changing pills seemed worth the effort. A couple of those brightly-coloured items might pick her up, propel her out of the door to a place where there were lights and music only to slam her back down to earth in the desolate early hours of the morning. These days, the pleasure of going up hardly seemed worth the pain of coming down.

Barefoot, in a dark red kimono, she ran a finger

along the mantelpiece in the high-ceilinged sitting-room. Her eyes scanned the invitations, some for Mr Clay Wentworth, some for Mr and Mrs Clay Wentworth, none for Mrs Zena Wentworth. She hooked a finger around the bronze figure of a horse and jockey driving for the line.

'Whoops,' she said, pulled it slowly over the edge so that it fell with a clatter on the marble fireplace below. 'Favourite's down.'

Zena picked up the bronze, noting without much interest that the jockey's head had been bent to one side, giving him a comical look as if he were wondering what all the fuss and effort were about. She ran a long finger down his bronze back, around the back of his bronze thighs, thinking vaguely of Paul Raven.

'Horses,' she said, looking at the painting on the wall, the ornaments on tables. 'Nothing but bloody horses.'

The house was unusually quiet. Emilio and Maria, the Spanish couple who lived in the basement and looked after the Wentworths, had gone out to some obscure spot in the suburbs where Spaniards met on their nights off. When Clay and Zena had moved into this house, shortly after their marriage, the idea had been that it would be filled with children. Now, ten years later, the quest for a family was over, giving Clay and that creepy old father of his yet more reasons to despise her.

Slowly Zena crossed the hall, ruffling her faded blonde hair like someone who had just awoken from a long sleep. She entered a small room which smelt of stale cigars – her husband's study, his little retreat. She sat on the leather chair, leaning back and placing her bare feet on the desk so that the kimono fell back, revealing her long slender legs. Yes – Zena ran a hand over one smooth thigh, and then the other – at least she still had good legs. Not that anyone cared.

There were two photographs on Clay's desk. One showed her husband on Skinflint, taking a water-jump. Zena smiled – it had taken quite a search to find a shot that made Clay look like a real jockey and even this one showed him with his mouth open like a goldfish – but it was good enough to be blown up and featured above his desk at the office. Poor, foolish Clay.

The other photograph was an old portrait of Sir Denis, taken shortly after he had received his knighthood. Against the background of what seemed to be a setting sun, he stared out at her with his cold tycoon eyes.

Creepy. Zena pointed a toe like a ballerina and pushed the framed photograph off the desk.

He had always hated her. He had distrusted her looks, the way she exuded pleasure in the good things of life. Even in the early days, when she had acted the proper daughter-in-law, he had shown her little respect, hardly bothering to talk to her, introducing her to his important friends with an apologetic mumble. Then, as it became obvious that she was unable to fulfil her most important function – to provide an heir for the Wentworth millions – he had ceased even to acknowledge her existence, drawing his son into the business and away from her.

Clay, as was his habit, took the line of least resistance. Torn between father and wife, he returned to the cold bosom of the family. He spent evenings with Sir Denis, still the little boy desperate to please Daddy.

Languidly, Zena pulled open the top drawer of the desk and took out her husband's Filofax. She flicked through the pages, forlornly hoping to find signs that Clay was more than a cypher in his father's plans. There were notes about race meetings, business addresses but – unless Clay had shown an intelligence and cunning uncharacteristic of him – not the slightest hint of adulterous behaviour. Zena sighed. Her husband had always regarded sex as yet another chore life had burdened him with.

A small scrap of paper fell onto her lap. It had been folded many times and contained a list of names, written in an unfamiliar hand. The first three items on the list had been deleted with a line. The last, 'Tanglewood', had been circled heavily with blue biro.

It took a few seconds for Zena to remember where she had heard the name Tanglewood. Of course – that had been the horse that had beaten Clay in his last race.

She looked more closely at the list and noticed, written faintly in a corner, in pencil by her husband, the words 'Dig For Glory'. They too had a line through them.

Zena put the Filofax back in the drawer, which she closed. She stood up and, fanning her face with the slip of paper, made her way out of the study and up the stairs to her bedroom. In her handbag was a small notebook, which she flicked through until she found what she was looking for. She dialled a number on a telephone beside the bed, then drummed the long fingers of her right hand as she waited. 'Bloody machine,' she muttered.

'Paul, this is Zena Wentworth,' she said. 'I think I have something which might be of interest.' She paused. 'It's to do with Alex. Perhaps you could call me as soon as possible.' She gave her number and hung up.

Smiling, she folded the piece of paper and put it in her bag. Maybe she was being disloyal to her husband. Perhaps the list meant something.

At least she'd be able to see Paul again.

It was a tremendous game – the best game Digby Welcome had ever played. The fat man puffed out his cheeks as he cupped his hands around a brandy glass, gazing into it as if he could read his future there.

It was almost eleven thirty. The kitchens were closing, customers were being turned away at the door. Soon the waitresses – including Diana and Juljana, both of them his girls – would be dividing up the evening's tips and going home to lives of sweet, if not entirely simple, domesticity. At about the same time, Roberto the manager would amble over to his table, sit down and spend a few minutes chatting with him. Business might be discussed – girls who needed Digby's help.

Other games – at school, in the army, on the turf – had tended to end in tears, those in authority frequently failing to share his sense of humour. But in this game, he was in control. He called the shots.

It had been so easy, such an obvious development of Digby's personal interests – money, food and, of course, people. In the early 1970s, after his career as a trainer had been terminated, Digby had taken to dining out in restaurants in the Kensington and Chelsea area. His easy charm and teddy-bear looks had encouraged the girls to chat to him. One – he forgot her name now – had, late one night, opened her heart to him. Her student permit had expired, the immigration people were after her, yet she would rather die than return to the grey and cold of Warsaw. She needed a husband within a week – she could pay £2,000.

Digby helped her. He knew plenty of Englishmen happy to lose their bachelor status for the three years required in return for instant cash. The girl had a friend with the same problem, which Digby also solved.

His strength was that he never asked too many questions. Where the money came from, for example, or whether the husbands he provided – some of whom were frankly rather dubious characters – demanded more of their new wives than mere cash.

Since then, he had become a familiar figure around the restaurants of London. It turned out that Eastern Europe was full of families who had sent their girls to make their way in the West, and London, of course, was not short of husbands.

Digby's unofficial marriage bureau had flourished and – even allowing for kickbacks to managers like Roberto – he had flourished too. The only disadvantage to this part-time job was that some evenings he was obliged to eat two or even three dinners and that, for Digby Welcome, was no great hardship.

He looked across the restaurant to where Diana was talking to the manager. She was a nice little thing – dark, slim, with a look in her eyes that promised much in the way of diversion – but these days Digby resisted the temptation to combine business with pleasure. Once he used to demand a non-fiscal bonus with some of his more attractive girls, but it hadn't been a success: the demands he made of them had been rather too sophisticated – too much of a culture shock – to be acceptable. After one tearful scene too many, he had decided not to jeopardize the business. There were experienced business girls he could call – girls who took him for what he was, warped and all.

The door opened behind where Roberto and Diana were standing, and a slight girl with short blonde hair entered. Digby was trying to remember where he had seen her before when he noticed, standing behind her, the face of a man he knew all too well.

Roberto was telling the girl that the restaurant was closed, but Paul Raven had seen him, and the manager smiled and gave a nod as if to say that any friends of Mr Welcome were friends of his.

The couple approached, the girl waiting for Paul to make his way slowly past the tables.

'Digby,' said Paul. 'Here you are. We heard this was one of your watering-holes.'

Digby scowled as the girl pulled back a chair for Paul, then sat down herself.

'This is my friend Angie,' Paul said conversationally. 'Angie, this is Digby Welcome. We met one another briefly at Wincanton the other day.'

'What do you want?' Digby avoided Paul's eyes. 'I was just going.'

'We know all about you,' Paul said quietly. 'Your little business looks like it will be getting some belated publicity in the press.'

'Business?'

'Your work as Agony Uncle.'

'I don't know what you're talking about.' Digby swirled the brandy around in his glass before drinking it back in one gulp.

'Invite me to one of your poker evenings,' said Paul. 'And we might be able to keep your nasty little secret quiet.'

An ingratiating little smile played on Digby's lips,

as if he couldn't believe his luck. 'They're not my poker evenings. They're Clay's.'

'Well, get me invited.'

Digby took a calling-card from his top pocket and scribbled an address on it. 'Next Thursday,' he said. 'I'll tell Clay you're my guest.'

Paul took the card and, glancing at it, gave it to Angie. Leaning heavily on his walking-stick, he stood up. He looked at the stick as if suddenly remembering something.

'How are they by the way? Still sore?'

Digby's face turned a darker shade of red. 'Very amusing,' he said.

After Paul and Angie had left, Roberto came over to the table. 'Nice girl,' he said easily. 'One of yours, was she?'

With a distracted stroke to his head, Digby muttered, 'No – just old friends, you know.'

'Can we talk business?'

But Digby was staring at the door of the restaurant like a man who knew his gravy train had just left the rails. 'No business tonight, Roberto,' he said.

'*Puttana!*'

The tall, thin man stabbed the table with a knife, leaving it quivering like an arrow until a passing waitress removed it with a muttered '*Idiota*'. The man watched her walk away. He was only young and his chiselled good looks had caused many a female customer of his small pizza parlour to return in hope

154

and lust, but his cold green eyes gave him a harsh, forbidding maturity.

He was sitting with two other men, one in his sixties who was examining his carefully manicured nails with a look of intense concentration, the other in his late twenties with a dark moustache, good-looking but with a pale, apologetic smile on his face. 'Giorgio,' he said quietly, 'we've only just begun.'

The young man, Giorgio, darted a look around the room. The last customers in the small cellar, a popular haunt among the young and upwardly mobile of Wandsworth, had gone home, leaving the three Italians alone, except for one waitress who was cleaning the tables. 'Every time she tricks us,' he said.

'We know where it is,' said the man with a moustache soothingly. 'Our little Polish friend has not responded well to his acid bath.'

'What about his wife?'

'We know where she lives. I could – '

'No.' The older man spoke for the first time. 'There's no point in that.'

'We're losing time, papa,' Giorgio said quietly.

'Salvatore has done well, Giorgio.' The grey-haired man picked at one of his nails with a fork. 'You know the layout of the factory, right?'

The man with a moustache nodded. 'But I can't be a VAT man again. She was suspicious last time.'

'Hurting the Polak's wife would be counter-productive. Perhaps we should turn our attention to other members of the syndicate. The man Wentworth. Or

Calloway. We know we can reach Welcome.'

'Time, papa!' There was anger in Giorgio's voice, and a hint of panic.

'We have three weeks.'

'There's another problem,' said Salvatore. 'I have heard that someone else is interested, is snooping about.' He reached into the inside pocket of the jacket of his dark suit and took out a photograph torn from a newspaper. He unfolded it, laying it in the centre of the table.

'Who's he acting for?' the older man asked.

Salvatore shrugged. 'He's some kind of jockey.'

'Jockey?' Giorgio said softly. 'What's a jockey got to do with this?'

'We had better discourage him,' his father said mildly.

Salvatore reached for the photograph. 'I'll ask if anyone has heard – '

'No!' Giorgio spoke sharply. 'There's no time for that.'

The waitress marched across the room and, with a reproachful look in the direction of the manager, began to clean the table. As if it were contaminated, she picked up the photograph, glancing as she did so at the dark features of Paul Raven.

'Mmm,' she muttered. '*Che bel tipo.*'

'Not for long,' said Giorgio. 'Not for long.'

Chapter 8

It wasn't the first time she had returned to Czechoslovakia since the day she had left to find her future in the West but, every time that she alighted from the plane into the greyness of Prague airport, a touch of claustrophobia, of a deep, psychic anxiety, gripped her.

Whatever the changes – to her, to the motherland, to the world – the dark, crumbling buildings and the weary, watchful eyes of the Czech officials always meant the same to her. It was a trap. This time she would not escape. The sins of her past – those deeply capitalist sins of greed, lust and selfishness – would come back to haunt her.

With the other passengers, she was herded into an airport bus, which smelt faintly of cheap, stale cigarettes and disinfectant. The engine sounded unhealthy and the driver drove with contemptuous speed towards the main terminal as if, whatever the politicians might say, the old disapproval of the soft, decadent ways of the West still endured. Around her, the other passengers seemed uneasy – perhaps the bus with its crazed driver would head out of the airport, take them without a word to another, more sinister destination. A middle-aged businessman tried a joke about local driving standards, but no one smiled and his words died on his lips.

Sitting on one of the few benches on the bus, Alice noticed, were two teenage girls, one of whom – with dark, cropped hair and fine features – she might, under other circumstances and in another country, have tried with a smile. Not here: it was strange how even her most natural instincts went into retreat in her cold, forbidding homeland.

In the main building, there were queues. The English thought they understood patience – they boasted about their queues – but they were amateurs compared to her countrymen. Here you stood in a line for everything: sometimes you queued for a permit to join another queue and, by the time you reached the front of it, you'd forgotten what you had wanted in the first place. Alice shivered – she hated coming back – and gathered her fur coat more closely around her.

On this occasion, she was met by a government functionary, a middle-aged man with shifty eyes and a coat too thin for the climate. 'Miss Flaishman?' he said, as she walked towards the queue.

'Markwick,' she said.

The man nodded. 'Please follow me,' he said.

It was better. Every time she returned, she was treated with more respect. Twenty years ago, the man would have called her by her surname, holding her eyes with the stare of a man with power over her, perhaps even allowing himself a speculative glance at her legs. Now she was in charge; he avoided looking at her. Conversation would be minimal.

The man nodded to passport control officials as he took Alice past the queue through the hall of the terminal and into a large car that was waiting at the entrance. Sensitive to the essential signs of social and political importance in Czechoslovakia, she noticed that the car was not quite the most luxurious available. Those had been reserved for the party officials and were now used by the new brand of politician scrambling for power under the free, post-communist constitution.

New. Free. Settling back in the adequate comfort of the car, Alice smiled. They were just words. Nothing had really changed.

On the way to the Ministry of Defence, the car drove past the huge government building where, all those years ago, Alice's mother had once worked. There was something desolate about it now as if its power to terrify had gone for ever. Alice stared at it without feeling any of the old dread and disgust. That ghost, at least, was dead.

Josef Petrin, her contact, was waiting in his large, chilly office when she was shown in by the official. He smiled, extending his arms in a phoney gesture of welcome which, when he saw the icy disapproval in Alice's eyes, became a brisk handshake. They exchanged pleasantries about the journey, as he escorted her to a chair in front of an ancient gas fire, which had been installed in the ornate fireplace.

'Now, Mrs Markwick,' Petrin smiled ingratiatingly. 'You cannot keep us waiting any longer. Tell me when we take possession.'

'Quite soon.' Alice spoke slowly as she placed her briefcase on a table in front of her and fiddled with the security lock.

'How soon?'

The question contained an undertone of impatience, perhaps even threat. Petrin was the new breed of official but, while his suit came from Savile Row, his shiny black shoes from Rome, and his slick smile owed much to Madison Avenue, he was not that different from his predecessors, only younger – in his late thirties – and marginally more plausible. Briefly Alice wondered whether he demanded intimate overtime from office cleaners. No, the modern way was a hunting-lodge, complete with young mistress, in the forest nearby – such was progress.

Alice took a folder out of her briefcase and gave Petrin a videotape. 'The tape I promised,' she said, choosing to ignore his questions. 'You have the machine?'

Petrin nodded and, taking the tape, crossed the room to a table on which there was a television and a video machine. He stood in front of the machine as a sequence of films was shown. Occasionally he gasped and laughed, like a little boy watching a circus.

'Excellent,' he said, after the television screen had turned to grey. 'You use peculiar clinical models but that is your choice.'

'We had our reasons.'

'And afterwards? Any problems with the post-mortems?'

'Nothing.'

'Of course, we need a human test. As you promised.'

'Humans talk.'

'We have humans that don't – or won't, if we ask nicely.'

'No. Leave it to us. We'll manage something.'

'Fine.' Petrin smiled once more like a barrister addressing a hostile witness. 'When?'

'You'll have your evidence in a week. If you're still happy, we deliver at the end of March.'

'Not before?'

'There's still work to be done.'

'And we're exclusive? That's what we're paying for. My colleagues will be very unhappy to hear of models going elsewhere. We're depending on you for this.'

Alice closed her briefcase with a click. 'Trust me,' she said. 'Remember I'm a Czech.'

'That's what worries me,' said Petrin, and they both laughed guardedly as he showed her the door.

There were three hours before her plane left for

London, but Alice had only one call to make. She told the driver to take her to the west side of the city, a square mile where the houses were painted and had heating that worked even in the winter when, as if by tradition, the power in the big housing blocks used to fail, sometimes for days at a time. This was where the foreign diplomats lived, and senior civil servants and politicians. There were few shops and no bars for the poor to gather and drink vodka and talk of future freedom. It was the acceptable face of the new Czechoslovakia.

At first, Alice's mother had objected when, as a condition of dealing with the government, her daughter had secured her a two-bedroom house in the suburbs. Since her husband had died some seven years previously, she had lived alone, depending on neighbours and the occasional visit from Tomas, her son, for company. The new house might be comfortable, she argued, but she would be lonely. But Tomas had a car these days and, aware that one day he might inherit the house, he had promised to bring his family to see her every weekend.

The car drew up outside the house and Alice told the driver to wait for one hour.

'Alzbeta.' The old woman opened the door and embraced her daughter, then held her at arms' length, stroking Alice's fur coat. 'My daughter.'

The two women sat in the kitchen drinking tea while Alice gave her mother a sanitized version of her work in London. Her mother, as usual, became tearful and asked her when she would be coming home for ever.

'One day,' Alice said, 'when I've made my fortune.'

'Money.' Her mother looked away, ashamed by the memories that swarmed in. 'It's always money in our family, isn't it?'

And, with the faintest shiver of repulsion, Alice agreed. Yes, it was always money.

At first, when Ginnie Matthews had written to Paul suggesting he ride out for her, he had assumed it was her idea of a joke. Although the doctors were pleased with his progress, he could still only walk slowly and his legs felt as unsteady and weak as those of a newborn foal.

Then, when Paul had rung her, Ginnie had explained that she had an old hunter in the yard called Monty who needed exercising. He was dead quiet and Paul would be able to sit on him and go where he wanted. He could even come up to the gallop and watch her horses working. To his surprise, the specialist raised no objections. Nor, less surprisingly, did Ron Charlesworth. Still he hesitated.

'Try it once,' Ginnie had said. 'What's the problem?'

At that moment, Paul knew what the problem was.

'I'll be there,' he said quietly. 'What time d'you need me?'

Under other circumstances, it would have been comical. Paul Raven, the ice-cool jockey, afraid of the idea of mounting a fat and ancient hunter. Yet as, early the following morning, Monty was pulled out and led by one of the lads to a mounting-block in the corner of the yard, Paul felt sick with fear. He climbed the steps of the block slowly, like a man going to his execution.

'Hold him up for the first couple of miles, then give one behind the saddle,' joked the lad. 'He's got a great turn of speed.'

As Paul hesitated on the block, the reins in his hand, Ginnie walked towards him. 'Step one of Raven's comeback,' she said loudly. 'Don't hang about, Paul – you're not at Charlesworth's now.'

Paul lowered himself across the saddle and slowly pulled his right leg over. Ginnie helped him adjust the stirrups. 'All right?' she asked.

Paul nodded, his face pale.

And it was. Although he felt weak, he followed the string out in the cold morning mist and, even when the horse in front of him had shied violently, causing his lad to curse at him, the old hunter had hardly turned a hair. As the string worked at half-speed over six furlongs, Ginnie had watched with interest, noting how they had all gone, and it crossed his mind that if he couldn't race again, then, despite all the problems, maybe he would try training. Cheltenham was now two weeks away and Ginnie had three fancied contenders for the big prizes – The Smiler for the Trafalgar House Hurdle, Harry's Champ for the National Hunt 'Chase and Skinflint for the Kim Muir.

Looking down the hill to the all-weather gallop, Paul noticed Skinflint, pulling hard, at the back of the string. 'He must have a decent chance,' he said.

'Yes.' Ginnie narrowed her eyes as if not entirely comfortable with the subject. 'The race has cut up badly.'

There seemed to be an easiness about the lads who worked for Ginnie Matthews. Behind the jokes about 'the missus' and her booming voice, there was none of the edgy competitiveness that Paul remembered from Charlesworth's yard. As the string made its way back, the sun showed through the mist and one or two of the lads had lit up cigarettes. The talk was of racing and horses and women. Paul smiled and patted Monty's neck. It was good to be back.

These days, although Alex's death was still at the front of his mind, so was his own future. His mother had taken to sending him letters advising him to find a desk job while there were still vacancies – she didn't actually spell out that soon Paul and his racing successes would be forgotten and he would be just another applicant, but she didn't need to. He had thrown away the pages from the local paper with jobs circled without even looking at them. Maybe one day he would become a tea-boy or an office clerk, but not yet.

Strangely enough, it had been Angie who had convinced him that only when he had settled his mind about what had happened to Alex would he be able to start a new life. She was working out her notice period at the hospital but, since the night Gavin Holmes had told them about Digby Welcome, she had become quieter, more subdued.

He thought of the message from Zena Wentworth on his answering-machine. It had been two days since he had heard from her but something – perhaps a wariness about her motives – had prevented him calling her back. Whatever Zena could tell him, Paul was convinced he could find out more by attending one of her husband's poker evenings.

On returning to the yard, his back was aching but he insisted on unsaddling Monty himself. The old hunter had done him more good than all the doctors put together, and for the first time Paul began to feel more like he had before the accident.

Zena Wentworth was bad at waiting at the best of times and now wasn't the best of times. The previous night Clay had stayed out late, having dined with his father and Lord Wallingford, another bent peer with property interests, at one of their dull gentlemen's clubs. On his return, Clay had been more monosyllabic than usual. She had even accused him of cheating on her. Clay's face had been such a picture of astonishment that she had had to laugh. Clay Wentworth an adulterer – there was certainly something comic in that.

Two days she had waited for Raven to respond to her bait but there had been nothing, not a nibble. After Clay had gone to bed, she had taken a pill and stayed up all night watching television. At six, she had had a bath, washed her hair, put her face on. By eight o'clock, she was in the Rolls heading down the M4.

She had been surprised to find that he was out, but her patience had paid off when, twenty minutes after she had parked outside his door, Paul had drawn up behind her in his car. Zena watched in her rearview mirror as he lifted one leg and then the other onto the pavement, before pulling himself out. She checked her face one more time, then opened the door.

'Riding again?' she asked breezily.

Paul looked surprised, and less than pleased, to see her.

She smiled and walked lazily towards him. 'You look good in your... togs.'

'Thanks.' Paul walked slowly to his door and Zena followed him.

'I drove down from London to see you,' she said.

'Why?'

'You didn't answer my call. I wanted to help you.'

Paul unlocked the door and hesitated as he opened it. 'Help me?'

'I admire you,' she said brightly. 'There aren't many wounded heroes where I come from. Can I come in?'

'All right.' Paul sighed. 'I have to be going soon, though.'

'Pity,' said Zena quietly.

As Paul put on the kettle, she sat at the kitchen table, crossed her legs and glanced into the sitting-room next door. 'Cosy.'

'It does. Why don't you tell me what you're here for.'

'Two reasons.' Zena opened her crocodile skin bag and took out a small folded piece of paper, which she laid on the table. 'What horse were you riding at Plumpton?'

'Dig For Glory.'

'I found this in my husband's desk. Why d'you think he's written the name of your horse on it?'

Paul turned and looked at the list of names. 'Did your husband write this?' he asked.

'No. That's a woman's writing. Apart from Dig For Glory, what are the other names?'

Paul looked more closely at the list and frowned. It was strange. 'Just horses,' he said quietly.

'Wasn't Tanglewood the horse that beat Clay at Wincanton?'

'That's right.'

'And it's the only one that's not been crossed out.'

'So it seems.'

Either Zena knew more than she was letting on or – and this seemed more likely – she was too stupid or uninterested in racing to see the connections between all the horses whose names had been deleted from the list. All had died in racing accidents over the past two months. As he gave Zena a cup of tea, he glanced at her, catching her eyes on his legs.

'They suit you, those jockey trousers,' she said.

'They're called jodhpurs – I never thought of them as a fashion accessory. What was the second thing?'

'Mmm?' she smiled, parting her painted lips.

'The second reason you came down here.'

In reply, Zena leaned forward and extended a hand across the table, placing it on Paul's hand.

'You know the answer to that,' she said.

He tried to withdraw his hand but found that her grip was surprisingly strong. 'I'm very good, Paul,' she said. 'Alex could have told you that.'

'Aye.' Paul wrenched his hand back. 'And look what happened to him.'

'I'm serious.'

'And so am I. Drink up your tea, Mrs Wentworth. I have things to do.'

'Mrs Wentworth.' Zena spoke coldly. She took a sip of tea then stood up, smoothing the front of her skirt down her thighs. She brushed his cheek with her long fingers. 'Mrs Wentworth wants you, Paul. And what Mrs Wentworth wants, she gets.'

Paul watched Zena as she strolled to the door, with a lazy swing of the hips, and let herself out without a backward glance. Outside, there was an angry purr and a squeal of tyres as the Rolls set off back to London.

What was her game? Paul was used to fending off the attention of libidinous older women but there was a dangerous, driven quality to Zena that worried him. He reached for the slip of paper, which lay on the kitchen table. After a moment, he picked it up and walked slowly through to the sitting-room. At his desk, there was a copy of Chaseform, a small plastic-bound book whose weekly supplements recorded every race in the calendar.

Apart from Dig For Glory, whose fate Paul knew all too well, there were four names on the list – Ballina Lady, Whataparty, Brut Force and, undeleted and with a heavy circle around it, Tanglewood. Paul flicked through the pages to find Ballina Lady's last race, the Philip Cornes Handicap 'Chase at Leopardstown. The summary beside her name was succinct. '*Always going well. Fell second last. Destroyed.*'

Whataparty had run on Boxing Day at Haydock Park and he too had failed to finish. His final entry read, '*Settled early, improved rapidly at half way. Led third last clear and going easily when fell last. Destroyed.*'

Paul recalled Brut Force's last race – his accident at Huntingdon had made the headlines in the sporting press. Once again Chaseform's summary was brief and laconic: '*Always with the leaders. Left in front at the third last. Ducked out at last bend. Destroyed.*'

There was no need to look up Tanglewood's form. Paul remembered the race well, Bill Scott tracking Clay Wentworth until they approached the last fence, then riding his horse out with hands and heels while, behind him, Clay did his imitation of a drunken band-master wielding the baton with impotent fury. Another image flashed across his mind – Angie, star-

ing with undisguised horror as the other horse in
contention, Drago's Pet, lay motionless a few yards
beyond the second last fence. He too had been
destroyed. Even in a sport where equine casualties
are the norm, it seemed too much of a coincidence.

Paul reached for the telephone and dialled. He
hadn't warmed to Gavin Holmes – there was something seedy and unhealthy about the man – but, for
the moment, they had a shared interest. The woman
who answered his extension laughed incredulously at
the idea that Gavin should be at work at ten. She'd
try to get him to call back when he made his customary late-morning pit-stop at the office before wander-
ing off to lunch.

Hanging up, Paul looked once more at the piece
of paper Zena had left him. The writing seemed
somehow familiar. He shuffled among the papers on
his desk before finding what he was looking for.

He put the letter he had received last week beside
the shopping-list of ill-fated horses. There could be
no mistaking the bold, round strokes, the way the
cross on each 'T' floated oddly above the perpend-
icular, the confident 'F' on the name Brut Force.

Few village gossips were as effective, as ruthless pro-
fessionally, as Joe Taylor. While others might happen
upon an interesting titbit which was broadcast, suit-
ably embellished, to anyone who cared to listen, Joe
hoovered up the gossip at Lambourn and passed it
on to one or more of his contacts. And, because horse

chat can often be converted into money, Joe made a good living.

The word about Paul Raven riding again was hardly vintage material – no one was going to get rich on a broken-backed jockey – but it had a bit of colour to it, brought a smile in a grim and grey month, so, as soon as he heard about it, within a matter of hours of Paul alighting carefully from Monty's back, he rang one of his journalist contacts. It was a soft story but it would make a paragraph in the morning's gossip column and provide Joe Taylor with a handy £25, so all things considered, Paul Raven's return to the saddle was good news for everyone.

A profound restlessness assailed the heart of Digby Welcome. It was nine in the evening and, instead of working, he had spent most of the day worrying about developments in his life. On a normal night, he would be out there on his territory, bringing a harsh and chilly relief to Dianas and Juljanas all over West London, setting up marital deals that would keep them one step ahead of Immigration. There was work to be done – just because the authorities in Eastern Europe were happier to export the young and ambitious than they had once been, it didn't mean their counterparts in England would ease control on human imports – but tonight Digby hadn't the strength to engage in his own peculiar form of social work.

He sat in front of a fake coal fire warming his neat

and chubby hands on the gas flame. Already he had tried different forms of distraction – a brandy and ginger ale, a quiz show on television, a few minutes on the crossword puzzle – but his mind kept returning to the mess of grimy deals and petty corruption that was his life.

If only his business and personal affairs were as ordered as the neat bachelor flat off the Old Brompton Road where he lived. Digby sat back in his armchair and closed his eyes to it all. With those glittering little points of greed extinguished, he appeared almost amiable, a red-faced, roly-poly character in an expensive tweed suit, the sort of man you might see asleep in a corner of one of London's better clubs – a card, a joker, a gentleman.

Digby drummed the short, well-manicured fingers of his right hand. Wearily he opened his eyes and reached for a telephone on the table beside him, placed it on his knees. He dialled Clay's private number – the number to which crazy Zena had no access – and waited.

'Clay,' he said eventually. 'Can you talk?'

There was a brisk and not entirely friendly reply from the other end of the telephone. Whatever else he was, Clay was no gossip. Besides, few people spent more time chatting to Digby Welcome than was strictly necessary.

'Ran into that chap Paul Raven the other day. Mmm. Met him at the sports.' On occasions like these, Digby's voice became plummy and distracted.

'No, didn't say a word about poor little Alex. He seemed to have heard about our Thursday nights. I said he could come along, try his luck.' He winced comically as Clay, with a certain impatience, presented his objections. 'I don't know, old boy. Felt sorry for him, I suppose. His back and all that kit. Perhaps a spot of gambling would take his mind off it.' An effete and deeply insincere chuckle shook Digby's frame. 'I don't know where he gets his money,' he said. 'Maybe the Injured Jockeys' Fund is more generous than we thought. That's his problem. Hmm. My guest, of course. I hear what you're saying, old boy, but I can't believe that one night can do any harm. Well done, good kit, see you on Thursday.' Digby hung up. 'Fucking bastard,' he drawled with quiet vehemence.

What he had never understood was how men like Clay – or indeed women like Alice Markwick – managed to get through life without the disastrous, crippling setbacks that seemed to afflict him. While his career could be seen as a juddering switchback ride, theirs was a straight line, an inexorable upward graph. He was brighter than they were – brighter, at least, than Clay – yet there was something about him that invited distrust and, after distrust, disaster.

He reached into a drawer and took out a box of expensive cigars which he kept hidden in case one of his rare guests at the flat expected to be offered one. He lit up, puffing at the cigar restlessly as if, within

174

moments of indulging himself, he wanted it to be gone.

He thought of school, army, his racing stables. The pattern was always the same. Up, then down. Boom, then crash. Order, then confusion. The business in which he had been engaged over the past decade or so had been good to him but now – Digby knew to the core of his substantial frame – it was all about to go wrong.

He was sensitive in that way, with the crook's instinct for the job that he shouldn't do, but always will.

Briefly, Digby considered ringing Alice Markwick. He didn't like the woman but if his other business interests were about to hit the rocks, it was important that his investment in Markwick Instruments paid the spectacular dividends that he expected. 'Alzbeta,' he said quietly. How she had changed over the years.

Laying the cigar in an ashtray, Digby pulled himself out of the armchair and walked slowly towards the bedroom.

Something bad was coming. He just knew it.

The organization had many divisions, each of them catering in a highly efficient way for different forms of human weakness. Drugs, ranging from the recreational and mind-expanding to the more serious and death-dealing, was an ever-buoyant area. Fraud, funny money games played with neat, hi-tech sophistication, was demanding more and more attention.

And, of course, there was sex – there was always sex.

Maria Curatullo checked her make-up in the mirror of a Maida Vale flat, then looked, with a brisk professionalism, in the leather carrier bag on the floor beside her. Seven days she had been waiting in this grey city where the men watched you with dirty-little-boy stares and the women scurried home from work as if they had sand in their knickers.

Maria had worked most of the cities in Europe. She liked Paris, which was like a flighty and expensive mistress; she was always happy to return to Frankfurt, a sharp and ambitious teenage whore of a town, ready for anything at the right price. Rome, of course, was like her – a big, generous woman of the world who understood pleasure. But London? She was a sour old widow, shrivelled up with repressed and twisted desire. Only for very special cases did Maria come to London.

The dark Rover that waited for Maria Curatullo outside her flat might have belonged to a senior sales director of an international firm, just as the young man in suit and tie who sat in the driver's seat might have been a professional chauffeur. The organization liked to look after its executives.

There was no need to give the driver the address to which he was taking her. The words '*Al lavoro*' were good enough. The waiting was over, the time-killing expeditions to shops or cinemas were behind them. The young man, an apprentice in the organization, risked a glance at his passenger in the rearview mirror. Despite the night outside, the signorina was wearing dark glasses.

Behind the shades, Maria's face showed no interest in the streets of London as they sped by. Once, when the Rover stopped at a red traffic light, two men in a nearby car stared across, laughing uneasily at her menacing sexuality. Maria ignored them. With the self-knowledge of a true professional, she knew that her eyes were most effective when hidden. Without dark glasses, she was no more than a handsome woman with a knowing look, a wife even; with them, she was forbidden and dangerous.

From the early days, when she was recruited as a teenager to work for the organization, she had fallen into the habit of giving her punters nicknames. It made the work easier, these private labels. The job tonight was on 'Il Grassone', the fat one.

Maria pulled the leather hold-all closer to her at the thought of the task ahead. Once she had needed no more than her own body but, as the years went by and she became known for experience and skill rather than youth and beauty, she needed props, a bag of tricks. Some of the older women she saw stepping into limousines in Mayfair, or Les Halles or on the Via Veneto, were practically carrying suitcases. In that sense, Maria considered that she was lucky. Sex was no longer her exclusive area of expertise – she had diversified, made herself useful to the organization in another way.

The car pulled up and Maria told the driver that

she would be an hour, maybe slightly more. Relaxing at last, he watched the signorina as she walked up the steps towards the block of flats. She still had good legs – the man smiled – despite the miles on the clock.

Maria pressed a button on the intercom at the entrance. 'Mr Welcome,' she said, 'Ees me.'

There was a pause of some seconds before the door clicked open.

By the time the lift had taken her to the third floor, Il Grassone had left the door to his flat a little ajar. With a slight sense of foreboding – you never lost the smallest frisson of fear the first time with a new man – Maria pushed the door and entered a small, dimly lit hall.

'I was expecting Nicola.'

Il Grassone was standing at the entrance to the sitting-room, his hair slicked down, wearing a maroon silk dressing-gown – an English client of the traditional variety.

Maria slipped off her coat and threw it over a chair. 'Nicola ees eell. You got Maria,' she said huskily. 'I go away?'

He stood there taking in the statuesque body in the black Armani dress. She was too big. Too old. Too much of a woman.

'Did you talk to Nicola? About me?'

'Yes, Deegby. I talk. I know.' She stepped closer to him. They never changed their minds – once they had made the call, slipped the leash from their sick and feverish desires, there was no going back.

'So you know how you are required to oblige me?'

Il Grassone had stepped back, as if afraid of being touched. She knew nothing of this Nicola, except that, just this once, she had been taken off the case; but experience told her what the man needed.

'Oblige me? What means this?' she asked.

'Bloody hell, they've sent me someone who doesn't even speak English.'

Maria glanced at her watch. 'You want conversazione, I fetch someone else,' she said.

'No.' Il Grassone's pleading, glittering little eyes told their own story. Anger was precisely what he wanted.

'Maria.' He seemed to cower slightly. 'I've been a very naughty boy.'

'To bedroom,' she said like a school matron. 'Get ready for Maria.'

Il Grassone ran a nervous tongue over his lips, then turned towards the bedroom.

'*Fai presto!*' she hissed, reached for her leather bag. *Dio*, these Englishmen were all alike.

Her right arm ached. She was getting bored. For twenty minutes she had been working on Il Grassone who lay face down on his bed, the acres of white flesh now striped with red marks from the whip. As he whimpered, it wobbled like some disgusting English summer pudding.

He had had his fun. He was relaxed. It was time for business. 'Turn over, you fat peeeg,' she said.

179

Nervously, painfully, he lay on his back, exposing his vast belly and pitiful manhood to Maria's scornful gaze. His eyes, wet with tears, widened as she took two pairs of velvet-lined handcuffs out of her bag. 'That was antipasto,' she said, clicking them onto his wrists. Roughly, she wrenched the cuffs upwards and attached them to the bedhead. 'Now is time for main course.'

Caught between fear and pleasure, Digby whispered, 'Sorry, Maria.'

Briskly, she reached into the bag, this time bringing out a small cassette recorder which she placed on the bedside table, then an electric lead, a plug on one end, two naked wires on the other. With genuine alarm, Digby tugged helplessly at the handcuffs.

'*Allora*'. Maria switched on the cassette and, as loud disco music filled the room, plugged the lead into a nearby socket. Humming softly to herself, she looked into the hold-all once more and took out a piece of paper which she unfolded. 'I have to ask you some questions, Deegby.' She ran the hand holding the live wires across his hairless chest and down over his stomach. 'Ees true what you say. You were a vairy naughty boy.'

She turned the disco music up louder.

At the pizza house in Wandsworth, three men sat at the corner table. Conversation was flowing less easily tonight, as if all three of them sensed that what, they had assumed, would be a simple task, had proved to be a problem.

When the telephone rang at two-fifteen, it was Giorgio who walked to the bar, picked it up and listened. 'No,' he said eventually. '*Si.*' He hung up wearily.

'*Niente,*' he said, returning to the table. '*Assolutamente niente.*'

The three men sat in silence for a moment, before Salvatore asked a question, a casual afterthought.

Giorgio shrugged. '*Naturalmente,*' he said.

Personally, Maria had nothing against Il Grassone. He had been an easy patient, succumbing to electricity with only slightly more noise than he had made under the whip. And it was hardly his fault that he had been unable to give her the information the organization needed on the whereabouts of the Markwick machine, whatever it was.

Personally, she would have left it there but Giorgio had insisted and, above all, she prided herself on her professionalism.

Maria shifted slightly on Il Grassone's face. Luckily he was tired and, when she had settled on him, placing one foot each side of his great white stomach, he had writhed only for a few moments. She glanced at her watch. In half an hour's time she would be at the airport hotel for four hours' sleep before she left to catch her flight home. It would be good to get away from this odd, depressing country.

Il Grassone trembled once more and was still. Maria sighed. Sometimes she felt she was growing too old for the game. Once sitting on a man's face had meant pleasure, not death.

Neither the sex nor the killing came as easy to her as it used to.

For a few more seconds, she sat there heavily, lost in thought, like a middle-aged washerwoman astride a log. Then with a quiet, 'Bye-bye, Deegby,' she lifted herself off the dead man and prepared to leave for the airport.

Chapter 9

It wasn't Watergate, but it was interesting.

Eyes closed, Gavin Holmes braced himself as another wave of nausea broke over him – but it took more than a Force Nine hangover to deflect him from a story once it started to buzz. 'Touch of 'flu, is it, Gav?' Shirley, one of the younger reporters, called out as she walked briskly past his desk.

'There's a lot of it about,' he muttered, carefully placing a third finger and thumb on his eyelids, as if to check the eyeballs were still in place. He opened his eyes to gaze blearily at Shirley's legs as she walked away. Maybe her turn would come.

He heaved himself back in front of the word-processor to look once more at his notes. On the screen, he read

DEAD NAGS

Five names on list given to Paul, all but one dead.

Except for Dig For Glory, all ridden by amateurs.

All fell towards end of race, three at a fence, one on the flat.

Postmortem: only two taken to Newmarket Veterinary College. Contact there – Heather O'Connell – claims neither horse, Whataparty or Brut Force, showed signs of substance in the bloodstream. Heart and lungs appeared to be entirely healthy.

Quote: 'It's a dangerous game and the majority of serious falls occur over the last half mile. Our conclusion was that these fatalities were the sort of thing that happen in National Hunt racing, no more, no less.'

Gavin sat back and massaged his eyes once more. It was just the sort of remark which, a week ago, he would have used but since then his area of interest had changed. 'The sort of things that happen in National Hunt racing.' That was yesterday's scandal. He punched some keys on the word-processor and more notes appeared on the screen.

Linked characters??

Clay Wentworth. Background – see Who's Who 1991. Chairman of Wentworth Properties and amateur jockey. Riding on the day Dig For Glory killed (not in same race). Also in race won by Tanglewood, the only surviving horse on the hit list. Ambitious?

List found in his possession?

Raven claims that Alex Drew used to play poker with him.

Strange (strained) relationship with wife Zena.

It wasn't much to go on. Gavin was as prepared as anyone to doorstep the great, the good and the guilty in pursuit of a story but the connection with Alex Drew's death seemed tenuous, even – Gavin remembered seeing photographs of Wentworth on financial pages – unlikely. He tapped in one more word onto the computer report.

Weak?

Gavin's notes on Zena Wentworth and Digby Welcome took him no further on the case. Zena, a former model, was said to have had a drink problem which developed into a fidelity problem – there was nothing new or unusual there.

Digby, the late Digby, was more interesting. According to Gavin's police contacts, the murder of Digby Welcome was being treated as a sex and robbery case. The flat had been turned over, a few items and possibly some cash had apparently been removed. The received opinion at Chelsea Police Station was that a business girl had got greedy and had graduated from prostitution to murder. Not even the fact that Digby was handcuffed to the bed, that his poor, abused frame showed signs of a beating and electrocution to sensitive erogenous zones, had aroused particular interest. The world was full of punishment freaks. The velvet-lined handcuffs, it was said, were made in Italy.

Gavin sat back and closed his eyes. The thought of Digby Welcome writhing around in pleasure as some hard-eyed tart goosed him with electric wires did nothing for his hangover. But it wasn't Digby's death, which he put down to the journalistic version of Sod's law – your best lead always dies – that interested him, but the connection with Clay Wentworth. On the face of it, they were ill-matched characters with no more in common than an interest in racing and, from what Gavin had heard, Digby was not one to spend time on normal social relationships. For him, friendship was always a means to an end.

There was another oddity. Paul Raven had discovered that Digby had put £3,000 on Skinflint to win, yet he was said to be funny about cash – after all, it had been chronic meanness that had finished his career as a trainer. Gavin didn't know much about racing but you had to be blind not to see that putting three grand on a horse ridden by Clay Wentworth in an amateur race was high-risk gambling bordering on lunacy.

Unless Digby had known that Tanglewood couldn't win, that after that race, the horse would be dead or injured and its name would be removed from Clay's list. As it was, Tanglewood won, although Raven had mentioned that there had been another casualty in the race.

He dialled Paul's number, but the boy wonder was out or busy with cute little Angie, because Gavin found himself listening to his soft northern tones on an answering machine. He decided to leave a message.

'These nags that bought it,' he said, as if they were in the middle of a conversation. 'What did they have in common which Tanglewood didn't? I was wondering if there was anything odd about the Wincanton race. The boffins at Newmarket are fucking useless, by the way. Give that darling girlfriend of yours a kiss or something from me . . .'

He hung up. Gavin preferred the company of women to that of men but he couldn't help admiring a man whose body had been broken but who was already walking, who was obsessively searching out the person behind his friend Drew's death and who, despite several disabilities – a lack of significant movement in the legs, a career in ruins, a family that came from north of Watford – had still managed to pull Angie O'Keefe. Gavin respected the man; in a world where words were cheap, his quiet determination was unusual.

He punched up more of his notes onto the screen.

OTHERS POSSIBLY INVOLVED

Ginnie Matthews (trainer)

Lol Calloway (rock star)

Alice Markwick (businesswoman)

With a grunt of effort and pain, Gavin stood up. He wandered across the large open-plan offices of the *Guardian* until he reached a group of desks where the staff covering the business pages worked. 'Sorry to wake you up, Peter,' he said to a man who sat, his feet on the desk before him, staring indifferently at the Teletext on the screen before him with the unmistakeable smugness of a journalist who has already filed his copy.

'I'm thinking,' said Pete Morrow, assistant business editor.

Gavin sat on the edge of the desk. 'What d'you know about Alice Markwick?' he said.

Kevin Smiley had once loved racing, but now he hated it. Fourteen years ago, he had left school with a dream in his heart of becoming a successful jockey. He had worked in a small yard near Leicestershire before trying his luck in Newmarket. He grew too heavy to get rides even in apprentice races, so he moved on yet again to a jumping stable outside Royston.

He was twenty-five before he began to realise that the dream was never going to come true. At first, he had thought it was his weight. Then he had convinced himself that the Head Lad disliked him. After that, he blamed himself – he was moody, sometimes giving the Guv'nor of the moment a piece of his mind.

Now that he was thirty, Kevin had discovered the truth that others had known for years. His problem was not on the scales, or in his character or attitude, but in the saddle. He wasn't exactly useless – sometimes he could look quite neat as he rode work – but he would never wear silks. He hadn't the judgement, or the balance, or the brains to ride competitively. His past, his present and his future were as a lad, not a jockey.

At first, he took his dissatisfaction out on the horses, prodding them with a pitchfork as he mucked out, jabbing them in the mouth as he rode them in the string. He became unpopular with the other lads, making trouble for them, bullying the younger apprentices, particularly if they showed a talent that he would never have.

Kevin was bent before he had come to work for Ginnie Matthews, supplying information, helping out when a certain runner needed to be slipped a certain untraceable substance with its morning feed. The fact that the Matthews stable was straight and the Missus trusted her staff implicitly changed nothing.

Kevin was part of racing's secret and corrupt network. He was a sleeper waiting to act on behalf of vaguely criminal elements. In return, he would receive money and, more importantly, experience the simple pleasure of doing someone harm.

'Morning, Kevin.' Paul Raven made his way slowly

across the yard on his way towards the Missus' house. 'Riding out second lot?'

'Nah.' Kevin looked away. 'You?'

Paul smiled. 'I'm giving Monty a half-speed over six furlongs,' he said.

'Right,' said Kevin, watching as Paul rang the bell at the Missus' front door.

Slo-Mo, he called him to the younger lads who were too afraid of him not to laugh. 'Here comes old Slo-Mo,' he'd say as Paul pulled himself out of the car before second lot.

He walked round to the tack room and reached for a bucket. Glancing around to check that no one was coming, he took some powder from his pocket and carefully poured it into the bucket which he half-filled with water.

He hadn't understood his instructions but he was confident that, somewhere along the line, he would be helping to cause a fair degree of pain and disappointment to some bastard who had it coming. Kevin smiled – it was good to feel wanted.

'How's Skinflint going?'

Breakfast with Ginnie Matthews was not a social affair – conversation tended to be minimal or non-existent – but there were two reasons why Paul had accepted the casual invitation, muttered the last time he had ridden out. The mixed grill cooked by the Irish maid was astonishing and Paul needed to resolve a question in his mind.

'Fine.' Ginnie hardly bothered to look up from her *Sporting Post*, tucking into the heaped plate before her as if she hadn't eaten for days. Manners had never played a great part in her life and, ever since she had lived alone, her breakfast behaviour had gone into a sharp decline. Through a mouth full of food, she added 'He'll win at Cheltenham if the jockey doesn't make a balls up.'

'The race has cut up badly.'

Ginnie nodded, as if to say that Paul had exhausted her supply of early morning conversation.

Paul persisted. 'Extraordinary how many of the fancied horses have gone wrong.' He looked away as the trainer did something mildly disgusting with a fried egg before shovelling it into her mouth. 'Died in fact.'

Ginnie glanced up and, below the thick make-up on her face, there appeared the hint of a blush. She finished her mouthful, reached for a napkin and wiped, not entirely successfully, the traces of egg from the sides of her mouth. 'Yes, I've noticed.'

Paul reached into the pocket of his jodhpurs and passed a slip of paper across the table.

'Who gave you this?' Ginnie asked eventually. She seemed more surprised than guilty.

'It doesn't matter. The writing's yours, isn't it?'

'Looks like it.' Ginnie pushed the paper back to Paul and busied herself spreading a thick layer of butter on some toast.

'The horses whose names are crossed out have all

been destroyed,' said Paul.

'Bloody hell,' Ginnie boomed. 'I may be keen on getting winners but I don't go around killing horses.' There was an edgy, unconvincing humour in her voice. 'The list is mine,' she added, 'but I didn't cross the names out.'

'What was it for?'

'An owner needed it.'

'Clay Wentworth?'

Ginnie nodded as she chewed on her toast. 'Some time back, Clay wanted to know the main contenders for the Kim Muir. I jotted them down for him.'

'Why Dig For Glory?'

'God knows. If you look at your piece of paper there, you'll see that name's in different writing. Anyway I wrote the list after your fall.' She glanced at her watch. 'Time for second lot. Or are you too busy playing detective to exercise poor old Monty for me?'

Paul stood up. 'How did he do it?' he said, almost to himself.

'It seems a bit efficient for Clay,' said Ginnie. 'I've always thought he lived like he rode – weak and ineffective.'

Paul smiled. 'He must have help.'

Ginnie walked briskly out of the door. Either she was a better actor than he would ever have believed or she was entirely innocent.

There were few advantages in being a part-time jockey on the mend, Paul reflected as he made his way out of the house towards the yard, but at least he was spared the drilling discomfort of riding out in the gloom and cold of first lot at seven o'clock. Now, as the lads pulled out the second string, a wintry sun was taking the bite out of the morning. There was another small privilege – Monty was tacked up for him by one of the younger lads.

As Paul approached Monty's box, a figure scurried out, carrying a bucket and sponge, whistling cheerily as he made his way back to the tackroom. Paul opened the stable door and, looking at Monty, noticed a dark stain on his chestnut hindquarters under the tail. Nothing unusual there – the Missus took a robust, old fashioned view of turn-out and had an eagle eye for dried sweatmarks behind the girth or a trace of muck on the hindquarters. The only surprise was that it was Kevin Smiley, not normally a perfectionist, who was attending to Monty.

The string had made its way past the farm buildings and neighbouring houses that backed onto the yard when Monty first swished his tail and lifted his hindquarters.

At first, Paul laughed. 'Who's been feeding up this old bugger?' he called out. 'He's trying to drop me.'

Pat, the Head Lad, who was riding in front of Paul in the string, looked around. 'You all right?' he asked.

Paul nodded. The old horse was jigging about like a two-year-old and, for the first time since he had resumed riding, Paul was nervously aware of his insecurity in the saddle. He laid a calming hand on Monty's neck and was surprised to find that, despite the cold, he was beginning to sweat.

There was a matter of seconds between Paul's realization that there was something wrong and the moment when it was too late to do anything about it. As the string turned right up a side road towards the gallops, Monty started to dance sideways, his eyes fearful, his mouth flecked with foam.

'Get off him, Paul,' Jamie called out. 'He must have something under his saddle.'

Paul kicked his feet out of the irons. The horse grunted, kicked the air and, before Paul could dismount, Monty had set off, first at a trot, then, snorting with pain, at a gallop away from the string. Like a clown on a circus horse, Paul clung to the mane, unable to grip enough with his legs to control the horse.

Pat set off in pursuit but pain had given Monty a surprising turn of speed and, before Paul could reach him, he had rounded a bend and was making for the main road.

Paul knew there was no choice. As pain wrenched his back, the wind whistling past his ears, he saw, drawing ever closer, the cars and lorries speeding along the road before him. Closing his eyes and doing his best to ball himself up as he fell, he dived to the left, hitting the ground a matter of yards before the main road.

Seconds later, Pat pulled up, alighting from the

saddle. He crouched down beside Paul, gently turning him over.

From the near distance, there was the sound of the blaring of car-horns followed by the unmistakeable sound of metal impact at speed.

Pat glanced towards the road, then back at Paul, registering the flickering of consciousness in his eyelids.

'Lie still,' he said. 'Don't move a muscle.'

Those who knew Alice Markwick well, a small and exclusive group, rarely guessed her true weakness. Although she had a deep and sincere affection for money, it wasn't financial greed. As for the trips to Heaven in search of someone young, firm and dressed in a leather skirt, that was controllable: her libido, while powerful and slightly odd, was not allowed to dominate her life.

The flaw in Alice's personal armoury was simple – she wanted to belong. All her life, she had been an outsider. Now, after two decades of work and discreet corruption, she felt it was time she became part of the inner circle where your place of birth was no more than an exotic extra, where the way you had made your money was irrelevant. Others slipped easily into Britain's legendary class system: why couldn't she?

She could have married again, of course, but that was an unacceptable option. For three years she had endured the demeaning reality of heterosexual sex. The day that she had stood by the coffin of Dr Eric

Markwick, she had promised herself that never again would she allow her flesh to be invaded by a repulsive male presence. Sex with Eric had been like submitting to a herd of eager slugs, one of whom was carrying an absurd and disgusting prong. No, never again – not even as a means to acquire the respectability she so longed for.

Alice sat in a deep armchair in her spacious and tastefully decorated Islington flat, flicking restlessly through a glossy magazine. It was about ten thirty; normally she would have been at the office for two hours by now but today, she deserved a morning off. Today she would take one step nearer society, *le tout Londres*.

She found herself thinking of Clay's father, Sir Denis Wentworth, whom she had met a couple of times. Like her, he had been an outsider, although he lacked her sophistication and looks. And, despite the fact that he was no more than a hard and humourless businessman, he had entered the magic circle with apparent ease. Why? Because he was rich? Because he was English? Because he was a man? Certainly charm had had nothing to do with it.

The bell rang. Checking her appearance before a large mirror, Alice walked to the intercom. 'Who is it?' she asked.

'Gavin Holmes. *Mail on Sunday*.'

Alice pressed another button. 'Top floor,' she said.

It had only been a matter of time. With her looks and contacts and professional success, fashionable exposure in the right places had to come. When the man from the *Mail on Sunday* had rung her at the office and asked whether she would contribute to a series of profiles called 'Me and My Roots', she had jumped at the chance. A Sunday magazine, complete with colour photograph – it was too good to be true.

'Mrs Markwick?' the man at her door had the unhealthy pallor that she associated with journalists. He extended a hand. 'Gavin Holmes. So kind of you to spare the time for our little feature.'

'What about the photographer?' Alice asked.

Gavin shrugged apologetically. 'He'll call you later to arrange a time for the pictures,' he said, entering the flat and making his way into the sitting-room. 'We'd only have been in each other's way if he'd come this morning.'

The man talked. As Alice gave him coffee, hoping that he would note that it was the best Italian blend served in softly hand-painted porcelain manufactured in Longchamps, she listened to him explaining at length the rationale behind the piece. It wasn't muck-raking, he said, more lifestyle, a positive, life-affirming, upbeat story full of human touches, surprising, intimate, that would reach –

'Why don't you just ask me the questions and we'll take it from there?' Alice smiled, settling back into her seat like a charming English hostess. Noticing the flicker of sexual interest in the journalist's eyes as she leaned forward, she took off her shoes and curled her legs under her, affording him a better view of them.

She smiled. A ladies' man; this was going to be easy.

Gavin took out a notebook. 'Perhaps you could tell me about your childhood in Prague,' he asked.

'Ah, Prague.' Alice allowed a shadow of unease, suggesting painful memories, to cross her face. 'I was born into a poor working family. My father worked in a factory. My mother, a beautiful woman, was an office-cleaner. It was a hard life...'

She spoke eloquently, her husky, slightly accented voice presenting the vivid picture of her youth which she had perfected over the two decades in which she had been in England.

The journalist jotted notes onto his pad. 'So you came to London. What sort of work did you do?' he asked without looking up.

'Au pair. Washing-up. Translation.' Alice smiled. 'The usual things.'

For a few minutes, Gavin asked questions about London in the sixties. It was wild, wasn't it, something of a party? Alice was evasive. Not in her circles, it wasn't. As if talking to himself, Gavin spoke of the fascination the old permissiveness held for *Mail on Sunday* readers. The music, the drugs, the laughter.

'You're asking if I had lots of boyfriends? The answer is no,' Alice said more coolly.

'Did you know Digby Welcome?' The question came out of the blue, attended by an innocent smile.

Alice frowned. 'The name seems somewhat familiar,' she said eventually. 'Have I read something about him?'

'He was murdered recently. I read somewhere that he had introduced you to your future husband.'

Alice felt the colour draining from her cheeks. She leaned forward and took the journalist's cup. 'More coffee?' she asked. 'I'm rather pleased with this blend. Rozzo di Palermo. Bought it in Harrods Food Hall.'

Gavin smiled, but made no note on his pad.

'I thought this was a lifestyle piece,' she said lightly.

'Colour. A little mention of Welcome would give the piece what we call "contemporaneity". The feature editor likes that. So you knew him?'

'I worked in a restaurant. I think Welcome might have invited me to the party where I met Eric. It was a long time ago.'

'And you kept in touch?'

'Good Lord, no. The man gives me the creeps.'

Gavin frowned, allowing a moment of silence before speaking again. It was clear that Alice Markwick had nothing more to say on the subject of Welcome.

'So,' he said. 'Tell me about your husband.'

'Ah, Eric.' Alice relaxed, a distant look in her eyes. 'A sweet, brilliant man.'

It was another half hour before Gavin Holmes left the flat. Although Alice knew little of journalism – she rarely bothered to read beyond the financial pages of *The Times* – the interview had surprised her. She had been expecting something rather gentler, a light-hearted tour of the flat, some harmless chat about her past, her work methods, where she shopped. Instead Holmes had asked prying, insistent questions about the work carried out by Markwick Instruments. He had been alarmingly well-briefed.

Then there was Digby Welcome. How on earth had he known about that?

There were certain memories which Alice had tried over the years to erase from her mind – useless, negative memories of events which, even these many years later, made her feel sick to the stomach.

Staring out of the window, she heard once more the smug and sinister tones of Digby Welcome – 'your guardian angel, my dearest', he used to call himself in the early days. And, of course, he was right. If Digby hadn't been there to rescue her from the smoky Knightsbridge restaurant where she was working, she would never have reached where she was today. Marriage wasn't a problem; but Eric, by some freak of chance, had been perfect. He was brilliant, he was gullible, he fell in love easily and – the best kept until last – died at an early age, leaving his firm to Alice.

Once Digby had something on you, he never let go. At first, it had been easy – Alice shuddered as she thought of Digby's skin netted with the red lash marks from her whip – but, as if he had understood that hitting a man was a positive pleasure for her, he had given that up, taking instead some share options in the firm. The fact that, because of his mysterious demise, Digby Welcome would not be picking up his share of the big pay-off caused Alice no disappointment whatsoever.

Her instinct told her that there was something not quite right about Gavin Holmes. She picked up the telephone book and, having leafed through its pages, walked to the hall telephone and dialled.

'Features editor,' she said.

At the other end, the phone rang for some time before a woman picked it up. The features editor was in conference at present, she said.

'My name's Mrs Markwick, I'm sure you could help me.' Alice put on her most ingratiating voice. 'Your man Gavin Holmes has just been interviewing me for your "Me and My Roots" feature. He told me I'd be visited by a photographer. I really need to know when he's coming round.'

'Holmes?' The woman at the other end seemed confused. 'I think he's on the *Guardian*. He doesn't work for us. Anyway we wound up that feature last month. Who did – '

Alice hung up. It wasn't often that she was taken in by a man and she didn't like it. She dialled another number.

'I think I've found Petrin's guinea pig,' she said.

Clay Wentworth put down the receiver as if it were a piece of rare china, and tapped his rolled gold biro on the desk. He didn't like Alice Markwick and he certainly didn't like depending on her. There was no point of contact – not class, not sex, not humour. All

201

that bound them together was the project on which they both, in different ways, depended. She was too cold, too hard – she seemed to relish the danger of their plan, the pain it caused to others. He thought of her luckless employee, Zametsky. Alice had known that there was some connection between what had happened to him and her own dubious plans, yet she had insisted it had been an accident. Zametsky had, for some reason, seemed too afraid to tell the truth. In the end, it had been Clay who had sent his wife £1,000 in cash. The money was nothing when your face was missing but it made him feel slightly better.

'Lunch.' His father stood at the door of the office, leaning on his walking-stick. As usual, his short frame and glittering blue eyes emanated wordless disapproval.

Father and son went through to the boardroom of Wentworth Properties plc, where a plump and nervous girl, the daughter of a shareholder, served them with a beef casserole taken from some Cordon Bleu cookbook for executive lunches. As usual, Sir Denis's portion was microscopic and, after the girl had gone, he looked at his meal with distaste before poking at a piece of meat and fastidiously putting it in his mouth. His old jaws worked slowly.

Sometimes, during these meals, Clay would look down the length of the long mahogany table and think, 'Die, you stupid old bastard, choke on it.' Then he would think again. Not yet. Not quite yet.

'Who was she?' Sir Denis spoke little these days so that, when he did, his words came out in a slow guttural rasp, like the voice of a Dickensian villain.

'Who, father?'

'On the phone. In the office.'

'Just business.'

For a moment, the boardroom was silent except for the sound of silver on china.

'Business.' Sir Denis pushed a bit of meat around his plate. He understood Clay well enough to know that no mere matter of profit or loss would preoccupy him for long. His son had never understood the importance of money. 'You're poking, I suppose,' he said.

'No, father. I'm not poking, as you call it.'

Chewing slowly, Sir Denis looked at his son with chilly contempt. 'I don't suppose you are.' An odd, birdlike sound, somewhere between a laugh and a death rattle, came from him. 'Never much of a poker, were you?'

A flush of anger appeared on Clay's cheeks. He could just about take his father when he was lecturing him about company matters; when he moved into the personal area, he was impossible. Ever since Lady Wentworth, a quiet, blameless woman, had died in the early 1970s, Sir Denis had lived in a flat in Knightsbridge alone apart from the butler who looked after him. The spartan simplicity of his life had allowed him to comment, almost always unfavourably, on Clay's domestic arrangements.

'Ditch the bitch,' Sir Denis said as if reading Clay's thoughts. 'New young wife. Children. That's what you want.' A drop of dark gravy hung on his lower lip. '*She's* poking, you know.'

'Told you that, has she, father?' Clay pushed away his plate. 'You talk about poking with my wife?'

'Ditch her. You'd make an old man very happy.'

Maybe, when this was all over, he would. Living with a crazed, pill-happy, middle-aged woman was almost as depressing as working with his cold and sinister father.

He watched as Sir Denis toyed with his meal. It would be another fifteen minutes before Clay was free to return to his office.

'Maybe I will,' he said, thinking of freedom, a new start in life. It wouldn't be long now.

This story had led to some of the worst places – a cold stableyard, the backstreets of Willesden, and now the casualty ward of a run-down rural hospital. It wasn't what he'd become a journalist to do.

Gavin walked down the ward to a bed beside which sat Angie, a ray of beauty in a grim, off-white world.

'Gavin,' she said, smiling. 'Kind of you to visit.'

'My pleasure,' he lied. Reluctantly, he turned to the bed where Paul lay. 'You prat,' he said. 'What is it with you and horses?'

It had been twenty-four hours since Paul had been admitted. His face was decorated by vivid bruises and his right arm and shoulder were bandaged up. 'It wasn't an accident, Gavin,' he said quietly.

The journalist pulled up a chair and slumped into it. 'What do the docs say?' he asked.

'That he was a bloody fool to be riding in the first place,' said Angie.

Paul smiled weakly. 'It could be worse,' he said. 'Light concussion, fractured collar-bone. The back's shaken up a bit. I fell in the right way.'

'You seem to have lots of practice.' Gavin produced a packet of cigarettes and was just about to light up when he remembered where he was. Swearing softly, he put them away again. 'While you've been trying to kill yourself, I've been making myself useful.'

'A trainer called Ginnie Matthews made that list,' Paul interrupted. 'She gave it to Clay Wentworth.'

'You think she's involved?'

Paul shook his head, wincing slightly. 'She suspected something was going on but I'm sure she wasn't involved.'

'Yet it was at her yard that you had your accident,' said Angie. 'It seems a bit of a coincidence.'

'No, maybe Paul's right,' Gavin said. 'There seems to have been very little gambling involved in these races. I think the people behind it are outside racing.'

He told them of his visit to Alice Markwick, pointing out the connection between her and Digby Welcome.

'Markwick and Welcome used to go to Wentworth's poker evenings,' said Paul. 'But why were they involved in killing horses?'

'To help Clay win races?' Angie remembered the tall man she had seen in the bar at Wincanton. He had hardly seemed the ruthless type.

'And how?' Paul asked.

Gavin smiled triumphantly. 'As part of my profile, I asked Alice about the research being done by Markwick Instruments. It's into the use of lasers in surgery – particularly in eye surgery. She was evasive, claiming that she was a businesswoman who knew little about the technical side.'

'Eyes,' said Paul quietly. 'That's how they did it. They blinded the horse they were after as it approached the fence.'

'No, I checked with Newmarket,' said Gavin. 'According to the lab, there was nothing irregular about the horses' sight.'

'How do they do it then?' Angie asked. 'And what's their next target?'

'I've got to get to that poker school,' Paul muttered.

Gavin smiled. 'I wish I could help but both Alice and Clay would recognise me.'

'No,' Paul said. 'I'll go.'

'We need to get to Alice Markwick. Find out how they're blinding the horses – I'm sure that must be what they're doing.' Gavin sounded evasive, as if he had an idea which slightly embarrassed him.

'But how?' Angie asked.

'There is one way.' The journalist was looking at

her in an odd and slightly alarming way. 'But it's ever so slightly tacky.'

'Surprise us,' said Paul.

There were times when Kevin Smiley cursed the day his father took him racing. He had been thirteen at the time and it had changed his life. The action, the atmosphere, the smell of courage and money – even though it was Haydock on a chilly Saturday, it had been enough to infect little Kevin. 'I know what I want to be,' he had said to his father, driving home that night. 'I'm going to be a jockey.'

And, sure enough, he wasn't.

As Kevin packed his few belongings into a suitcase, he thought of the cold mornings and casual humiliations that were the sum total of his racing career. 'You're fucking useless, Smiley,' one of the older jockeys had told him when he was still in his teens. 'You haven't got it.'

The bastard had been right. Whatever the 'it' was – that magic ingredient that turned boys into jockeys – he didn't have it. Kevin glanced at his watch and looked his last at the bedsit that had been home for the last couple of years. He was thirty. It wasn't too late to start again. He'd go to London, find a job. He'd tell his parents later.

Kevin felt an uncharacteristic pang of guilt. It was true that he had let a few people down. His mum and dad, who had always believed in him, Mrs Matthews, who had turned a deaf ear to those who had told her that Smiley was a wrong 'un and taken him on all the same.

He thought of the last time he had seen his employer. She had been talking to the vet the day after the business with Paul Raven. Later, as he cleaned tack, one of the lads told him the rumour going round the yard.

'Weren't no accident, were it?' he had said. 'Fuckin' vet only found acid on poor old Monty's hindquarters. No wonder 'e went fuckin' apeshit. Burnin' into 'is flesh, weren't it?'

'Acid?' Kevin had acted as casually as he was able.

'Slow acting. Reacted with horse's body sweat, is what I heard. The more he sweated, the more it fuckin' ate into him.'

'So someone did it on purpose?'

'You're fuckin' quick, ain't you?' the lad had said. 'The Missus'll find him, that's for sure. Can't have her darlin' Paul buried like that, can we?'

It was hardly a glorious note on which to end his career but, if he had learned nothing else in a life of ducking and diving, Kevin knew when to cut and run. He clicked the suitcase shut and, leaving the light on and closing the door, he made his way down the stairs.

His car, a Ford Granada, drew up within seconds of Kevin appearing at the front door of the hostel.

'Minicab?' Kevin asked, as the driver opened the passenger door.

'For Mr Smiley,' said the driver.

'That's the one.' Kevin put the suitcase on the back seat and climbed in. 'Swindon station please, mate.' He sat back and closed his eyes, relaxing at last. It was good to get away.

It took a minute or two for him to realize that the car was heading the wrong way.

'Sorry, mate,' Kevin said uneasily. 'I said Swindon.'

In reply, the driver accelerated, flicking an electric lock on his door.

'What's up mate? What are you up to?'

'Child lock,' said the driver, his handsome dark eyes watching Kevin in the rearview mirror. 'Child lock for a very bad boy,' he said.

For a moment, Kevin was confused. Then he sat back and asked quietly, 'What exactly d'you want from me?'

'Nothing,' said the driver. 'Assolutamente niente.'

Chapter Ten

The photographer sat in his rabbit-filled bunker, thinking about the future. It was a small room, brightly lit by strip lighting, with a workbench in one corner and, occupying most of the floor space, the animals' play area.

He had enjoyed designing their little assault course. It had reminded him of when he was a small boy in Warsaw, of the toys he would make in the small back room of his mother's apartment, except here the toys were alive and, for a while at least, warm.

Of course, the rabbits were predictable in the stupid, panic-stricken way that they responded to scientific stimuli.

'Want to play, Fi-Fi?' The photographer spoke in the well-bred undertone of a man who had spent much of his life in university libraries and laboratories. He took a white and brown rabbit from a cage, placed it carefully into a corner of the play area enclosed by wire and turned to a control board on his desk. Humming softly, he pressed a couple of switches.

The prod flashed red, then green, then white as it approached Fi-Fi, causing her to cower against the wire. As it touched her white fur, the shock of an electric current jolted the rabbit's body. The prod withdrew before, flashing brightly once more, it advanced again. Fi-Fi was relatively intelligent and soon the first bright flash induced her to leap backwards against the wire in the knowledge that where there was light, pain would follow soon afterwards.

The photographer opened a small door, allowing her to escape into the rest of the cage. For a minute or so, he watched as she dashed backwards and forwards in her new-found freedom. He liked Fi-Fi – her rabbitty will to survive made her a good target. He reached for the camera on his desk.

It was too heavy, in his opinion. Zametsky had developed the prototype and had been indifferent to the photographer's complaint that, while it looked like a camera, a security guard or customs official merely needed to hold it to be suspicious. These people were trained to look for bombs and, although the camera was far more dangerous than mere explosives, its weight was a serious design flaw. Zametsky had smiled. Cosmetics, he had said, could come later.

Fi-Fi's efforts were tiring her. With a soft 'tut' of impatience, the photographer activated two more prods, one of which caught her, enlivening her performance. He weighed the camera in his hand, then took aim and shot.

The noise was good. The click and whirr was just like a real camera. Fi-Fi kept running, only this time she hurled herself against the wire. The photographer activated the flashing lights on the two electric prods. Frantic as she was, the rabbit made no effort to avoid them, running blindly into the first one and then the other. In a relatively short time, she lay in a corner, her sides heaving with exhaustion. The photographer moved the prod slowly towards her. It flashed red, green and white, but Fi-Fi no longer reacted.

Perfect. The photographer left the prod flashing before the rabbit's unseeing eyes and checked his watch. Four minutes. Fi-Fi would come round within the next sixty seconds.

At first, he hadn't believed that there was no trace, that the beam of Zametsky's gismo could penetrate the corneal cortex and freeze the iris without long-term damage. It was a miracle of technology, a laser that incapacitated yet was untraceable. The photographer felt proud to be a part of it, privileged.

There was a scrabbling from the cage as the life came back to Fi-Fi's eyes and she saw the flashing horror before her.

The photographer smiled at the rabbit's clownish double-take. Throwing the switches on the control board, he said, 'Good girl,' and opened the run and picked Fi-Fi up. Her eyes, if anything, seemed brighter than they had been before the experiment.

Smoothing down her ears, he put the rabbit back in her cage.

It was good. He was ready for the next job. The photographer hoped it would be on something more interesting than a horse.

It had been a long time since Zena Wentworth had been needed. Now and then, she might get a call from one of her part-time lovers who, in that presumptuous way that men had these days, told her that he needed her now, right now – but that wasn't need, it was boredom, like you needed a gin and tonic, or a holiday in the sun.

Paul Raven wasn't like that. When he rung her and explained that he needed her help, she was almost down the stairs, in the Rolls and on her way before he had explained the precise nature of his need. When he did, she had hesitated, briefly unsure, assailed by a certain illogical loyalty to her husband.

Then she agreed. Bloody hell, she had needs too.

Paul had seemed surprised that she intended to visit him. She could phone him, he said.

She had insisted. She had something to give him.

Zena parked the Rolls down the street from the flat and walked briskly, her mink coat hanging off her shoulders, towards the flat. She rang the bell, tapping her foot impatiently as she waited.

After what seemed an age, the door opened and Paul stood in a dressing-gown, his right arm in a sling, and leaning heavily on a walking-stick.

'Sorry,' he said. 'I've got a bit slower since I last saw you.'

'Your poor face.' Zena made to reach out for him, then, remembering that Paul was uneasy with flirtation, stopped herself.

'Better than it was.' He turned slowly back into the flat. 'Only been out of hospital a couple of days.' He made his way through a small, comfortable sitting-room. 'I'll have to talk to you in the bedroom. Doctors have told me not to move about for a while.'

'Who looks after you?' Zena picked up a framed photograph on the table. It showed Paul upsides over a hurdle at Cheltenham. The other jockey she recognized as Alex Drew.

'Angie comes by after work.' Paul made his way into the bedroom and, with some difficulty, eased himself into bed. 'I feel bloody daft,' he said. 'Make yourself a coffee if you like.'

'I won't bother.' Zena took off her fur coat, threw it across a chair and sat on the end of the bed. 'The next meeting of the poker school is at this address.' She opened her bag and handed him a piece of paper. 'I suggest you ring Clay and explain that Digby invited you before his... accident.'

'You won't be there yourself?'

'I'm not welcome. My husband says I talk too much. Don't take it seriously like I should.' She smiled. 'Our marriage isn't close.' She looked at Paul, who had his dressing-gown wrapped around him to his throat, and smiled.

'What was the other thing then?' he asked, eager to break the moment.

'Apart from an invitation, there's one requirement for joining Clay's poker school. You have to have a minimum of a thousand pounds in stake money.'

'I'll borrow it,' Paul said.

Zena took an envelope from her bag. '*Voilà*,' she said. 'Your entrance ticket. Two thousand pounds.'

Illogically, Paul felt a surge of anger within him. 'It's your husband's money.'

'Don't be so ridiculously old-fashioned. We're married. We share. He goes to work, I look after the domestic side – send Christmas cards, book restaurants, that sort of thing.'

'He earned it.'

Zena laughed harshly. 'My husband has earned nothing in his life. He's waiting for his darling daddy to topple off the perch. The money comes from the highly dubious enterprises of Sir Denis Wentworth.'

Paul felt uneasy at the woman's casual intimacy, the way she was half-lying now at the end of his bed, pinning down the blankets so that he was unable to move his legs. 'I couldn't gamble with your husband's money,' he said.

'Why are you going to Clay's poker school?' Zena asked, casually kicking off her shoes.

'Because I want to know what happened to Alex. I have a feeling your husband was involved.'

'What scruples you have. You think he might have been involved in finishing your racing career and causing your best friend's death and you can't bring yourself to use his money against him.'

'You're very bitter.' Paul tried to move his legs but, now that Zena was kneeling at the end of the bed, he felt powerless. His shoulder was aching and suddenly he wanted to be alone.

'Use Clay's money. Nothing would give me more pleasure.' There was a sparkle in Zena's eyes as she leaned forward, proffering the brown envelope with her left hand. As he took the envelope, she shifted quickly, trapping his free hand beneath her. Paul gasped. Zena reached under the blankets and, before he could do anything about it, slender, knowing fingers were working their way up his bare thigh under his dressing-gown. 'Or almost nothing would give me more pleasure,' she added.

'Don't.' Paul looked at her coldly, then shuddered as her hand darted upward and found him. Zena closed her eyes ecstatically. He said, more threateningly, 'Get your hand off me.'

'Don't be like that,' she said, with a catch in her voice. 'I like you very much, Paul. You won't have to move.'

Paul swallowed hard. Trying to move his hand merely caused a searing pain in the other shoulder. To his horror, he felt his body responding.

'Everything else in working order, I see,' she purred. 'I'd really like to get your bit between my teeth.'

As she leaned forward, Paul gritted his teeth

and jerked his left hand free, brushing her off the bed. 'I'm not interested in being raped,' he muttered.

Zena stood by the bed, barefoot and contrite. 'Not even... ?' She gave an eloquently suggestive pout, her tongue across her upper lip.

'Bugger off out of it,' said Paul. 'And take your money.'

She put on her shoes and slipped into her mink coat. She walked over to a mirror and, checking and making some minor repairs to her make-up, she seemed cooler now, philosophical, as if such things happened to her every day.

'I'll leave the money,' she said lightly. 'You'll need it.' Without looking back, she swayed out of the bedroom.

Paul relaxed at last and closed his eyes with relief that she had gone. He glanced at the envelope still in his hand before becoming aware that Zena was back, standing at the door.

'Let me know if you change your mind,' she said. 'I have a feeling that we could be *very* good.'

The squire of Lenbrook Hall was out shooting on his estate. So far that afternoon he had zapped three rabbits, a couple of hares, five pheasants and a couple of smaller brown birds which he hadn't ever shot before. 'Not zapped, Lol,' the squire muttered to himself as he approached a cottage. 'Bagged.' He banged on the door with the butt of his shotgun like a sheriff making a house call, 'Ere, John,' he called out.

An old man wearing moleskin leggings and slippers opened the door. 'Mr Calloway,' he said. 'How did you get on?'

Lol thrust a black dustbin liner forward. 'That's what I bagged, John. Not a bad bit of bagging, eh?'

With a hint of a sigh, the old man opened the dustbin liner. 'Very good, Mr Calloway.'

''Ere, what's 'em little brown fellas, John? Grouse, are they?'

The gamekeeper held up a small bird. 'They would be mistle thrush, Mr Calloway.'

'Get away.'

'Tricky devils to shoot, sir.'

The squire looked disappointed. 'On the bird-table, weren't they,' he said sulkily. 'You can keep them. The old lady gets heavy about bodies in the kitchen.'

'Thank you, Mr Calloway.'

'Cheers, John.'

To tell the truth. Lol wasn't sure about that old bastard. There was something leery about him, like he was laughing up his sleeve all the time. He was good at his job, ensuring that the animals on the estate were plump, docile and slow, but he had an attitude problem: no respect. If the squire of Lenbrook Hall didn't deserve respect, who did?

Lol broke his twelve bore, took out the two cartridges and put them in the pocket of his Barbour, as he slouched across the lawn towards the house.

Although the owner of what the papers called a 'luxury Elizabethan mansion', he still didn't feel entirely at home there. Still, what with the leisure complex at the back and the conversion of the library into an indoor swimming-pool with jacuzzi en suite, it was getting there. He opened the french windows into the sitting-room and, leaning the twelve bore against the television, kicked off his green Hunter boots and trudged towards the kitchen.

'Cooee, darlin', I'm home,' he called out in the hall. There was no reply. 'Out playing Lady Fuckin' Bountiful, down the village, I suppose,' he grumbled.

Back in the seventies, Suzie had been the hottest groupie around. She was class, could do things that that geezer Kama Sutra had never dreamed of, and nice with it. You didn't mind waking up beside Suzie which, in Lol's extensive experience, was rare in a groupie.

But, ever since they had moved to the hall, she had been different. The middle-class background she had once been so ashamed of had re-established itself. Village fetes, the fucking Women's Institute, sending the kids off to nobby private schools. She had even objected when he changed the name of the house from Chevenham Grange to Lenbrook Hall, after his bassist Len Brook who had tragically died inhaling his own vomit back in 1969. Worse than all that, Suzie had become sniffy about the better things in life, like mind-expanding drugs. Lol laughed quietly. Now the only thing that was expanding was her bum.

Lol paused in front of the large oak mirror, which Lady Muck had bought for an arm and a leg the previous year. He pushed the deer-stalker to the back of his head and, as if to compensate for his bald pate, fluffed out the big brown locks around his collar. Whistling a song from the sixties, Lol pushed the door to the basement where he had built a games room. A touch of snooker, that's what he felt like; maybe a spot of indoor croquet.

It was as Lol was pouring himself a whisky at the customized cocktail bar in the corner that he became aware that he was not alone. Beyond the glass case containing his guitar collection, across the stretch of purple astroturf with yellow croquet hoops, there was a rocking-chair he'd bought in San Diego. It was rocking.

Stealthily, Lol backed towards the billiard table, keeping his eye on the chair. The door clicked shut behind him. 'Mr Calloway?' The voice was mellow and relaxed, like the voice-over for a coffee advert. There was a slight accent there. Lol turned slowly. From behind the door, a man in his early thirties stepped forward – his dark, even features, carefully tended moustache and well-cut suit suggested respectability, but the man's build, his broad and muscular hands, were not those of an office worker.

'Who the fuck are you?' Lol asked.

In reply the man stepped forward, picked up the billiard cue that was lying near Lol's right hand and broke it across his knee. Casually he threw the two bits onto the astroturf. 'I don't like snooker,' he said.

'How did you get in? The gate's locked. There's security.'

'Why so shy?' The man in the dark suit sat on the edge of the billiard table. 'You need security?'

'Fans. Autograph hunters.'

The man laughed humourlessly. 'There didn't seem to be many when I climbed over. Maybe the gate's too high for their bath chairs and walking-frames.'

'You didn't tell me who you are.'

'Call me Signor Salvo. I'm here to get your support for a good cause.'

'My wife – '

'Shut the fuck up and listen.' The man paused, as if slightly taken aback by his own outburst. 'I haven't got all day,' he said more quietly. Placing both hands on the side of the table, he lifted himself up like a gymnast on the parallel bars, landing on his toes. He walked over to Lol's guitar collection.

'All you got to do is give me some information,' he said. 'Then I'll leave you alone.'

Lol glanced towards the door. He might make it – a dash upstairs to the old twelve bore in the sitting-room – but then again he might not. With Signor Psycho here, it was no time for heroics.

'I believe you belong to a business syndicate.' Salvatore's hands were in his pockets now. 'You have an interest in a certain product being developed by Markwick Instruments.'

Lol shrugged.

'Right. My employers want your product. We want it exclusively and we want it very, very soon – before it gets into the wrong hands. And you're going to help, right.'

Lol was no stranger to violence – he had been yards away when his bouncers had clubbed an over-enthusiastic Hell's Angel to death during the 1970 tour of the States – but he didn't like it at first-hand, one to one. Suddenly he felt old and afraid.

'I have a lot of business interests,' he said. 'Maybe I am involved with Markwick. Why don't I talk to my people...' He hesitated as Salvatore ambled over to the purple croquet lawn and picked up the heavy end of the broken snooker cue '...and get back to you.'

Salvatore tapped on the glass in front of the guitars. It was like the window of a music shop, with no less than ten gleaming instruments on their stands. 'Are you going to open this or am I going to smash it?' he asked. 'I'm interested in music.'

'They're of purely historic interest, but – '

A sharp crack, followed by a tinkle of falling glass interrupted him. Salvatore put the snooker cue down and kicked in the rest of the glass. He reached into the display and took out a large red guitar, with the vulgar, extravagant curve of an old American car. Lol took a step forward, like a mother anxious about her child, but paused, as Salvatore froze him with a look. 'I've always hated rock and roll,' he said conversationally, picking clumsily at the strings.

223

'Different strokes for different folks, eh?'

'Jazz, that's what I like.' Salvatore turned the guitar over and tapped its shiny back. 'You know who the last decent guitarist was?'

Lol frowned, desperately trying to think of jazz guitarists. 'Pat Metheny? The blind Canadian geezer?'

'Django Rheinhart, dickhead.' Salvatore was holding the 1955 Gretsch by the neck as if it were a baseball bat.

'Ah,' Lol smiled. 'The gypsy.'

'*Not a gypsy*!' The guitar was held aloft a brief second before it fell like an axe, shattering on the side of the billiard table.

'Cool it, Luigi!' Lol had seen a few smashed guitars in his time – in fact, he'd stomped on a few himself as part of his stage act, but this was different. 'Jesus, man,' he sobbed, 'Scotty Moore played that axe.'

'Not a gypsy.' Salvatore turned the wrecked instrument over with his toe. 'A romany.' He seemed calmer now. 'And my name's not Luigi.' He glanced at the display case, as if choosing which guitar to destroy next. 'You feel like talking now?'

'I'm an investor in Markwick, that's all,' Lol said quietly. 'I don't know what's going on. There's this thing called Opteeka B – sort of camera-type gismo that their boffins have been working on.'

'We know all. What's the timing?'

'They've got a prototype they've been testing. They're going to sell it to some Czech geezer. Alice

Markwick's information was that the Ministry of Defence here and the Pentagon were a bit iffy about a weapon that blinded people.'

'When's it being handed over?'

'Soon.' Sorrowfully, Lol picked up the remains of the old Gretsch. There was a guy in Ealing who reconstructed guitars but, apart from the neck and the chrome machine-heads, this one was a goner. 'I'm just the money,' he said. 'They don't tell me nothing.'

Just the money. As Lol examined the mess of wire and wood, turning it over in his hands, memories of his ill-fated investments of the past crowded in on him. The independent record company. The rock magazine. The film company. All he had wanted was a safe home for his royalties, a bit of financial security, yet every time it went wrong. Opteeka B had seemed too good to be true, too easy. 'I'll help you if I can get my money back.'

'We might give you some compensation,' Salvatore said, 'when we take possession.'

Lol nodded wearily.

'You tell us where to find it, okay? I'll call you in a week's time. If you speak to the others – Markwick, Wentworth, Raven – it won't be your Gretsch that's destroyed. Remember what happened to your friend Digby.'

'Raven? Who's Raven?'

'The jockey – he isn't with you?'

Lol shook his head. 'Never heard of him.'

'One week.' Salvatore walked to the door. 'You're with us now, Lol.'

'Right.'

'By the way, what are those tests?'

'I dunno. Horses, mostly.'

'*Horses*?' Salvatore laughed. This was going to be like taking a toy from a baby. 'Be in touch, Mr Rock and Roll.'

'Sure, man.'

With a final look of contemptuous pity, Salvatore turned on his heel and left.

The place was going downhill and no mistake. Goods in the shops seemed shabbier and more expensive, the assistants less respectful. You held up your hand on a corner in Regent Street and taxis swept by as if a better class of passenger, with a bigger tip, awaited them around the corner. The locals had an edgy, defeated look to them as they went to work. In the evenings, the restaurants were virtually deserted, and the windows of the residential flats were illuminated by the glow of a million television screens. Outside there were beggars – disgusting, black-toothed creatures, toting some dog or baby, as they extended a grimy hand from their cardboard shelter in the entrances to shops. Policemen walked in twos, with surly expressions on their faces. The traffic moved with the speed of a glacier. Public transport was a joke in exceedingly poor taste.

'Two months ago.' Josef Petrin drummed his fingers on the counter of a gentleman's tailor in Savile Row. 'Surely to goodness you people can manage to put together a tweed suit in such a time.'

A grey-haired man with apologetic eyes, hunched by a lifetime of measuring inside legs, explained that there had been 'flu among their employees, and layoffs. If Mr Petrin could give them another fort-night –

'Heavens above, man. I could be anywhere in two weeks' time. I really can't build my schedule around the health of your staff.'

The tailor simpered some more. Maybe ten days was possible, quality was so important, it was vital not to hurry the final work on the suit.

With some difficulty, Petrin extracted a date from the man and left the shop exuding righteous indignation. There was no doubt about it – London was in terminal decline.

By some miracle, a black taxi deigned to stop for him. 'The Ritz,' he said.

The taxi-driver, a youth with the cropped hair of a football hooligan, nodded moodily. Whatever happened to the cockney, Petrin wondered as he settled back in the cab – the cheery red-faced character full of vulgar working-class charm, the bloke who addressed you as 'Guv'? Nothing was simple any more.

The tea-room at the Ritz was full of Arabs and ancient women but, after a five minute wait, Petrin was shown to a table. Without waiting for Green, who would inevitably be late, he ordered tea.

He was on his second scone before Bernard Green, an overweight producer of what they called 'Talks' at the BBC, flapped into view and, with much huffing and puffing, slumped into the chair opposite Petrin.

'Bloody meetings,' he explained.

Petrin decided not to give Green the benefit of a smile but poured him a cup of tea. The producer eyed the scones like Bunter, the famous English schoolboy whose adventures Petrin had read while at university. 'Help yourself,' he said drily.

'So.' Green took a scone onto which he heaped a mess of butter and raspberry jam. 'How goes life in Prague now that you're liberated from the embrace of the Bear?'

It was always like this – the paunchy Englishman pretending, perhaps to himself, that they were meeting on BBC business. Petrin smiled at last. He enjoyed the irony of playing host to this unhealthy-looking fool, so old for his forty-odd years, wearing the cheap ill-fitting suit. Mao had been wrong – power does not grow out of the barrel of a gun but out of carefully maintained political contacts. 'Less has changed than you might think, Bernard,' he said. 'You'll be glad to hear.'

A look of unease crossed the Englishman's face. On Petrin's last trip to London, Bernard had casually suggested that *perestroika* had swept away the need for secret alliances. Petrin had dismissed Bernard's pathetic attempt to resign his commission with an airy wave of the hand. Astonishing as it was, he was quite a big wheel in the BBC, his radical past now no more than a distant memory – distant, but not forgotten. 'There's always room for unofficial diplomacy,' he said, adding more firmly, 'We still need you.'

Bernard was building up his cholesterol level, shovelling back scones and cakes with the determination of a man who'd like to be struck down by a heart attack before tea was over. 'What do we want to know?' he asked.

'There's a woman called Alice Markwick who runs a company specializing in lasers. She has a rather ingenious device which we covet.'

'A device of aggressive intent?'

'If you mean a weapon, yes. We're due to take possession within the next few weeks. I have a suspicion that Mrs Markwick might be contacted by someone else.'

'Like who?'

'As I say, it's an ingenious piece of technology. There might be interest from the Americans, or the French, or even some branch of private enterprise.'

Bernard winced. 'Weapons,' he said heavily. 'Haven't we outgrown weapons yet?'

'Maybe at your Television Centre they value your inquisitive spirit, your charmingly ineffective liberalism,' Petrin said more sharply. 'We just want you to do what you're told. The weapon, as it happens, has considerable political credibility. It's not in the least bit messy.'

'What do you – ' Bernard hesitated. 'What do we need to know?'

'Who the opposition is. Can we trust the Markwick woman? Is this thing any bloody good? Perhaps you could discover these things without alerting ten camera crews and the national press.'

Bernard nodded.

'I'm here for a few days.' Petrin stood up. Lowering his voice slightly he said, 'Let's not have one of your legendary British cock-ups this time, eh?'

Bernard ran a broad finger across his plate and licked the crumbs off it.

Not telling Angie about his visit from Zena Wentworth was the easiest decision Paul had ever had to make. Since his fall, she had been trying to persuade him that to risk future injury trying to discover what had happened to Alex Drew was putting death before life, the past before the future. Gavin's sleazy scheme to entrap Alice Markwick had alarmed her further. The news that Zena Wentworth had attempted to rape Paul on his bed of pain might have been the final straw.

'Welcome to the evil empire of Crazy Mary.' Angie held open the door of her Mini as Paul, whose arm was still in a sling, heaved his legs round and out of the car. He looked up at a discreet sign reading 'The Empire Club'. There was a burly uniformed doorman standing by the entrance of the club, stamping his feet in the cold.

'Looks respectable enough to me,' Paul said.

Angie smiled and slipped a hand through his free arm. 'Wait 'til you meet Mary,' she said.

It had been her idea to come up to London the night before the poker game. It would get Paul away from the flat, she said, tune him into the ways of the metropolis. They were staying in the Putney flat of an old school friend, whose work as an air stewardess took her away much of the time. Then there was the briefing session with Crazy Mary.

'We're here to see Mary Chivers,' Angie told the doorman. 'The croupier.'

The doorman showed them down the stairs, into a large room full of roulette and backgammon tables. Apart from a few cleaners, the place was deserted. The smell of the previous night's cigars hung heavily in the air.

The short, dark girl who walked towards them in a navy blue suit and flat shoes might have been a stockbroker.

'Hi, Chiv,' Angie said. The two girls brushed cheeks in greeting. 'This is Paul.'

'Hullo, Mary.' Paul extended his left hand.

'It's a bit grim at the moment.' Mary glanced around the brightly-lit room. 'We're only closed for three hours out of twenty-four. The punters will be back this afternoon.'

They went to a small office where, over coffee, the two girls talked of friends from school. As far as Paul could gather, most of them had gone wrong: one worked for a discreet and exclusive escort agency, another had run away to Spain with an ageing bank robber, a couple had hurried into marriage and out the other side.

'What was this, a reform school you went to?' Paul interrupted at one point.

Mary shrugged. 'Convent girls,' she said, as if no other explanation was necessary. 'You wait – you'll discover Angie's hidden vices in the end.'

'I've discovered a few already.'

Angie blushed, but smiled with pleasure. 'It's Mary here who's the fast one. Don't be taken in by the respectable suit.'

'Croupiers have to be above suspicion,' Mary said. 'One hint of a relationship with a punter and you're out.'

'That's why they call her Crazy Mary.'

The croupier frowned, as if surprised by the nickname. 'You become a bit of a control freak working in a casino. Once every few months, I take time off with some of the other girls to work on transatlantic cruises.' She shrugged. 'I seemed to have acquired something of a reputation.'

'She'll try anything once,' said Angie.

Paul smiled nervously. He felt ill at ease with this casual talk of misbehaviour.

As if she sensed that now was not the moment for confessional reminiscence, Mary opened the top drawer of the desk and took out a new, unopened pack of cards, which she unwrapped. 'Right,' she said, shuffling the cards like a magician. 'Crazy Mary's crash course in stud poker.'

Chapter 11

There were times when Ginnie Matthew's love affair with racing went through a rocky patch, when she envied those friends of hers whose children were growing and whose husbands, becoming balder and duller by the minute, at least provided a stolid kind of security.

It was four o'clock on a chilly afternoon in late February. The racegoers at Lingfield Park were drifting home after a day's racing which had provided the Matthews yard with a disappointing third in the novice hurdle and a faller in the two mile 'chase. She walked briskly towards the stables where Skinflint and a decent five-year-old called Above Par were being saddled up for some post-race work. There had been two spare places in the horse-box and, once the Lingfield authorities had given her permission to gallop two of her horses on the track after the last race, she decided that Skinflint – and, more significantly, his jockey Clay Wentworth – would benefit from one last outing before Cheltenham.

'Looks well, don't he?' Pat, the Head Lad, stood beside her as Clay led Skinflint out of his stable.

Ginnie stepped forward and patted the horse, running a hand down his shoulder and his front legs. 'Could be worse,' she smiled, knowing Skinflint had never been in better condition. The Kim Muir had come just at the right time for him – but the same could be said of the Cheltenham Gold Cup, which was to be run the day after. The greed of owners, the vanity of amateur jockeys – Ginnie sighed, as she watched Clay Wentworth hold up a leg so that Pat could give him a leg-up into the saddle. He looked soft, slightly overweight and nervous; not for the first time, Ginnie found the comparison between Skinflint and his jockey painful to contemplate. At last she had a top class horse in the yard – and it was doomed to be ridden by Clay Wentworth.

From the next door box, Dave Smart led Above Par, checked his girths and hopped into the saddle. Dave wasn't the greatest jockey of all time but he was a good professional, honest and tough. He deserved the ride on Above Par in the Ritz Trophy at Cheltenham.

'See you in front of the stands,' she said.

Watching them as the two horses made their way onto the race-course, Ginnie found herself reflecting that although Skinflint was her favourite horse in the yard, she would have mixed feelings if he won at Cheltenham. There was something tainted about his success this season. It was as if his progress was inextricably linked with the misery of others – horses that were destroyed, the suicide of Alex Drew, the ending of Paul's career.

'Wish I'd entered that horse in the Gold Cup,' she said to Pat, who was walking beside her.

'With Mr Wentworth on board?'

'No,' Ginnie sighed. 'He'd need a jockey.'

It was never the professionals who caused her problems. It was when outsiders became involved, dabbling in racing for their own peculiar reasons, that it became confusing, demoralizing. Bent jockeys, corrupted stable lads – there was inevitably the hand of someone outside racing working them, misguided, greedy amateurs.

'I heard from Kevin Smiley's parents yesterday,' she said. 'They seemed to think what happened to him was our fault.'

'It wasn't suicide, that's for sure.'

The trainer and her Head Lad walked on, each thinking of the inexplicable death of Kevin Smiley. It was clear, even to the police who had seemed reluctant to treat his drowning as murder, that it was Kevin who had put acid on Monty's hind legs that morning. Possibly he knew the gravity of what he was doing; more probably, he took the money without asking questions.

A local mini-cab company had confirmed that he was due to be taken to the station that evening, but when the car turned up, there had been no sign of him. Next morning his body was found floating in the River Kennet, some eight miles away. A post-mortem had revealed alcohol in the blood and bruising to the side of the head consistent with a heavy blow.

'Who was he working for, that's the question?' Pat said.

Ginnie looked down to the racecourse, where Clay and Dave Smart were walking in a circle, waiting for her. 'Whoever it was seemed to be after Paul,' she said. 'And if they could do that to him, bumping off poor little Kevin was hardly going to worry them.'

'But why Paul?'

'Why indeed?' Ginnie thought of the note she had written for Clay, of Paul's determination to find the person behind Alex's death. Yes, sometimes she wished she had never set foot in a racing yard.

She glanced back to the grandstand, where a group of race-goers was lingering, watching her two horses through binoculars as the crowds thinned. A few would-be journalists and professional gamblers, but the majority would be the clueless addicts of racing whose dreams of a great gambling coup would never be realized.

'No shortage of spies, I see,' she said.

It was true. Ginnie never gave her horses trials. The punter and journos doing overtime at Lingfield would discover no more than what the more knowledgeable of them already knew – that the Matthews yard never sent a runner out for one of the big prizes who wasn't jumping out of its skin with health and fitness.

Sitting by the rails, hunched on a shooting-stick like an ogling vulture, sat Sir Denis Wentworth.

'I see Daddy's here,' Pat muttered.

Ginnie laughed. 'All teeth and smiles, as usual,' she said. The relationship between Clay and his father was a mystery. Neither particularly liked the other but, wherever the son went, the father seemed to follow. Yet Clay never objected. A generous interpretation would be that a cold, undemonstrative kind of family love was at work but there was no hint of affection in Sir Denis's pale watery eyes as he watched his son.

Ginnie stood beside the old man. 'Looks well, doesn't he?' she said.

Sir Denis moved his jaws as if he had been given something unpleasant to take. 'Very,' he said eventually.

'Hack on round to the two-and-a-half-mile start. Pull them up and let them get a breather and then carry on the rest of the way round.' She called out to Dave Smart and Clay. 'You can let them stride out the last couple of furlongs but don't go mad.'

As the two jockeys cantered their horses to the far side of the course Ginnie heard a guttural mumble emanating from Sir Denis. He might have been clearing his throat, or maybe making some comment to himself. The words sounded suspiciously like, 'Bloody fool, he is.'

She decided to ignore him. Ginnie had more important matters to worry about than Wentworth family relationships.

It was his first visit to a British racecourse and Gavin Holmes wasn't impressed. The afternoon had seemed to consist of a lot of standing around punctuated occasionally by equestrian events of highly questionable entertainment value. A large majority of the racegoers were the type of Englishman, goofy and over-confident, that he had until now thought were an endangered species. They honked, they drank, they talked about horses, they honked some more.

'Get on with it, you stupid *bastards*,' he muttered to himself, stamping his feet on the ground to keep the circulation going. Clay Wentworth and the other jockey seemed to be taking an age to do whatever they intended to do.

A ferret-faced little man, an ex-jockey, perhaps, looked up at him in slight surprise. Gavin smiled apologetically.

The only way he had managed to survive the afternoon was by putting away a bit at the bar. Bucks Fizz, during those brief early moments when he had felt he should behave himself; champagne to celebrate the completion of the first race; brandy and ginger ale, followed by brandy. It was one way to spend an afternoon at the races – in fact, it was the only way.

As the two horses had pulled up on the far side

of the race-course, Gavin put the binoculars he had borrowed from a colleague at the office to his eyes. He had difficulty focussing them, or maybe it was his eyes that couldn't focus any more.

To work while terminally pissed was a basic journalistic requirement. Over the years, Gavin had taken this skill one step further so that now he could only work while pissed. During the afternoon he had chatted easily with barfly racegoers, concentrating on the career and character of Ginnie Matthews. Was she ambitious? Was she ruthless? Was she bent?

The general consensus, gleaned from an in-depth survey at the Lingfield Park bar, was that Mrs Matthews was marvellous, bloody *marvellous*. Troubles in the past, of course, with that shit of a husband of hers, but good old Ginnie hadn't let that hold her back. Bent? Good God, no – she was straight as a die.

'Here they go,' said the ferret beside him in the grandstand. Gavin managed to focus his binoculars accurately enough to follow the two horses as they galloped down the back straight. Maybe, to the cognoscenti, the way the animals were moving had deep significance, but to him they looked like any other horses doing the sort of thing that horses do.

Gavin let the binoculars drop, and looked down to the rails where, broad-backed in her sheepskin coat, Ginnie stood between one of her employees and an old man Gavin guessed was Sir Denis Wentworth.

After the fourth race, he had ventured out of the

warmth of the bar down to the sort of clubhouse from where the jockeys appeared. One of Ginnie's horses had taken third place in the race which had just finished and he managed to talk to her briefly outside the winners' enclosure.

'Mrs Matthews,' he had said. 'Gavin Holmes, *Guardian*. D'you have a moment?'

'Holmes? Are you new on the racing page?'

'It's a general feature. We want to profile your owner, Clay Wentworth. A half-page on a businessman at play, that sort of thing.'

Ginnie Matthews had frowned. 'Businessman at play? Doesn't sound very *Guardian* to me.'

'It's a departure,' he said, noting that she was more perceptive than most of the people he had met racing. 'How is Mr Wentworth preparing for his big race at Cheltenham?'

'You'd better ask him that.'

'I have a meeting with him later. He suggested I watch him ride here, then we could talk afterwards. But you could tell me if, say, he goes to watch the horses he'll be racing against.'

'For example?' Ginnie seemed more interested now.

'Brut Force, was it?' It was lucky he had done his homework. 'Ballina Lady. Whataparty.'

The trainer looked away, then said more quietly, 'The businessman at play, eh?' There was nothing evasive about the way she had looked at him. 'Why don't you ring me this evening and we can talk about this at more length?'

It had not been the remark of a guilty woman.

'Look at that fucker go.' The ferret standing beside him in the grandstand muttered to himself. The two horses, Gavin saw, had just entered the home straight but, while Dave Smart was niggling at Above Par, Clay seemed to be having difficulty holding Skinflint. By the time they passed the stands, Skinflint was eight lengths to the good and still pulling.

'What a flying machine, eh.' Watching Skinflint go through his paces seemed to have cheered the man standing beside Gavin. 'He's got a wally on board, he's giving the other horse a stone and a half and he still trots up. Talk about a good thing for Cheltenham.'

'Right.' Gavin glanced at his watch. It was time to ask the wally a few pertinent questions.

As the taxi moved slowly through the streets south of the River Thames, caught up in the late afternoon traffic, Josef Petrin stared out gloomily onto the damp streets outside. Ant-like, the workers scurried into the underground stations, grabbing evening papers, ignoring one another in their feverish need to get home to television, a drink and some ghastly English meal. 'Don't hold your breath,' the taxi-driver had said. 'Bad time of day to be heading out of the centre of London. Early rush hour.'

Petrin smiled wanly. Did they really call this crawl a 'rush-hour'? Not for the first time, he found himself wondering whether his country's relentless move towards capitalism was such a good idea. There may have been queues and shortages in Prague, free speech might have been somewhat curtailed, but at least there was a kind of security in hopelessness. Here in London, no one was satisfied with his lot – jealousy, greed and resentment seemed to seep from the very brickwork.

The cab jerked forward as his driver neatly headed off a car trying to filter onto the main road in front of him. 'English – very bad drivers,' he said over his shoulder. 'Very dozy, right?'

'Right,' said Petrin.

'You wanna watch yourself down where you're going, mate,' the driver said.

'Yes?'

'Bandit country. Walk down the street in that overcoat, in those shoes, carrying that briefcase, and you'll be in dead schtuck, mate. Brixton, Stockwell – mugging's like the local industry down there. Everybody's at it.'

Petrin looked at his slim, expensive black briefcase. Perhaps it had been rather naive to venture out of central London with it.

'They have mugging where you come from, have they?'

'No,' said Petrin in a tone he hoped would discourage further conversation. 'Not yet.'

He wasn't nervous as he noted, as he neared his destination, the increase in litter on the streets – paper, tin cans, not to mention debris of the human kind – just mildly concerned. It was not that he was incapable of looking after himself – you didn't work your way up from the factory floor to the senior reaches of government in Prague, as he had, without learning about self-preservation, but he disliked fuss. Over here, the press was not as accommodating as it was back home.

'How long you going to be?' asked the cab-driver.

'Ten minutes maybe.'

'Tell you what. Pay me for the trip and I'll wait outside for you.'

'That would be most kind,' said Petrin.

The street in Brixton where the Zametskys lived was pleasingly grimy. The old communist in Petrin – part of him that he rarely mentioned these days – took satisfaction in reflecting that it was for this that the man Peter had fled his motherland – this was his precious freedom. The taxi drew up outside a forbidding two-storey house with dustbins tipped over by the front door and a window boarded up.

'Sure you've got the right address?' asked the driver.

'Yes.' Petrin stepped out. This was home sweet home for Mr and Mrs Zametsky.

As soon as he stepped into the cold, high-ceilinged room with its peeling wallpaper and yellowing posters, he knew it was going to be a depressing experience.

'Peter.' The plump Polish girl with the peasant eyes spoke softly. 'We have a visitor.'

He had never been a squeamish man when he was young, yet these days Petrin found he avoided visiting friends in hospital. Driving by an accident just outside Prague and seeing the body of a lorry-driver laid out beside the road had made him feel really quite nauseous. He put it down to middle age.

So he hesitated when he first saw the thing on the bed. It was particularly unfortunate that, while the parts concealed by a suspiciously off-colour blanket had presumably been unaffected by the accident, his hands and, more disgustingly, his face, were horrifically disfigured.

Hairless, wearing dark glasses, his flayed skin red and shiny on the cheekbones, Peter Zametsky was making an odd sound through the lipless void that was his mouth.

'Hullo, Mr Zametsky,' Petrin said, drawing up a chair some way from the bed. 'My name is Josef Petrin. We've not met.'

Klima, his wife, sat on the bed and laid a soothing hand on the scarred right hand. 'He wants me to stay,' she said. 'He's been very nervous of strangers since the accident.'

An angry sound came from the figure on the bed.

'Sorry, darling.' Klima smiled apologetically as she turned to Petrin. 'My husband believes it was no accident. You aren't the police, I suppose?'

In a way, thought Petrin. 'No,' he said.

'Somebody did this to my husband.' The woman's pale and placid features showed signs of animation. 'He was visited in hospital by a man, threatening to do worse. Even though the nurse gave them a description, the police have put it down to the effects of the acid.'

Peter made another incomprehensible noise.

'Yes,' said his wife. 'They think he's mad.'

Briefly, Petrin considered confiding his disappointment with the state of Britain, perhaps comparing it to the new vitality of Eastern Europe, but he restrained himself. It would seem like crowing; another time perhaps.

'I'm an acquaintance of Mrs Markwick,' he said. 'I'm here to offer some help.' Laying his briefcase on his lap, Petrin opened it and took a sealed white envelope which he gave to Klima. 'Please open it,' he said.

The woman blushed as she saw the £50 notes, as though she had already done something mildly immoral to earn it. 'It's money, Peter,' she said. 'This gentleman's giving us money.'

'A thousand pounds.' Petrin smiled. 'Not much, but a start perhaps. It's a sort of insurance payment.'

Peter stretched out a hand. His wife gave him the envelope. He said something, then hurled the money across the room.

'The money doesn't come from Mrs Markwick,'

Petrin explained smoothly. 'It's not compensation or guilt money.' From a distant room, he heard a baby cry. 'I'd keep it if I were you.'

Klima walked across the room where the £50 notes had spilled out of their envelope onto the bare boards of the floor. 'What do we need to do?' she asked.

'Alice and I are old friends. For some time now, we have been discussing the acquisition of her secret project, the development – ' he nodded in the direction of the shape in the bed ' – thanks to Dr Zametsky, of Opteeka B.'

There was a question from Peter, which his wife interpreted. 'He's asking how you know about Opteeka B,' she said.

'I am Alice's client. As you probably know, she has been talking to the Czechoslovak government. Once Opteeka B has completed its tests, I take possession of the prototype and the design plans. My problem is that I very much fear that there are others who may sabotage my agreement.'

'The people who did this to Peter.' Klima was holding the money as if, at any moment, she would have to hand it back.

'Precisely. They're remarkably unpleasant people. Civilians, I suspect. Whereas we would mass-produce Opteeka B for entirely legitimate military use, these people are nothing less than criminals. I dread to think what they have in mind.' The sound of the child crying was beginning to irritate Petrin. 'D'you want to fetch the baby?' he asked. 'I'm in no hurry.'

Klima hurried out of the room, returning moments later with a child, red-faced from its wailing. Without a word, she unbuttoned the front of her dress. Petrin looked away queasily but not before he had caught sight of a billowing, blue-veined breast.

'So.' As Klima looked from her baby to Petrin, her face became edgy and mistrustful. 'What do we have to do for the money?'

'It's yours.' Petrin smiled, forcing himself to look at the baby. 'It was the least we could do. You could – ' he hesitated, as if a thought had suddenly occurred to him ' – maybe earn a little bit more.'

For a moment, the room was silent but for the sound of the baby as it sucked noisily. Petrin swallowed as his sensitive nostrils were assailed by the sweet, sickly smell of mother's milk.

'Yes,' he said. 'If you were able to tell me how Opteeka B is going to be tested, and where. That would help me forestall any last-minute hitch in the arrangement with Markwick Instruments.'

'What about Mrs Markwick?' Klima asked. 'Why don't you ask her?'

'It's complicated. She denies there's a problem of security.' Petrin opened the briefcase and took out another envelope which he weighed in his hand thoughtfully.

'He's got some more money, Peter.'

There was an odd moaning sound from the bed. Peter Zametsky took off his dark glasses and, with the red stubs of his fingers, wiped a tear from his light grey, sightless eyes. He repeated the sound more loudly.

'Paper.' Klima stood up, holding her baby to her. 'Yes, that's right. You'll need some paper.'

It was twenty minutes, not ten, before Josef Petrin closed the heavy door behind him and, with just one glance down the street, stepped into the taxi.

'Sorry,' he said. 'My business took a bit longer than expected.'

'All right, squire.' The taxi-driver put down his evening paper and started the engine. 'The meter was running so I wasn't worried.'

'Of course.'

'Where can I take you then?'

'The Ritz.' Petrin had seen enough of Brixton to last him a lifetime. 'As quick as possible.'

On this story, Gavin had given himself so many false identities that he had almost forgotten who he was. Deception was part of the job, of course – it went with the territory – but he preferred distorting a few facts on the page to inventing aliases for himself. Written lies were somehow easier to live with.

Gavin poured champagne into the glasses of Clay and Sir Denis Wentworth, then filled his own, fighting back his need for a brandy. 'Cheerio,' he said raising his glass. 'Here's to Skinflint at Cheltenham.'

Lifestyle expert he had been with Alice Markwick; now he was a human interest journalist, contributing to the business pages. Gavin took out his spiral-bound notebook and smiled. What he did for his art.

'Fire away.' Clay Wentworth sipped at his drink with the air of a man who has better things to do than be interviewed by the press. 'Which area d'you want to major on?'

'Your hobbies. Horseback riding, for example.' Gavin smiled as Clay looked pained.

'It's rather more than a hobby,' he said. 'And we call it racing.'

The man wasn't bright, Gavin decided as he asked a few routine questions, noting down Clay's highly predictable answers, and there was something oddly immature about the way he occasionally glanced at the old curmudgeon, his father, before he spoke. It was almost as if he were a schoolboy rather than a grown man approaching middle age and the chairman of a company.

'You've had a spot of luck with the opposition,' Gavin said, 'A racing friend of mine said the Kim Muir was going to be easier to win than many expected.'

'I'd prefer to win on the racecourse against the best opposition.'

'So you'll be hoping this – ' Gavin referred to his notes ' – this Tanglewood doesn't suffer any untoward accidents?'

For a moment, Clay looked up sharply, as if he were about to depart from a carefully prepared script, but then the look of urbane boredom settled back on his face. 'Ron Charlesworth looks after his horses,' he said, 'I'm sure there will be no problem.'

The bar was empty now, and the barman was making enough noise as he washed up the glasses to suggest that he was planning to close up soon.

'Why d'you do it, Clay?' Gavin asked easily. 'I mean you've got everything – you run a company, you're not a teenager any more. It's *dangerous* riding those things, isn't it?'

Clay Wentworth looked out at the racecourse on which darkness was now falling.

'In a way, it's like business,' he said. 'You have to have the right product, your horse, if possible with a unique selling point that will cut it in the marketplace. Speed, stamina, courage. Then you've got to gather the right team about you – from Ginnie Matthews, who I see as a sort of Technical Director, down to Joe, the lad who does my two horses. Without the right executive team – the "boardroom mix", I call it – the product has no position in the marketplace.'

With a thoughtful frown, Gavin made a note in his notebook. It read 'Bollocks'.

'Then there's the personal challenge. The preparation for the launch of your product, the race. You have to be ready, fit. You have to know about the opposition. And on the day, it's all about concentration, skill – and, of course, keeping your nerve.' Clay looked pleased with his little speech. 'Then it's all down to luck.'

Gavin smiled. 'And there was I thinking you rode horses for fun,' he said.

'There's that as well, of course,' Clay said coldly.

More out of politeness than through some journalistic hunch, Gavin turned to Clay's father, who was sipping impassively at his champagne. 'What about you, Sir Denis?' he asked, raising his voice slightly. 'What do you think of your son's love of racing?'

The old man turned to look at Gavin with cool distaste. 'Whatever gives my son pleasure, gives me pleasure,' he said.

'Right.' Gavin made another careful note on his pad.

'Daddy?' he wrote. 'Check out Daddy.'

Although the walls in the Victorian row of houses were solid, Peter Zametsky could hear the thud of reggae music from the people next door. It was still early evening; by two in the morning the wall would shake.

Not that Peter minded. At least he could still hear things. The sound of other people's partying reminded him that he was alive.

He could feel, too. Right now, he felt the weight of two inprints on the bed, only one of which was familiar.

'He's asleep,' Klima said. She seemed to be fussing around with a blanket. 'He loves to sleep on your bed.'

He felt her touch the other weight, which was much

lighter than the baby, and heard a rustle of paper. Money. Klima was counting the money again.

'It seems too easy, *moje kochanie*. I'm frightened. I think we should tell the police.'

Peter made a sound in his throat which a stranger might have taken for a cough.

'Don't laugh, Peter,' said his wife. 'There's something wrong. If this man was dealing with Mrs Markwick, why did he come to you? And whoever heard of a Czech paying out £5,000? Not even in vouchers – in cash.'

Peter extended a hand and ran it through the notes as if they were a pool of warm water. Of course, Klima was right. The deal stunk. But what more could be done to him? The Italian who had taken away his face must know that he could give him no more information. As for the Markwick woman, her behaviour hardly merited loyalty. Not a single visit while he was in hospital and no mention of compensation above his salary.

'Someone's going to get hurt,' said Klima.

Peter made a sound, both anguished and angry. It meant, 'So long as it's not us, I don't care.'

'*Kochanie.*' Klima touched his hand. 'I hope you're right.'

Alcohol was brainfood for Gavin. The same substances that would render another man comatose – indeed, rendered Gavin comatose when he wasn't working – propelled him forward when he was working on a story. Admittedly, the propulsion often took him by a strange, indirect route, full of odd and inexplicable stop-ins, but that was good. Booze made him an instinctive reporter, who relied on an unsteady sixth sense that took him to destinations that mere logic would never find.

After the ordeal of passing twenty minutes with the Wentworth father and son team, feigning interest in Clay's banal, non-committal replies, he had needed a top-up before he went home.

'Give us a real drink, my friend,' he muttered to the barman, after saying his goodbyes to Clay and Sir Denis.

'We're closed, sir.'

Gavin held up a £10 note. 'If you've cashed up, no need to give me the change.'

The barman took the money and, with remarkably little grace for a man who had just received a tip, said, 'I'm locking up in two minutes.'

There was something odd about Clay Wentworth. Gavin had met a few sportsmen, professional and amateur, in his time; invariably, they came alive when talking about their sport. With Clay, it seemed forced, almost rehearsed. If riding nags at speed over bits of wood gave him no pleasure, then why did he do it? And the father seemed utterly uninterested in racing. Gavin gave a little shudder of satisfaction as the cognac burnt its way down his throat.

Maybe it was social. Yet the jokey questions Gavin had posed about the high-profile entourage of spectators Clay brought to watch him race – Lol Calloway, Alice Markwick, the late Digby Welcome – had been received with glazed indifference. 'They're friends,' he had said. 'They like a day at the races.'

It didn't wash. Gavin thought of Alice Markwick and of what he had heard or read about Welcome and Calloway. None of them were the types to spend afternoons at chilly racecourses for the sake of friendship. Money – that was what interested them all. Yet there seemed to be no gambling factor at work here.

Draining his glass under the hostile glare of the barman, Gavin slipped off the barstool and swayed palely for a moment. He extended a queasy hand to the bar to steady himself.

'Think I might have overdone it.' He smiled apologetically at the barman.

'You've had a heavy afternoon.'

'Too right, mate.' Gavin buttoned his bomber jacket.

'I trust you're not driving.' The barman polished a glass self-righteously. 'Drink and drive, you know.'

'It's not the drink that's the problem,' Gavin said. 'It's the fresh air. An afternoon of that's enough to make anyone feel woozy.' He shook his head like a man trying to shift some unpleasant thought from his mind, then made his way out of the bar, bumping against a couple of tables.

The racecourse was deserted now although there was the sound of voices coming from the Press Room, which was thoughtfully located close to the bar.

'Poor bastards,' Gavin muttered, thinking of the journalists urgently filing copy about how one nag ran faster than another. 'What a way to earn a living.'

At the bottom of the stairs, he looked onto the course where a tractor was already harrowing the turf between the fences. It took a moment of concentrated effort to remember where the car park was but then, seeing a couple of cameramen lugging their equipment behind the grandstand, he followed them. The car must be somewhere in that direction.

'Better call Raven,' Gavin said to himself. Paul had mentioned that Zena Wentworth had managed to get him an invitation to one of Wentworth's poker evenings. The boy was smart enough to extract information as effectively as the regulars would extract money from him.

Gavin was wondering vaguely at what price to Paul's innocence Zena's cooperation had been obtained as he tottered into the car park. There were only a few cars there and his car was near a van into which the two cameramen were already loading their equipment.

'And so we bid farewell to picturesque Lingfield Park,' he sang out softly as he fumbled in his jacket for his car keys. He wouldn't be going racing again in a hurry, that was for sure. Too many horses. Too much standing up. Above all too much fresh air.

'Mr Holmes?'

At first, Gavin thought that the words had sounded

within the alcohol-drenched recesses of his brain. He hesitated by his car.

'Do you have a moment?'

He turned, swaying slightly. The two men by the van appeared to be filming him – one, a small man wearing jeans, was training a video on him, the other was raising a large stills camera to his eye.

'Hullo, what's this then?' Gavin straightened his tie in a humorous way. 'Profile of Gavin Holmes, investigative journalist at work? Fame at – '

The camera held by the second man made a sound like a toy car being started, high-pitched and comical. Gavin looked into the lens then he felt himself thrown back against his car.

'What? *What*?' he heard himself saying feebly. At first, he thought the blackness came from a blow on the back of the head, yet the force had come from the front, hurling him backwards. 'What?' His arms felt behind him for the roof of the car and he sagged, his head lolling forward, like a boxer on the ropes. It wasn't a pain in his eyes, it was an ache, an anaesthetic tingling. Gavin rubbed them, as if to take away the darkness. Then he felt the knife against his throat.

A voice said, 'Move.'

Gavin pressed back against the car, 'What d'you want from me?' he whispered.

'Get away from the car.'

In the blackness all around him, Gavin moved forward. 'I can't see,' he sobbed. 'What the fuck have you done?' He needed to get away. Perhaps back on the course there would be someone who could help him. Arms outstretched like a sleepwalker, he took what he thought was the direction of the car park.

The blade of the knife touched him on the base of the throat, more gently this time. 'Turn,' said the same voice, with its odd foreign accent, 'Go the other way.'

Gavin turned back towards the car but, in his blindness, he must have wandered to its left because his hands felt the high brick wall against which the car was parked. He felt his way along the wall to the left. Maybe he would reach the road. There were no more orders from the men. Gavin sobbed with relief as he heard the engine of the van being started somewhere behind him. They were leaving him, thank God – sightless but alive. He fell against another car. Turning, he made his way back along the wall. If he could reach his car, maybe he could let himself in and lock the door until help arrived.

The van was driving away, yet seemed to hesitate, as if it were manoeuvring itself out of the car park. 'Don't let them come back,' Gavin sobbed. To his right, the van revved louder.

For perhaps two seconds, he realized what was going to happen. The van was coming towards him, reversing, it sounded like. Gavin broke into a run but it was too late. His last scream was drowned by the sound of the engine and the crash of metal against human flesh and brick.

* * *

The photographer jumped out of the van and, without a glance at the body by the wall, wiped some traces of blood from the back of the van with the damp cloth he was carrying. There was no need to arouse unnecessary suspicion.

'Off we go,' he said as he jumped back into the passenger seat.

The van left the car park at speed.

Stroking the Opteeka B, the photographer found that it was still warm. Carefully, he put it back into its aluminium case and locked it, pocketing the key.

'That's some machine,' said the driver, turning down a side road. Within two minutes, the van would be dumped and he and the crazed professor here would be making their way back to London in separate cars.

'Video?' said the photographer.

'It's all there.' The driver nodded to a hold-all on the floor of the van. 'I think you'll find my camera work is more than adequate.'

The photographer didn't answer. He was not a sadist, and being a party to the loss of life gave him little pleasure but, right now, he was exulting.

He hadn't seen a thing, the poor bastard. Fi-Fi was good, but this was better. It had been the perfect experiment.

Chapter 12

It was the entrance of a loser, a lamb to the slaughter, a patsy – but that suited Paul fine.

'Mr Raven.' Clay Wentworth was the first to react as Paul stood at the door, having been shown in by a butler. He had been sitting in a deep armchair but got to his feet like a public schoolboy whose housemaster has just walked into the room. 'What a surprise.'

Paul smiled. 'I meant to ring,' he said. 'Poor old Digby Welcome invited me some weeks back. I meant to be here last week but I had an accident.'

The arm had only come out of its sling yesterday and a stab of pain darted through his shoulder as Clay shook his hand with a muttered, 'Never knew you played.'

'I have a lot of time on my hands.'

Clay glanced at Paul's walking-stick and, for a brief moment, seemed embarrassed. 'You know we have a no-railbird rule.'

'Sorry?'

'We don't allow railbirds – kibitzers.' The smile on Clay's face lost some of its friendliness. 'Non-playing spectators,' he explained.

Paul grinned goofily. He had been warned by Mary that he would be tried out with some recondite poker slang. Her advice had been to play the innocent. 'No, I'm here to play,' he said, patting the side of his jacket. 'I've got enough for the, er . . .'

'Pot?'

'Pot.'

'How exactly did you know where we were playing?'

'Zena,' said Paul significantly. 'We're friends.'

There was a tension in the room that was not entirely explained by his presence. As Paul was introduced to the four other guests, he noted that they seemed wary, like people forced together who have little in common but their habit. Alice Markwick he recognized. Then there was a stockbroker, a barrister with florid skin and a loud voice and a man called David who said he worked in a bank.

'A bank?' Paul acted surprised.

'Not that kind of bank,' said Clay coldly. 'Drink?'

Most of the gamblers seemed to have Perrier or wine. 'A whisky would be nice,' said Paul.

'We're just waiting for our last player,' Clay said, handing him an over-generous whisky. Uneasy small talk had been resumed among the other guests.

'I was a friend of one of your regulars.' Paul

lowered himself carefully into a hardback chair. 'Alex Drew.'

'Alex.' Clay shook his head. 'Terrible business.'

It was another five minutes, during which Paul sat, contributing only occasionally to the stilted conversation, before Lol Calloway appeared, complaining about the traffic into London.

'Lol, you know everyone except Paul,' said Clay. 'Paul Raven.'

The balding rock'n roller winked, clicked his tongue and made an oddly old-fashioned six-shooter gesture with both hands. 'How ya doing, man?' he said.

'I'm doing well,' said Paul.

With a palpable sense of relief, the party moved to a table in the corner, and ceased to be an ill-assorted social gathering. The Wentworth poker school was in progress.

'We normally play Texas Hold 'Em,' Clay said, pulling up an extra chair at the table for Paul. 'That all right with you?'

Paul furrowed his brow. 'Just run it through for me, will you?' he said.

'Standard seven card stud. Each player's dealt two cards – five communal cards are revealed. You bet after the deal, the flop, the turn and Fifth Street.'

'Flop? Fifth?' Paul allowed a look of panic to cross his face. 'I'm sure I'll pick it up as I go along.'

Let them think you haven't a clue, Crazy Mary had said. Every poker school needs a supply of pigeons, plump and clueless. Play two or three games like an amateur and they'll be falling over to get at you. Then you hit them.

Ignoring his instinct to take the early games slowly, fold early and get a sense of how the others played, Paul laid £50 on the first game, despite being dealt a phenomenally poor hand. The flop gave him a low pair – two sevens – and when Alice, unable to keep the sparkle of triumph from her eyes, turned over a triple queen, Paul gasped in astonishment, revealing his pathetic hand with a wimpish 'Whoops!'

After two more games like this, played with transparent ineptness, Paul sensed a stir of interest around the table. It had been some time since fresh money had been introduced to the school. Even if the new man lacked big funds, his participation in the game would help the pot. Even Lol Calloway had a chance to stay in play that much longer.

'Tonight doesn't seem to be my night,' Paul said, as Clay Wentworth won another hand in which Paul should have folded but had stupidly insisted on playing.

He had lost £350 of his £2,000 when, with the banker, he retired to the other side of the room to sit out a couple of hands. Feigning a mood of deep gloom, he managed to discourage conversation as they sat by the fire.

So this was what had set Alex on his way to destruction. It seemed inconceivable, absurd. Paul had read somewhere that the serious gambler, the addict, is acting on a deep psychological need to punish himself – that, however much he wins, he'll return to the table for the throw which will finish him. Certainly there was more to Alex than his loud and cheerful manner revealed. Yet he never gambled on horses. All Paul's sources – Jim Wilson, the valet, the other jockeys, Ginnie Matthews – had agreed that he had no contact with bookmakers. And in racing, there was no jockey who placed illegal bets regularly without at least some of his colleagues knowing.

'Seems to be my lucky night,' Clay Wentworth muttered from the table as, with a languid hand, he pulled in the pot for another game.

'You're not a regular then?' the banker interrupted Paul's thoughts.

'No. I'm having a bit of difficulty with this Texas Hold 'Em thing.'

'Goes in runs, like everything.' The man stared gloomily at the fire. 'How much are you in for?'

Paul resisted the bait. 'Enough,' he said.

'Are you lads in or out?' Lol Calloway called from the table. The banker threw his cigarette into the fire and wandered back to the game.

'Next one and I'm in,' Paul said.

Crazy Mary hardly lived up to her nickname when it came to poker tuition. No one could have been saner or cooler. She knew Clay – he was a regular at most of the gaming clubs and a better than adequate social player. He liked seven card stud, and Mary had guessed correctly that Texas Hold 'Em would be the favoured game at his poker evenings.

'It's one of the easiest games to play,' she had said. 'But to make money at it, you have to be good.'

Paul had learned the moves – how to make like a high roller while playing tight, how to watch for 'tells' in other players, the jargon and in-talk. Mary had laughed when he had told her that, unbeknownst to Clay, he would be playing against his own money. The fact that, win or lose, Wentworth would be out of pocket, thanks to his wife's contribution, gave Paul a confidence that the other players lacked.

'But play as if it was your money,' Mary had advised. 'Too much confidence and you can go on tilt.'

It was almost one before Paul began to play seriously, by which time he was down to £700. The few games he had won, he made seem like fluke victories and celebrated them with excessive good spirits. By now, the banker had lost interest and, muttering something about throwing good money after bad, he pocketed his remaining cash and bid the school farewell. Clay's look of disapproval at this early departure suggested that he wouldn't be invited in the future. Calloway had lost more heavily than Paul and seemed to be what Mary had called 'steaming' – playing with wild lack of judgement. The barrister was making money but Miles, the stockbroker, had descended into something of a sulk.

Paul glanced across the table. Alice Markwick had seemed distracted and was marginally down on the evening. The biggest winner, of course, was Clay.

'I hope those aren't your life savings you're blowing there,' he said amiably to Paul as Miles dealt them in for another round.

Paul thought of Wentworth's wife and her long, prying fingers. 'No, but I earned it the hard way,' he said.

'Let's hope you don't lose it the easy way.'

It was strange. Clay must have been £2,000 up on the evening, yet there was something restless and unhappy about him. Paul sensed that it had something to do with his presence.

Clay glanced at his cards and, without a moment's hesitation, pushed out £700. Alice, Lol and the barrister folded but Paul, following his instinct, called, matching Clay's bet. To his left, Miles glanced at him with some surprise before folding.

The man made an unconvincing bully, Paul thought as, for a moment, he held Clay's stare. All his life he had been surrounded by solid, strong men – his father, his business rivals. He had seen the look on their faces as they closed the deal, turned the knife on some poor sap. But when he had to tough it out, like now, the merest hint of uncertainty, of a deep inner weakness in his soul, betrayed him and spoilt it all. As he went all-in, trying to break Paul, he was like a bad actor playing Macbeth.

Paul held two eights in the hole. The flop had brought an ace of diamonds, a jack of spades and an eight of spades.

Somewhere, in the poker textbooks, Clay must have read that once you've earned the respect of your opponents, you can frighten them into folding even if your hand is weak. The other players had reacted according to the book. Paul hadn't.

Impassively, Clay turned over his cards, revealing that he was holding an ace, jack, queen and king, inferior to Paul's trip of three eights. Abandoning the dewy-eyed amateur act, Paul pulled in the pot with the smallest of smiles. To his surprise, Clay left the table, as did Alice Markwick.

The idea had never been to make his fortune and Paul played the next two games tightly, folding early as he tried to catch the conversation from where Clay and Alice sat by the fire, but they were talking too quietly.

It was almost three in the morning before Paul was able to take his moment, by which time Lol Calloway had bowed out with his normal string of obscenities. Miles was playing well, but Alice had lost interest, limping in late and low in those games where she didn't fold. Clay was down by a few hundred but appeared to have unlimited funds backing him.

The buck was with Paul, and by chance, he dealt himself the sweetest hand imaginable – two kings, followed by a flop of a king, a five and a four. After Alice and Miles had folded, Clay chewed his bottom lip in a pathetic attempt at a bluff, then pushed £1,000 into the centre of the table.

Paul hesitated for a minute or so. Then he raised

with all the money he had before him, confident that, even if Clay had aces wired in the hole – two aces – he was on a loser. The last two cards to be turned, a nine and a queen, sealed his fate.

Clay went for the full bluff, raising Paul by another £2,000 with a triumphant little smile. 'We work on the basis of IOUs in this school,' he said. 'Two weeks to pay.'

For a moment, there was silence in the room. Lol ambled over from the fire where he was sitting. 'You are one hard bastard, Clay,' he said quietly.

Paul looked at the two kings in his hand like a man reading his own death sentence. 'IOU?' he said. 'I hadn't realized I could run up debts.' Suddenly he found himself thinking of Alex. It was this easy to be caught in the gin-trap of indebtedness. The harder you pulled, the tighter you were held.

'You're with the big boys now, Paul,' Clay said. 'This isn't a social event.'

At poker, as in racing, there are amateurs and there are professionals. Paul swallowed, playing for time, allowing the tension around the table to build up. And professionalism was more than a question of skill and knowledge; it was a state of mind. Although Paul's experience of poker was limited to a few light-hearted games with the other jockeys and a two-hour lesson with Crazy Mary, he thought like a winner. Clay Wentworth was an amateur to the marrow of his bones.

'Perhaps,' Paul said, reaching into the inside pocket

of his jacket, 'I could bring this into play.' He threw a scuffed and faded piece of paper onto the pile of money. 'It's worth £2,000 of anybody's money.'

Clay leaned forward and picked up the piece of paper, a list of horses' names, most of which had been deleted. At last, there was panic. 'Where did you get this?' he asked, quietly.

'Win the hand and it's yours.'

Paul glanced around the table. Alice had looked away but seemed disturbed by the turn of events.

'What on earth's going on?' Miles asked. 'Is that an IOU?'

'Of a sort,' Paul said. He stared hard at Clay. 'Accepted?'

Clay nodded. 'Tricky little bastard, aren't you?' he said, turning over his two cards to reveal two jacks.

Paul flipped over the two kings. As he reached out for the pot, taking the piece of paper first of all and returning it to his inside pocket, he said, 'It's been copied, Clay – and two people know I'm here.'

'We need to talk about this – privately,' Clay said. 'The game's over.'

'That game's over,' said Paul. 'The other is just beginning.'

They should have stopped shooting. Alice Markwick stood on the steps of Clay's house in the early hours of the morning, and felt lost. The night had passed in a dream of poker hands, low birds and bantering conversation. Had she lost money? Did Paul Raven know about Opteeka B? Was Clay at this very moment revealing secrets that could destroy him and her? She didn't care.

They should have stopped shooting.

Alice wasn't aware of the whine of a milk float, approaching her from down the road. It stopped ten yards away and, with quite unnecessary jauntiness, a young man in his early twenties jumped out of the cab, took two pints from a crate and, whistling, walked towards the entrance to Clay's house. "Ullo,' he appraised the dark, slender woman standing on the doorstep with a cheeky up-and-down look. 'Heavy night, darlin'?'

Alice looked at him slowly. 'They should have stopped shooting,' she said.

There was a roar in her ears. Alice wasn't drunk, although she had tried during the evening to dull the pain with the occasional vodka tonic. With a huge effort of concentration, she remembered where she had parked the car and, as the milk float moved away, she walked slowly down the street, feeling for the car keys in her handbag as she went.

Sometimes it felt lonely on the small, deserted island that she had chosen to inhabit. She wasn't made for relationships, for confidences, for the ghastly domestic messiness of cohabitation, so after the death of Eric, she had kept the world away from her little island. At times like this, she regretted it. She wanted to talk to someone. There were girlfriends, of course, but they belonged to another world – a world of music, laughter and easy gratification. If she rang them, they would misunderstand what she wanted.

Alice unlocked the door of her Aston Martin and drove carefully back to the flat in Islington.

She knew what she had to do when she arrived. Without even checking her answering machine, she walked into the sitting-room in which all the lights had been left blazing. Behind a mediocre nineteenth-century landscape painting there was a safe which, tapping out a number on its security board, she opened. The videotape lay there, like an unexploded bomb.

She had to see it just once more.

Alice poured herself another vodka tonic from a cocktail tray in the corner. Her television and video were designed into a bookcase and, having inserted the tape, she sat on the sofa and, curling her legs underneath her, watched the recorded last moments of Gavin Holmes one more time.

Despite inept camera-work, it was clear that Opteeka B had passed this, its most important test, with full marks. One moment he was standing there, unsteady but in control, in front of his car, the next he was as blind and helpless as a newborn kitten.

Alice gripped the glass. This was what she wanted, she told herself. It would provide a future free of the insecurity which had haunted her since she was a little girl in Prague. She would never have to suffer in the way that her mother had suffered. Freedom came with a price-tag attached.

On the screen, Gavin was feeling his way towards the exit of the car park. Then, with the knife at his throat, he was turned back to the wall.

The violence she didn't like. Even while Opteeka B was being developed, she would sometimes wake at night, ambushed by visions of how her brain-child would be used. If she could have won a lifetime of security with a device to save a child's eyesight, or assist in major operations, nothing would have made her happier, but of course that was impossible. Life paid badly; it was with death that you made a killing.

Tears filled Alice's eyes. She wiped them away angrily, forced herself to watch the screen.

Like a rabbit blinded by a searchlight, the man blundered along the wall, then turned back. The speeding van filled the screen, but the roar of its engine was not loud enough to obliterate entirely Gavin's last scream of terror. The experiment was proved, there was no need to keep filming. As the van moved forward, the camera trained on the journalist's twitching, bloodied body.

Dry-eyed now, Alice stared ahead of her. Petrin had his evidence. It would soon be over.

'They should have stopped shooting,' she said quietly.

'Perhaps I ought to tell you that my wife and I have no secrets.' Clay Wentworth sat at the mahogany desk in his small study and puffed at a large cigar he had just taken from a silver box. 'We tell each other everything.'

Paul looked up at him from a deep armchair. Clay had recovered his composure somewhat since the final game in the night's poker school. He had bid farewell to the other guests with cool courtesy and before ushering Paul downstairs to his small room with the weary disapproval of a schoolmaster.

'So it came as no surprise that you were in possession of that particular piece of paper,' Clay continued.

'You accepted it as a bet. You must want it back.'

'What a pathetic thing to do.' A look of irritation crossed Clay's face. 'Your little moment of melodrama. Yes, of course I'd like it back.'

'You can have it.'

'But you've got a copy.'

'The photocopy of a scrap of paper is hardly going to serve as evidence.'

Clay leaned back in his absurd leather executive chair, like a bad actor in a soap opera. He was probably an amateur at business too, Paul reflected. The layout of his dark womb-like little study suggested a deep insecurity. The guest chair was lower than Clay's so that Paul had to look up at him. The desk lamp was positioned to dazzle him. Doubtless a psychiatrist might say something about the big cigar Clay was toying with as he spoke. Despite his position and his money – or perhaps because of them – the man was a loser.

'You have a deal in mind, I suppose,' Clay said. 'Some sort of cheap blackmail.'

'You'll have the list back, once you've told me what happened to Alex Drew.'

'Alex?' Clay looked surprised, as if he had forgotten that the man had ever existed. 'I really didn't know him well.'

'He came to your little evenings.'

'Bloody awful gambler, your friend. Ran up debts of fifty big ones.'

'And committed suicide.'

'It's happened before.' Clay puffed at his cigar and waved away the smoke as if, with it, he could make memories of Alex fade. 'You knew the boy, Paul,' he said reasonably. 'He lived for racing, but he had his weaknesses – women, the need to be seen in the right places. I liked him. He begged me to let him join us on Thursday nights; I thought I was doing him a favour.'

It was almost four in the morning and, as he listened to Clay Wentworth trying to lie his way out of trouble, Paul felt a profound weariness. 'I'm not interested in this bullshit,' he said, 'Tell me – '

Clay held up a hand. 'I covered his debts, that's how much I liked him. He owed me around thirty – the rest was to other members of the school. I asked him to go to his parents but he was too proud. Tragic. I wish I'd been able to talk to him.'

Outside the window, a blackbird with a faulty body clock had started singing in the darkness. For a brief moment, Paul thought of his friend – Alex, joking as the string pulled out at Charlesworth's yard; Alex, talking to Jim Wilson in the weighing-room; Alex, his face a mask of pale determination as they circled around the starter before a race.

Misunderstanding his silence, Clay added, 'It was a terrible shock to all of us.'

With the clarity of vision that comes with the graveyard shift, Paul saw that it wasn't greed for money or social acceptance that had led Alex to his death. It was weakness – the weakness of Clay Wentworth that somehow infected all around him.

'I'll tell you what I'm going to do,' Paul said softly. 'I'm washing my hands of this whole business. I'm going to hand this small piece of evidence – ' he patted his jacket pocket ' – to the Jockey Club. Just in case they reach an opinion that no respected amateur could possibly be guilty of driving a professional jockey to his death, I'll also tell the police everything I know. What happened to me. What happened to Alex. And what happened to the horses on the list. Then, just to make sure, I'll give the story to a journalist friend. Between them, they'll discover the truth about Mr Clay Wentworth and his friends.'

'Journalist?' Oddly, Clay seemed most alarmed by the least potent threat in Paul's armoury.

'Nobody you know,' Paul said. 'I've found out enough about Alex's death.'

'You know less than you think,' Clay muttered flatly.

There was a soft knock at the door. Before either man could react, it had been pushed open and a dishevelled figure in a white silk nightgown and a dressing-gown half hanging off a slender shoulder, stood at the entrance.

'Zena, what a nice surprise,' said Clay coldly.

'How did it go, Paul?' Zena asked woozily. 'Make lots of money, did you? Spend my investment wisely?'

'Yes.' The interruption was doubly annoying. Clay had seemed on the point of cracking. His wife's determination to reveal that he had been gambling against his own money was an unwelcome diversion. 'We were talking about Alex.'

'Oh, Alex.' Zena entered the room, running a hand through her hair. Whatever she was on, pills or booze, had done little for feminine allure, and the make-up around her eyes seemed to have smudged or run earlier in the night. 'One of our first victims, wasn't he, darling?' She smiled in the general direction of her husband as she sat on the edge of his desk, affording Paul an unavoidable view of her thighs.

'You're drunk. It's late. We're busy,' Clay said. There was a tightness in his voice that Paul had not heard before.

'I screw 'em, you kill 'em, isn't that right?'

'Alex committed suicide.' Clay glared at his wife but, behind the threat, there was something shifty and defensive. 'There's no need to bother Mr Raven with this.'

'I'm sure Mr Raven –' Zena smiled crookedly at

277

Paul and waggled a bare foot in his direction ' – would love to know this.'

Paul waited.

'Did you know a man called Gavin Holmes, darling?' Zena said suddenly. 'Journalist on the *Guardian*, nice man, bit of a lush – ' she paused ' – good lover, though. Killed today. Accident at the races. On the news it was. They say he was pissed, but we know better than that, don't we, darling?'

'Is this a joke?' Paul asked. 'Is Holmes dead?'

'Crushed against a wall. Went to Lingfield Park. Weren't you at Lingfield today, darling?'

With a sudden movement, Clay stood up and, taking Zena roughly by the arm, propelled her, drunkenly protesting, out of the door. Paul heard snatches of angry conversation in the hall. Eventually, Clay returned, closing the door behind him.

'Sorry,' he said. 'She gets rather emotional sometimes.'

'Is she right?'

'I heard an item on the news about this man.' Clay returned to his desk. 'It's the first time I've even heard his name.' He smiled wearily. 'It's all history,' he said. 'I'll tell you about the list you have, and you can do what you like with it.'

'History?'

'Yes.' Clay seemed haggard, broken by the events of the evening. 'I wish I had never become involved.'

The tape on the answering-machine turned slowly.

The voice of Clay Wentworth, weary but not defeated, sounded in Alice Markwick's flat.

'... an executive decision, no more or less. I've thrown him off the track. He has discovered why Drew died, which is all he really wanted to know. I managed to persuade him that the journalist's death was some sort of weird accident. He's finished his little quest. He'll leave us alone now . . . '

Alice sat on the sofa, an empty glass hanging loosely from her hand, the blank grey television screen before her.

' . . . the unfortunate fuss this evening about my shopping-list,' the voice from the tape continued. 'I even managed to persuade him to leave that with me so it's a question of hanging on until Wednesday. After that, we're free of . . . '

As if awakening from a dream, she put the glass on the floor, stood up and turned the television off. She pressed a button, removing the videotape and locking it once more in the safe.

Clay was still talking as Alice switched off the light and walked slowly to the bedroom.

Chapter 13

It wasn't like they show on the silver screen, the gathering of wrongdoers at a small terraced house in Perivale on the outskirts of London. The picture of the Virgin and child above the mantelpiece was good, so was the way one of the young men, the one with a moustache, cracked his knuckles occasionally, but the rest, three Italians sitting in cheap chairs by a gas fire, was too light, too domestic, too English – more *EastEnders* than the Godfather.

'So,' Tino, the older man, smiled with satisfaction. '*Il Cavallo di Troia* is doing his work.'

'*Cavallo? Troia*? What you talking about, papa?' The grey-haired man's son Giorgio looked mystified, as did Salvatore who, for a moment, was distracted from his knuckle work.

'*Dio*, do they teach you nothing in English schools. *Il Cavallo di Troia*? The Trojan Horse?'

'What's this, some kind of racehorse, is it?' Giorgio asked.

The older man laughed, but he felt sad. Even in Naples, where he had been raised, children understood the rudiments of classical education. Here, it seemed, school provided a foundation course in getting into girls' knickers and listening to loud music but little else. Occasionally he looked at Salvo and his friends and wondered whether the problem was not more with them than with the system but he quickly dispelled the thought. No, there was something rotten in the heart of this country. 'It's a reference to Greek mythology but it doesn't matter,' he said. 'I meant Calloway.'

'Ah, Johnny Geetar,' said Giorgio. 'He rang me. He does his work well.'

'It's impossible to get the *machina* from the factory, papa,' said Salvatore. 'Calloway says it's kept in some kind of bunker, guarded by the guy who uses it. Short of getting hold of the Markwick woman, there's no way we can find out where it is.'

'So?' Tino looked surprised. 'What's the problem? You get her.'

'That's just it,' said Giorgio. 'We don't have to. Our Trojan whatsit has told us where it's going to be used next.'

'Cheltenham, Tuesday,' Salvatore interrupted eagerly. 'There's a big race meeting and, in one of the races, a horse called Tanglewood's running. They're using the machine to stop it.'

'Where?' Tino sat still, waiting for the boys to understand.

'Cheltenham, papa. We told you.'

'Start, finish. First fence, last fence, bend. It could be anywhere.' Exasperation entered Tino's voice. 'We don't even know what the fucking thing looks like.'

For a moment, there was silence in the room, apart from the sound of Salvo's mother washing the dishes, humming to herself, from the kitchen across the hall.

Tino sighed. '*Cazzo*, you're useless, you two. You're not going to make it by knowing how to use a knife, how to make a man talk, how – ' he glared at Salvatore ' – how to smash up guitars.' He tapped the side of his head. 'Think,' he said more quietly. 'If you want to survive outside the law, you have to use this, you know.'

Giorgio and Salvatore looked at the floor, resentful yet slightly afraid, like two errant schoolboys who know that a lecture is on the way but don't have the nerve to interrupt.

'This is our big break,' Tino continued. 'We can go on working our little patch in London, running the girls, pushing the dope, carrying out the occasional bank job. But England is small, you want to get away. *Dio*, I want to get away. West Coast of America, or Chicago, or maybe New Orleans. They understand there. And, with this, they respect us.'

'We've got large parts of London tied up,' Giorgio muttered sulkily. 'Isn't that enough?'

'Not for these guys. They are big time, the true brotherhood.' For a moment there was silence in the room, and the unspoken word 'Mafia' hung in the air. Apart from a few Sicilian connections, Tino's London network was no more than an unofficial mafia and mention of the word was regarded as boastful, or even bad form. After this, they would be able to embrace the name with pride. 'They need a passport, a ticket of entry,' Tino continued. 'If I can go to Signor Guiseppi Vercelloni in New York and present him with the perfect weapon – a camera which blinds temporarily – our links with America will be assured.'

'Where?' said Salvatore eventually. 'We need to know where the photographer will be.'

'I'll call Calloway,' said Salvatore. 'I'm sure he'll be pleased to hear from me again.'

'This Cheltenham thing – it's big?' Tino asked. 'Lots of people?'

Giorgio nodded. 'They say it's a big deal for English racing.'

'Excellent,' said Tino.

Occasionally Zena Wentworth suffered from serious regrets and right now, as she lay naked on pine boards while her back was massaged by a beautiful and muscular Turkish homosexual at an exclusive health club in Chelsea, she found there was no escaping them.

She regretted the abortions when she was a teenager that later prevented her having children. That was normal. She regretted her dependence on alcohol and recreational drugs. There was nothing new there. She regretted the day that she had met Clay

Wentworth, and even more the day that she married him. That regret was with her at every waking moment. She regretted not telling Paul Raven everything she knew about Clay and Alice Markwick. This was new, a fresh psychic wound that had opened a few hours ago.

She winced. 'You're a sadist, Adnan,' she gasped as the fingers of the Paradise Health Club's most popular masseur seemed almost to reach into her flesh and touch the backbone.

A light laugh. 'Mmm. You're close, Mrs Wentworth,' the Turk said coquettishly.

In her life, she had done so little that was good. She gave her mother and her father Christmas presents, she went to church on the occasions when it was expected of her but, apart from that, she and common decency had parted company years ago. No one asked Zena Wentworth to be a godmother to their children.

Now was her chance, the time for a single act of blazing charity that would signal a turning-point in her life.

She thought of the conversation between her husband and Paul Raven which she had listened to, sitting on the stairs, after Clay had told her to go to bed. By his standards, he had been almost honest. He had told Paul about the small clique of investors who had put money into Alice Markwick's firm. He had explained precisely why Opteeka B was such a valuable scientific breakthrough. He had even confessed to the on-site racecourse experiments. But that was where his honesty had ended.

'What about the future?' Paul had asked.

'It's finished. The Ministry of Defence took possession of it this week. Our little investment has paid off.'

Only fear and weariness had stopped her going back into the study and confronting Clay with his lie.

Paul had asked about Gavin Holmes.

We knew nothing of that, Clay had said. There are undesirable elements interested in Opteeka B. He very much feared that Holmes had become involved with them and had paid the price.

She hadn't been surprised when Paul appeared to believe the line that Clay had sold him. Alex's death was explained. He had his own life to think of. The world of secret weapons was nothing to him.

'Turn?' the masseur asked.

Her back and shoulders tingling, Zena rolled over. It was a moment that even she found slightly disconcerting as she lay naked, her flesh glowing with sweat, beneath the entirely indifferent gaze of an oriental god. 'Are you absolutely sure that you're 100% gay, Adnan?' she smiled.

The man's eyes flickered down her pale, slack body, as if to confirm the rightness of his sexual orientation. 'Correction,' he said, starting to work on her left calf and thigh. '110%.'

After she had left the Paradise Health Club, Zena drove at speed back to the house. Ever since she had been a teenager, she had driven fast through London but there was a precision and determination to the way she took the streets now. Adnan always had that effect on her, as if his powerful hands had the power to cleanse her of poisonous thoughts, to make her as fresh and clean as the skin of her body. The good resolutions rarely lasted longer than the effects of the massage but her few hours of virtue convinced Zena that she was not entirely lost.

She ran up the steps, the keys of the house in her hand. Letting herself in, she took the stairs to the bedroom and sat on the side of the bed. Breathlessly, she dialled Paul's number. He deserved better than to be deceived by her husband.

'Paul,' she said, leaning forward, her hand on her forehead like a Victorian morality painting called The Ashamed Mistress or A Confession. 'It's Zena. No, wait, don't hang up – ' She hesitated. 'There are two things you should know,' she said. 'You should go to Cheltenham on Tuesday. Clay's little game isn't over yet. They're going to stop Tanglewood.'

At the other end, Paul asked a question but, before she could reply, a finger had broken the connection. Zena looked up to see her husband standing before her.

When he spoke, his voice was gentle, just like it was in the old days, although there was no tenderness there now. 'And the second thing?'

Clay replaced the telephone and lifted her face towards him like a man raising a pistol.

'The second thing, my sweet deceitful darling?'

*   *   *

The BBC was not generous with its offices. Producers, even tubby, self-important producers like Bernard Green, tended to be given a quality of work station which, in any other business, a junior secretary would find unacceptable.

Bernard was gazing at the wall-chart in front of his desk wondering, not for the first time that day, how he was going to bring in a programme on Northern Ireland on time, under budget and in a form that would not offend BBC governors, their wives or dinner-party friends, when the dull green phone beside him gave an uneven wheeze of a ring.

'BBC Psychiatric Intensive Care Unit,' he said laconically. It was one of his favourite jokes. 'Mr Joseph? For me?' Then, with a double-take that shook his ample frame in the tight off-white shirt he was wearing, he sat up straighter in his chair. 'Ah yes, Mr Joseph. Send him up.'

He put down the telephone with a muttered, 'Sodding hell.' Standing up, he reached for a corduroy jacket that had been left on top of an old grey cabinet. He put his head out of the office door and said, 'Be a love, Irene, and fetch us two cups of tea. Unexpected guest. Yugoslavian journalist called Joseph.'

A tall woman with glasses and the forbidding look of a senior librarian glanced unaffectionately in his direction, but, like the overweight ornament on a cuckoo clock, Bernard had ducked back into his office.

'Hot, steaming piles of *shit*,' he muttered to himself. 'How dare he come to see me *here*?'

As usual, Petrin seemed entirely at home when he was shown into the office, charming Irene and even accepting the grey, weak tea in a styrofoam cup with a modicum of grace. As the door closed, Petrin looked around the tiny office. 'How cosy,' he smiled.

'I frankly find your pitching up like this at my place of work, unannounced, beyond – '

'Shut up.' Petrin allowed his smile to disappear like the winter sun behind grey clouds. 'I have no problem with my security. If you're on some sort of list of suspects here, then you only have yourself to blame. Can we talk?'

Sulkily, Bernard said, 'We don't bug people at the BBC.'

'Next Tuesday, you will have a camera crew at Cheltenham. You will be obliged to attend yourself.'

Bernard shifted himself in his chair and gave a hopeless little laugh. 'My schedule's ridiculously tight but I just might be able to move a few things around.'

'How co-operative of you.'

'The camera crew's out of the question.'

Petrin looked at him coldly.

'We have such things as unions over here,' Bernard continued. 'I can't just send a crew off to some race-course. There'd be questions. We're meant to be cutting back on – '

'I didn't expect this sort of attitude from you of all people, Bernard. Particularly given your years of service for us. Years – ' he paused significantly ' – of which I have extensive notes and tapes.'

'I deserve better than this,' Bernard said weakly. 'It could finish my career if it got out that I'd been working for you.'

'The alternative certainly will. The choice is yours.'

'What do you want these men for anyway? They're very difficult, technicians. Ask them to do something that's not in their contract and you've got a strike on your hands.'

'Men? What men?'

Bernard was paler than usual, and his face was greasy with sweat. The unpleasant smell of human stress filled the airless office.

'The camera crew.'

'Ah, I failed to make myself clear. I don't need your technicians. I want to borrow some equipment for the afternoon. And, of course, we'll need a pass.'

'We?'

'You and me, Bernard. We are the technicians.' The stink in the office was becoming really quite unbearable.

'It's not possible. There are all sorts of regulations to bear in mind.'

Pausing with his hand on the door-handle, Petrin said, 'Do it, Bernard, or the Director-General gets your personal file.' He opened the door and switched on a smile. 'Thanks so much for the restorative cuppa,' he said, winking suavely at Irene.

Sleep had never been easy since the attack in the

laboratory but, ever since he had accepted money from the man called Josef, Peter had found himself waking in the middle of the night, drenched in sweat. He dreamed of himself alone in a barren snowscape but when he touched the snow, it burnt his flesh like battery acid, and Klima was before him melting, her mouth wide in a soundless scream, her eyes uncomprehending as she disappeared and he was unable, despite everything, to make a sound, while he cowered from a hand pressing him into the evil, death-dealing snow and a child was screaming, his son –

'Peter, Peter, calm.' His wife held him down on the bed and, as the sobbing subsided, Peter Zametsky knew with utter certainty that he had to act.

'Let's go to bed.'

Angie looked up from the floor where she had been sitting when the phone rang, bringing the news about Gavin Holmes' notes, and saw that Paul was lost to her.

'Mmm?' he frowned.

'Make love, remember? Act like a normal couple for a while.'

Paul leaned forward and ran a hand slowly over her fine blonde hair across her cheek, tracing the line of her lips. 'I've got to warn Bill Scott.'

'Who?'

'He's riding Tanglewood at Cheltenham. He must know that they're trying to stop him.'

Angie laughed briefly. 'You always were a romantic, Paul,' she said. 'I offer you my body and you prefer to go and chat to another jockey.'

'It's not a chat.' A flush of anger suffused Paul's cheeks. 'Christ, you should know what can happen to a jockey in a bad fall.'

She looked away. Every time she believed that she and Paul were going to be able to live a life of some normality, he was dragged back into the murky side of racing. 'It will never leave us, the ghost of Alex Drew, will it?' she said.

'This is no longer about Alex. He was weak. Some unscrupulous bastards put pressure on him to put me through the rails. He couldn't live with his guilt. But there are the other horses.'

'Why not just hand all the evidence over to the Jockey Club or whatever it's called?'

'What evidence? A bit of paper. A late-night conversation after a game of poker. And, remember, this is Mr Clay Wentworth we're talking about.' Paul smiled bitterly. 'The respected businessman.'

'It will never end,' Angie said bleakly. She thought of the day she had realized, back at the hospital, that this was the man she wanted. Since then she had given up her career for him. She had become involved in a sport she had once believed was inhuman. She had given him – a small thing but her own – her virginity.

'A few more days,' he said, as if reading her thoughts. 'Then it will end one way or another.'

Wearily, she nodded. 'So we collect Gavin Holmes' notes, then what?'

Paul looked at her almost impassively. 'You collect the notes, I go to see Bill. Time's against us now.'

Angie stood up and reached for a light green shoulder bag she had left on a chair nearby. 'This is how they do things up your way, is it?' she asked. She let her arms swing ape-like before her and said in a Neanderthal voice, 'Me macho man, you little woman run around for me, right?'

Paul looked into her angry, hurt eyes. 'This is important,' he said quietly but, as she turned away towards the door, it occurred to him that maybe nothing was as important as to hold her lithe and slender body close to his. 'There'll be time for love later,' he added.

But she was gone.

The photographer had been surprised to get a late commission only two days before the final experiment, and not entirely pleased. He was a professional; he needed to prepare himself for the payoff, not run about the country doing last-minute errands for her ladyship.

'I wouldn't have asked you,' she had said. 'But I need someone I can trust.'

That was fair enough. When it came to tact, keeping schtum while all around him were shooting their mouths off or asking stupid questions, the photographer had few equals.

'You won't need any assistance, will you?' she had asked sweetly. 'After all, our man isn't exactly going to run away.'

So he had agreed to keep it simple, keep it in the family.

Mrs Markwick had been curiously distracted, confiding secrets which normally she would have kept to herself. There was a small hitch, she had said, Raven was taking an unhealthily close interest. He needed to be de-activated for a few days.

De-activated? What the hell did that mean?

Mrs Markwick had explained. He was to be brought back to the bunker beneath the office, and kept with Fi-Fi for a while. Mrs Markwick would find someone to guard him. The price of his freedom would be carefully explained to him – one word to the authorities and immobility would be the least of his problems.

A bit elaborate, wasn't it? Surely it would be simpler to –

But no. Something had happened to Mrs Markwick. Ever since the last, highly successful experiment, she had a look in her eyes the photographer had never seen before. Distant, almost wistful. She wanted no more killing. We fulfil our agreement with Wentworth, then it was farewell to Opteeka B and good riddance.

He didn't like it. Kidnapping was messy. It could go wrong.

The photographer sat in the driver's seat of an

old, battered Citroen parked outside the Blue Boar Tavern, Leatherhead. This was G and T country and, although it was Monday, the pub car park was full of company cars whose occupants were doing business the English way over steak and chips and an agreeable glass of Chateau Plonk. It wasn't going to be easy, breezing off with an unwilling individual, even one with wonky legs.

He's a boy, Mrs Markwick had said, an innocent and, as if to prove it, she had given the photographer Raven's number and told him to ring him. He was to be a friend of Gavin Holmes, a fellow journalist. He had some of Gavin's notes which the *Guardian* refused to touch. He owed it to Gavin to get them into the right hands. Could we meet? Say, the Blue Boar, Leatherhead. The car park, for security reasons. One o'clock, Monday, fine.

Candy from a baby.

The photographer lit a cigarette. It was five past one, and he was beginning to worry. The only person in the car park was a young girl with short blonde hair, wearing jeans and a light blue jacket. She seemed lost.

Then she saw his car and started walking towards it.

Until today, Paul's acquaintance with the young amateur Bill Scott had been restricted to occasional weighing room banter, but now, as he talked to him in his cottage near Wantage, he found that Bill reminded him of Alex Drew a couple of years back – the same enthusiasm for racing, the same diamond-hard will to win behind his easy manner.

'Let me get this right,' Bill said, sitting in towelling dressing-gown outside his sauna. 'You're saying that if I hadn't tracked Skinflint onto stands side at Wincanton, I'd have been brought down by some weird weapon that blinded my horse?'

Paul smiled. Described in Bill's broad West Country accent, the idea sounded even more absurd than it was.

'That's why Drago's Pet fell on the inner. They got the wrong horse.'

'Not very competent, were they?'

Sweat was still running down Bill Scott's face, the result of a final wasting session of the day. Although his weight on Tanglewood in the Kim Muir posed no problem, he had another ride earlier in the afternoon for which he would have to do ten stone two. 'The only reason I was tracking Skinflint was that my horse doesn't like to be left alone. Drago's Pet was fading so it made sense to go with Wentworth, even if he was taking the longest way round.'

'Not that competent,' Paul said, 'but ruthless. Three other horses fancied for the Kim Muir have been taken out. They claim that they've proved what they needed to prove, and that nothing will happen at Cheltenham, but I don't trust them.'

'You think they'd try something? At the National Hunt Festival?'

'The bigger the crowd, the easier the job.' Paul shrugged. 'I hope I'm wrong but the fact is, with Tanglewood out of the way, Skinflint's a certainty.'

'So what do I do? Watch out for a missile-launcher by the second last and duck?'

'How d'you normally ride Tanglewood?'

'Hunt him along for the first couple of miles, then start improving. He's a clever sort so jumping's no problem – I can place him anywhere. As I say, the only problem is that he goes to sleep where he hits the front.'

'That's perfect. If you can keep him covered up as long as possible, they'll have to get at you over the last couple of fences. Stay in the middle of the course to make yourself a more difficult target.'

Bill looked doubtful. 'It's a three mile 'chase at Cheltenham. If Skinflint's ten lengths up at the third last, you're not going to get me holding him up to avoid getting zapped.'

'You're right.' Paul stood up. Like any serious jockey, Bill Scott understood that danger went with the territory. Missing the chance of a winner at the biggest race meeting of the year because of the obscure threat of some secret weapon was hardly likely to appeal to him. 'Do me one favour, though. Try to stay on the stands side coming up the straight. I'll cover the inner.'

'I'll try,' Bill said, although the look on his face suggested that he had more doubts about Paul's sanity than his own safety.

'You're going to beat Skinflint tomorrow,' Paul said, hesitating by the front door. 'Do it for Alex, okay?'

Bill smiled indulgently. 'You just watch me,' he said.

The man in the Citroen had long grey hair and there was a high colour to his big rounded features. He looked like a film director who had once been big in the sixties, or a moderately successful second-hand car dealer or – yes, or a journalist. He opened the window to the car as Angie approached.

'Mr Davison?' she asked.

The man seemed suspicious of her. 'I was expecting Paul Raven,' he said.

'I'm Paul's friend,' she said. 'He's had to go somewhere and asked me to collect the material.'

'Wasn't the arrangement. I told him I wanted to see him personally.' The man glanced towards the girl's car, a Mini. There was no one else with her.

'You can trust me,' she said, a hint of desperation in her voice.

The man hesitated. 'Get in,' he said reluctantly, nodding in the direction of the passenger seat on which there was an orange file.

'Can't you just give it to me?'

'Forget it.' He started the car.

'No.' Angie walked round, opened the door and, as she stepped in, the man picked up the file to make room for her.

With the engine still running, he said, 'I need to explain this stuff to you.' Opening the file, he took out a small pistol. 'Sorry,' he said. 'I wanted your boyfriend but you'll have to do.' Pointing the gun at her, he leaned across and, with his left hand, locked the passenger door. 'We've got to make a little trip,' he said. 'All right?'

Angie sat back in the seat and closed her eyes. 'Thanks, Paul,' she said quietly.

Before – long before – he heard from them, Paul knew something had gone wrong. He cursed himself for not checking the journalist who had called with the *Guardian*. Not only had he failed to see the trap, but he had sent Angie into danger instead of him. As darkness fell, he recalled their last conversation, her sad, defeated words. 'It will never end.'

And why had he exposed her to Christ knew what risk? In order to warn an amateur jockey that someone was going to stop him winning a horse-race – an amateur who, it turned out, suspected him of being deluded.

He called Angie's flat. There was no reply. Her friend in Putney hadn't seen her. Crazy Mary was working on the early evening shift. Finally, he contacted the manager of the Blue Boar. No, he had seen nothing strange, the man replied impatiently.

'A friend of mine was meeting someone in your car park,' Paul explained. 'She seems to have disappeared.'

'Oh yeah?'

'She was in a Mini, registration A663 BLB. Is the car there?'

Sighing, the man put down the telephone. 'It's here,' he said when he returned. 'But no sign of your friend.'

Paul put down the phone. He should call the police. And say what? My girlfriend was meeting a stranger and hasn't been seen for a couple of hours? The world was full of disappearing girlfriends.

He was reaching for the telephone when the doorbell rang. He hobbled across the room and flung open the door.

The first thing he noticed was that the man was wearing dark glasses despite the fact that night had fallen. Then the face – or what was left of it. The man made an eerie gurgling sound.

A woman stepped forward out of the shadows. 'My husband says we have to talk,' she said.

Chapter 14

Stress affected her in a strange way. She knew other people who became tetchy and ill-tempered, or who resorted to intense alcohol therapy, or who simply slept. Right now, Alice wished she was like them.

But she wasn't.

Her heart was beating like that of a teenager going out on her first date as she drove across London from the flat in Islington to the office. The chain of events over the last twenty-four hours had filled her with dread – to lose the deal at this late stage because of some interfering little jockey seemed absurd. Yet the word from Clay was unambiguous. His silly bitch of a wife had tipped Raven off. He had to be stopped.

The hitch, followed by the solution.

He wasn't that smart, falling easily for the lie about Gavin Holmes and his notes. She had no worries about sending the photographer. After all, Raven's legs were still weak. The photographer was strong. He was also armed.

The hitch, followed by the solution, followed by the fuck-up.

Alice gripped the steering-wheel with anger as she thought of the call summoning her to the office.

'She's here.'

'She?'

'Raven sent his girlfriend.'

She had cursed. Then it all became clear. So the jockey has sent his lover into the lion's den. Very heroic. Perhaps it wasn't so bad. In fact, perhaps it was better.

'What shall I do with her, Mrs Markwick?'

'I'm on my way,' she had said.

She parked the car in the forecourt, uneasily aware that tomorrow's last experiment was no longer uppermost in her mind, that her hands were clammy. She checked her face in the rearview mirror, then stepped out of the car and walked briskly towards the darkened offices.

May she be fat, she said to herself as she unlocked the door and ran up the steps towards her office. May she look like a horse. She walked into the executive bathroom and unlocked what appeared to be a cupboard. May she have cropped, greasy hair. She descended a dark spiral staircase and pushed open a heavy metal door. At first the bright strip lighting blinded her after the darkness, then she saw the photographer at his desk, the gun on the blotter before him. He glanced across the room. May she have unfortunate skin.

The girl was tied to a chair, her arms bound at the wrists, each of her feet tied to the legs of the chair. She was small and slender and, when Alice first looked at her, a curtain of fine blonde hair concealed her face. Then she looked up, fear and anger in her light blue eyes.

Damn. It was as Alice had feared. The girl was perfection.

She really wished that stress didn't affect her this way.

As soon as Angie saw the woman standing at the door, smiling at her in that peculiar way, she knew she was in trouble. At first, she hadn't understood. The man with the gun and killer's eyes, the trip to London, her legs tied together with rope, the brightly-lit room that smelt of rabbits – none of it made sense. But now she began to see it all.

'Mrs Markwick,' she said. 'Would you mind explaining what all this is about?'

Alice ambled forward, picked up the ugly, black pistol that was lying on the desk, ran a finger down the silencer that was on the barrel and put it back carefully as if it were a piece of antique china. She dressed well and expensively, Angie noticed, and the long dark curls which might have seemed ridiculous on a woman of her age gave her a sort of cold stylishness. 'How d'you know my name?' she asked in a low voice, in which a foreign accent was just detectable.

'I've seen you at the races with your friend Clay Wentworth.'

'He's not my friend.'

'You haven't answered,' said Angie. 'Why are you doing this?'

Alice pulled up a wooden chair which she placed in front of Angie. 'You're hardly in a position to be asking me questions,' she said, as she sat down. Angie shrunk back from her. There was something faintly alarming about this woman, the way she sat too close so that Angie could smell the expensive scent on her. There was a rustle of silk as she crossed her legs. 'You don't look very comfortable,' Alice said, a hint of mockery in her voice.

Angie's shoulders ached and the back of the chair was biting into the flesh of her upper arms, but she said nothing.

'As it happens, this matter can be easily resolved,' Alice said. 'I would like you to make one call to Mr Paul Raven. Then you can relax, we'll take off the rope and let you go – maybe tomorrow night.'

'What am I supposed to say?'

'I don't want him to go racing tomorrow. I have a little project which, I'm told, interests him. There will now be … an alternative attraction.' Alice lingered over the word then, as if returning to more practical matters, she said, 'At four o'clock, he will receive a call at his house. It will tell him where in London he will find you.' She smiled. 'That's all. No money. No information. He'll just have to miss the races.'

'He'll tell the police.'

'Not if he likes his little girl, he won't. If anything

goes wrong at Cheltenham, your friend will not be getting you back in the condition he last saw you.' Alice hesitated. 'Personally, I had hoped Gavin Holmes would be our last casualty.'

Angie looked away. There was an unsettling intimacy in Alice Markwick's smile.

'One call?' Alice gave a girlish pout. Without taking her eyes off Angie, she added, 'Maybe you need a little encouragement. Maybe you'd like to see our performing rabbits.'

Behind her, the photographer reached for his camera. 'Fi-Fi?' he asked.

'Yes,' said Alice. 'Fi-Fi.'

It took a long time to get the truth out of Peter Zametsky. The strain of the past few months and the fact that he was unable to enunciate in a way that was comprehensible to anyone but his wife meant that his account of the development of Opteeka B, the deadly experiments demanded by the Markwick Instruments' main investor Clay Wentworth, and the deal with Czechoslovak Intelligence was halting and unclear. But gradually, through the translation of his wife Klima, the truth unfolded.

In the end, Paul knew everything except what he needed to know most. Who was holding Angie.

'My husband says he has not the address of Clay Wentworth,' Klima said.

Paul shook his head. 'They wouldn't keep her there. It's too obvious.'

They listened as, for almost a minute, Peter gasped and gurgled, what was left of his face showing increasing animation.

When at last he finished, there was silence, as if Klima was reluctant to convey what Peter had told her.

'The people who did this to my husband,' she said eventually, 'they too want Opteeka B. Is possible, he's thinking, that they find you as rivals. Perhaps they have your girlfriend.'

Paul reached for the telephone and dialled a number. 'Ginnie,' he said. 'Angie's disappeared. I think it's something to do with the race tomorrow. Give me Wentworth's number.' He jotted down the number on a pad, promising to keep her in touch with what was happening. When he dialled Wentworth, there was an answering machine.

'Wentworth, this is Paul Raven.' He spoke quietly and firmly. 'My girlfriend was meant to be meeting a journalist today. She's gone missing. If this has anything to do with you – *anything* – you should know that the police have been informed. You have my number. Ring me when you get in, whatever time it is.' He put down the telephone and pushed it away. 'We'd better wait,' he said. 'Maybe she's trying to contact me.'

It was the scream he heard first.

They must have been holding the telephone close to her mouth because, as Paul picked it up, the receiver reverberated in his hand. At first it seemed an alien, unrecognizable sound but as the scream subsided into sobs, he knew it was Angie.

'Mr Raven?' A man's voice came onto the line. 'We have your girlfriend. She will be released tomorrow afternoon if you do what we require.'

'Yes?'

'You should wait by your telephone tomorrow. At precisely four o'clock, you will receive a call from us which will tell you where you can find her. Go to Cheltenham or talk to the police and your friend will pay the price.'

'I'll do it,' Paul said quickly.

'Maybe you would like to talk to her – in case you think we're not serious.'

Angie seemed quieter now, almost sleepy. She whispered something which at first Paul couldn't catch. Then she repeated it. 'I...can't see,' she said. 'I...can't see.'

The phone went dead.

For a moment, Paul stood, the telephone in his hand. Then he put it down slowly. 'They've done something to her eyes,' he said.

With an odd croak of excitement, Peter Zametsky stood up, speaking quickly and incomprehensibly to his wife.

'We have to go,' Klima said finally. 'My husband knows where they are keeping her.'

It was like waking from a dream. Angie moved her

legs slowly then gently touched her eyes. There was a distant roar within her head and an ache behind the eyes but, when she opened them, she was dazzled by the light. Someone was touching her wrist. A woman with a distant, soothing voice.

She assumed that she had fainted. Memories of the night's events seemed as though they had happened somewhere else, and to someone else. She remembered the gun, being tied to a chair, the sinister dark-haired woman with the Eastern European accent. Then there was the rabbit, at one moment able to avoid the vicious electric pole wielded by the man, the next unseeing and panic-stricken. Its body had seemed to shudder when it had run blindly into the prod before collapsing. What had the man said as it lay, twitching in its death throes. 'Fi-Fi's last experiment,' he had said, almost sadly.

The low moaning sound that Angie heard as her head cleared seemed close. Then she realised it came from her.

'It's all right,' the voice said. 'You're all right now.'

For some reason, she was afraid to open her eyes, as if the blinding machine, the fake camera, was still directed at her. It had been like a blow to the head and, after the shock had receded, the true horror had begun.

'Open your eyes, my sweet.' The voice was almost a whisper now. 'You're safe.'

Through half-closed eyelids, Angie saw a hand, its long index finger stroking the dark red weal on her left wrist where the ropes had been, as if to smooth away the pain. She raised her head slowly, and opened her eyes.

'All over.' Alice Markwick's face was close to hers. Her sight restored, Angie saw in cruel detail its every contour – the tributaries of wrinkles leading into her wide eyes, the flecks of dark on the cold grey of the irises, the covering of down on her upper lip, the maze of tiny red veins at the base of her nostrils, the dark red tongue moving between the thin, glistening, grooved lips as she spoke.

'He's gone now. I've sent him away, Angie. I've untied you now that the business part's over.' The cold hand tightened on Angie's wrist. 'It's just you and me now. The night is young.'

Angie leaned back, pressing against the chair, but was too weak to escape Alice's insistent grip. 'What do you want from me?' she asked.

'Company. Girl talk. The usual things.'

The woman was mad. That much was certain. Since her hit-man, the man who had captured her, had gone and Paul had been set up for the following day, she had changed beyond recognition from professional woman to husky-voiced vamp. 'I want to hear all about you,' Alice was saying. 'Every little thing.' Angie thought she preferred the professional woman.

Over Alice's shoulder, she saw a hypodermic needle lying on the desk.

'Yes,' Alice said, following her eyes. 'I gave you a little jab while you were unconscious. It's a relaxant, nothing alarming. Now – ' She walked behind Angie's chair ' – if you'll excuse me a moment.'

Closing her eyes wearily, Angie said nothing. Fear had given way to a desperate need to sleep. Her head fell forward. Somewhere distant, she thought she heard a rustle, like the sound of falling clothes.

'Angie.' A hand cupped her chin and raised her head. She must have lost consciousness again. 'How do I look?'

Alice Markwick turned girlishly in front of her. Instead of a business suit, she was wearing a sheer black velcro dress over black tights. Her dark make-up was absurdly over-dramatic.

'You look like a witch,' Angie sighed.

Alice laughed and opened a small black handbag that was hooked over her arm. 'A devil more like.' A pair of handcuffs dangled from her hand. 'And you're my disciple.'

'What are you talking about?'

Alice stepped forward and touched Angie's face with the handcuffs.

'It's party time, my little one,' she said. 'I'm going to take you out on the town. We're going to celebrate in style.'

Like her husband, Klima Zametsky was seeing nothing, but that was because, as Paul's Saab hurtled through the streets of London, her eyes were tight shut. The country roads at eighty and ninety miles an hour she could take; Paul's town driving was another matter. She had gone beyond fear and nausea into a state in which she merely waited for the sickening crunch of metal, the searing pain and blackness of the inevitable crash.

'We're approaching a large roundabout with signs to Wembley and Willesden,' Paul said urgently. 'Which way?'

Peter made a sound which he interpreted as 'Left'.

As the car took the corner with a squeal of tyres, Peter added another instruction.

'The turning right after the Blue Turk pub,' Klima said faintly. 'Second right into the industrial estate.'

When they arrived, driving slowly past the offices of Markwick Instruments plc, there were no cars parked outside and no lights from the inside of the building.

'Now what?' Paul stopped the car around the corner and hesitated for a moment. He was hardly in a position to climb in through a window, and, of his passengers, one was blind, the other frozen with fear. 'Is there a back entrance?' He turned to look at Peter who was in the back seat.

Before his hairless, unseeing face, Peter held two keys.

It was a version of hell, Angie thought, as she stood unsteadily at the entrance to a large, dark room whose strategically placed lighting revealed murals of spectacular obscenity. In the centre of the room was a small, brightly lit swimming-pool surrounded by fake pillars and marble steps. The place was noisy and crowded and occasionally wild laughter could be heard above the pulsating music.

'Welcome to Slaves,' Alice said to her. 'London's wildest club. You'll love this, little one.' She stepped forward, tugging the handcuffs which connected her left wrist with Angie's right.

Angie stumbled forward. Her head was clearing but this felt like a dream – the Greek, neo-classical decadence, the noise, the pungent smell of marijuana. A tall black woman with a shaven head wandered past them, trailing a dog lead at the end of which, held by a black leather studded collar around the neck, was a subdued, slightly plump woman in her thirties. Both mistress and slave glanced at Angie appraisingly.

They found a table near the swimming-pool and a young waitress in a revealing toga took their order.

'I don't see any men,' Angie said quietly.

'Butch, fem, mistress, slave – they're all here,' Alice said, her eyes sparkling with pleasure. 'This is the first time I've been able to come with a partner.'

Angie looked at a trim, short-haired couple, one in a leather shirt, the other in a denim suit, and wondered vaguely who was meant to be dominating whom.

'You're crazy,' she said.

Fleetingly, as the three of them stood in Alice Markwick's office, Paul wondered what kind of woman it was who developed a bizarre secret weapon, planning to sell it back to the country from which she had fled, and who, for inexplicable reasons of her own, had become involved with Clay Wentworth.

Then he heard a sound from the adjoining executive bathroom.

'My husband wants you to follow him,' whispered Klima.

Feeling his way along the wall, Peter led them through a hidden door and down a steep spiral wooden stairway. The three of them paused before a heavy metal door, beyond which no sound or light came. Paul took the key and silently turned it in the lock. He pushed open the door and stepped inside.

Behind him, Peter groped for a switch that turned on the harsh strip lighting.

The first thing that Paul saw was a dead white rabbit lying in a run on the far side of the room. Then, near the desk, two wooden chairs sat facing one another. Beside one of them, there lay two coils of rope.

Peter said something as his hands ran over the open door of a wall safe by the desk, then groped inside its dark interior.

'The Opteeka B camera is gone,' Klima translated.

Near the ropes a small pile of women's clothes lay in a heap on the floor. Paul picked up a dark blue jacket, then let it fall over the chair.

'Angie's?' asked Klima.

Paul shook his head.

A dreary monotone emanated from across the

room where Peter stood. Klima seemed embarrassed, briefly lost for words.

'What's he saying?' Paul asked.

Klima blushed. 'This woman,' she said. 'My husband thinks that she likes girls.'

It was a strange paradox, to feel free at Slaves, but that was how it was with Alice. She had been here before but never with a partner and Slaves was not a place for meeting new friends. Most of the few loners there liked to watch and Alice had never been a watcher.

She noticed the covert glances in their direction, the way the other women looked at them. She smiled at Angie who was staring ahead of her. They made a good couple, one of them dark, tall and dominant, the other young, blonde and adorably submissive. 'Happy?' she asked.

'Take this absurd thing off my hand,' Angie said. 'I feel ridiculous.'

'Why should I trust you?' Alice asked, a flirtatious trill in the voice.

There was no alternative. For the first time that evening, Angie looked her full in the eye. 'You can trust me,' she said softly.

'You like it here?'

'Very much.'

Alice looked at her suspiciously. Was it possible that this sense of freedom had clouded her judgement – that the knowledge that, within twenty-four hours, her future would be secure had allowed her to relax her guard?

Angie seemed to have moved closer, so that her face was inches away from Alice's. Moments ago, she was pale and unsteady; now the colour had returned to her cheeks.

Slaves had that effect on a girl. 'Unlock me,' she said, 'and maybe we can get away from this noise.'

Alice ran a hand gently down Angie's forearm, toying briefly with the handcuff around her wrist. 'D'you like champagne breakfasts?' she asked.

'My favourite.'

'Then a quiet day at the flat, watching television?'

'The races?'

Alice laughed softly. 'Of course, the races. The Kim Muir Steeplechase. Then it's back to your little friend.'

'Please.' The girl's blonde hair was almost touching her face now. Alice imagined she could feel the warmth of her flesh. 'Unlock me.'

Alice looked at her sideways. 'I'm not sure about you.'

'I – ' Angie went through a pantomime of girlish embarrassment. 'I went to a girls' boarding-school, you know.'

'What happens there?'

'It makes this – ' Angie nodded confidingly in the direction of the throng of chain and leather gathered across the swimming-pool ' – seem like the fancy-dress at a church fete.'

Alice sipped her glass of wine thoughtfully. She had always prided herself on the erotic instinct that alerted her to girls who were broad-minded in every sense. As soon as she had seen Angie, tied so heart-breakingly to the chair in the office basement, she felt an affinity that was more than the mere tug of attraction. At first she had put it down to the stress of the moment but now, as she filled her glass yet again, she was sure she was right. 'How strange,' she said, looking deep into Angie's eyes, 'that something so bad could lead to something so good.'

'So bad?'

'I didn't want it, not all the nastiness and violence and lying. I just wanted to make enough from my husband's firm to retire, and live the life I was meant to lead. But – ' Alice waved the free hand which held her glass, spilling wine on the table ' – there's no money in lasers. You think there is, but there isn't. Not peaceful, friendly lasers. So when Zametsky, out of some weird scientific curiosity, began researching into optics, I encouraged him. It needed extra investment so I brought in Wentworth and Calloway.'

Angie listened patiently to the older woman's rambling account. Doubtless Paul would be expecting her to be taking notes but right now Angie had only one thought on her mind – to get away from this drunk, and very possibly insane, lesbian. 'What about Digby Welcome?' she asked, more from a need to keep the conversation going than out of genuine curiosity.

'That was something different, a sort of long-term

blackmail. He introduced me to my husband when I first came to London. Welcome knew rather more about my past than was good for him.'

For a moment, the two of them sat in silence, Alice lost in the fog of memory, Angie deciding when best to raise once again the question of unlocking the handcuffs.

'All over tomorrow,' Alice said suddenly. 'One last obstacle – one last little death – before I hand over the whole thing to someone else. Or rather – ' she smiled crookedly ' – three last obstacles.'

'Maybe we could celebrate together?' Angie whispered.

'Would you?' Alice seemed almost tearful. 'You'd stay? After the race?'

Angie raised the wrist held by the hand-cuffs. Frowning, Alice reached for her bag and produced a small key. Fumbling drunkenly, she released the lock.

'Thank you,' said Angie, rubbing her wrist.

'Poor you.' Alice lowered her head to kiss the deep red mark, closing her eyes as if to shut out the noise and vulgarity all around them.

She never saw the wine bottle raised above her like an executioner's axe, catching the light as it fell, shattering with implacable fury on the back of her skull.

Angie ran through the dark streets of Islington. Freedom was a taxi-ride – a ten-minute drive to Mary's flat. Monday was an early night for her and, even if she were entertaining a man friend, she would normally be at home.

Her head was quite clear now but she was trembling from shock. If the need to escape from Slaves hadn't been so pressing, she might have fainted herself as Alice slumped forward, blood pouring from the back of her head. Luckily the regulars at the club regarded violence between partners as normal. By the time they had realised that this was rather more than an advanced love game, she had slipped away.

She turned onto a main street and, seeing three men walking on the far pavement, she slowed to a walk. In London vulnerability could attract the wrong kind of attention. Images from the evening crowded in on her. The death throes of a rabbit in a brightly lit basement. The impact of the camera, throwing her backwards. The slender finger, tracing the rope mark on her wrist. The crazed dark eyes, unfocused by desire and alcohol, staring at her longingly in the club. Snatches of conversation – nastiness and violence and lying, all over tomorrow, one little death, celebrate together –

As Angie shuddered with revulsion, a black taxi, its light shining like a beacon, turned a corner towards her. She held up her arm and it pulled up beside her. She gave the driver Mary's address and settled into the back seat, still breathing heavily.

One little death. Now what did that mean?

Chapter 15

Of the approximately forty thousand assembled at Cheltenham racecourse on the afternoon of Tuesday 12 March for the first day of the National Hunt Festival, slightly under half were there because of an abiding interest in racehorses. The rest were in attendance for professional, social or ritual reasons. For the pickpocket or the society hostess or the Irish clergyman, Cheltenham covered three red-letter days in the diary. To miss it would be unthinkable.

Tino Marchesi liked seeing the English at play – in fact, as he strutted across the grass in front of the grandstand in his green checked suit and trilby, a new pair of binoculars around his neck, he felt almost English himself. He wondered vaguely whether in America, where he was about to become a leading member of the brotherhood, such occasions as the National Hunt Festival existed. He hoped so. They reminded him of the good things in life – friends, sportsmanship, nice clothes, money.

Behind Tino, his son Giorgio slouched moodily with his friend Salvatore. The older man glanced back and smiled. Sometimes he despaired of the younger generation. Both wore bulky long leather coats and dark glasses and looked around them as if at any moment they could be jumped by some hit-man among Cheltenham's army of tweed and cavalry twill. If they had been wearing signs reading 'Hoodlum' and 'Gangster' around their necks, they could hardly have made their backgrounds more obvious.

'Relax,' said Tino. 'You're frightening the race-goers.'

The three men found a bar but, to Giorgio's disgust, they had to fight their way through a crowd of loud and happy middle-aged men and women before being served. It was a strange and unwelcome sensation to be one of a crowd. In London, they were given space at the bar and were served almost before they had ordered.

'So.' A glass of champagne in his hand at last, Tino looked at the racecard. 'Ours is the last race. Will our guitar-playing friend Mr Calloway be here?'

Salvatore smiled broadly, displaying a vulpine set of white teeth. 'He had to rehearse, he said. "Gonna give it, like, a miss, man." '

'But he's told us everything we need to know.'

'One of the last three fences. We take one each. After they make their move, we grab the machine and disappear,' said Tino. 'No macho stuff, okay? No violence.'

'Sure.' Salvatore nodded, while Giorgio looked disappointed.

Tino sighed. Today was not going to be easy.

'Ey!' Salvatore said angrily as a tall woman swathed in mink pushed past him, carrying two glasses before her like a mother in a parents' day egg and spoon race.

'Sorry, darling.' Zena Wentworth looked over her shoulder at the dark young man in a black leather coat.

'The noise, my dear,' she muttered to herself as she progressed through the crowd. 'The *people*.'

This was definitely the last race meeting she was ever going to attend. Apart from its few advantages – being able to wear mink without getting dirty looks and the chance to chat with friends from London, for example – Cheltenham was every bit as depressing as Plumpton or Wincanton.

With some difficulty, she fought her way through to a corner where Sir Denis Wentworth sat, staring at the throng around him with evident disapproval.

'Here we are,' she said, placing a whisky and soda before him and sitting down. 'Whoever said the middle classes knew how to behave in public had never been to Cheltenham on Champion Hurdle day.'

Sir Denis looked at her, his face a picture of apathy.

'It's like a rugger scrum back there,' Zena added, nodding in the direction of the bar.

The old man sighed, then raised his glass. 'Chin-chin,' he said quietly.

'Here's to Clay's last race,' Zena smiled.

'Hmm?' Momentarily Sir Denis seemed interested.

'He told me this morning. Win or lose, he's hanging up his boots. I don't think his heart is in it, to tell the truth.' She sipped at her drink, an orange juice, and grimaced. 'Clay gives up racing, I go on the wagon – it's quite a day.'

'You give up booze?' Sir Denis sniffed. 'Fat chance.'

'No booze, no substance abuse. I'll be a new woman.'

Zena smiled brightly but her father-in-law looked away as if to confirm that whatever she did, however she reformed, his view of her would remain the same. Christ, she needed a drink – an afternoon spent with Sir Denis Wentworth would have a methodist reaching for the vodka. Not for the first time she wished that Lol and Suzie Calloway were there – even Alice, who had behaved so oddly recently, would have broken the monotony. It was a puzzle why Clay's little fan club had deserted him at what could be his finest hour.

'There's something else I'm giving up,' she said.

Sir Denis glanced across the table with a weary *now*-what expression.

'Yes,' said Zena. 'I'm giving up Clay. I've decided to leave him.'

For a moment, there was silence between them. Sir Denis took another sip of his whisky, swilled it around his mouth, and swallowed it as if it were cough medicine. Then he smacked his lips and, for the first time that Zena could remember, he smiled, revealing yellow teeth and pale gums.

'Excellent,' he said.

'It's no good,' Angie said, as she walked slowly beside Paul up the slight incline towards the weighing-room. 'I've tried to like all this –' she looked at the race-goers hurrying past them to see the first three horses in the Champion Hurdle enter the winners' enclosure '– but I guess I'm just not a racing person.'

Paul laughed. 'You've hardly had the best introduction,' he said.

'I still feel sorry for the horses.'

She was paler than usual after last night, Paul decided, but otherwise she seemed to have survived her ordeal at the hands of Alice Markwick without ill effects. She had been tearful when she arrived at Crazy Mary's flat to find Paul was waiting there too. After visiting the Markwick offices, he had sent the Zametskys home and then, on a hunch, had rung Mary, who had suggested he should stay at her flat. After an hour or so, Angie had arrived at the door, upset but unharmed.

'There's only one horse I'm worried about today,' Paul said, 'and that's Tanglewood. I've got to have a word with Bill Scott in the weighing-room.' He squeezed her arm. 'Stay here. I'll be out in a minute.'

He felt bad leaving her alone after what she had been through, but it had been her decision to come to Cheltenham and it was important to reach Bill with the information Angie had gleaned from Alice last night. One last obstacle, she had said – rather, three last obstacles. It made sense.

Jim Wilson was the first to see him. 'Can't keep you away from this place, can they?' he said. 'How's the back coming on?'

Paul waved his walking-stick. 'I'll be throwing this away soon,' he said.

'Good on yer, Pauly.'

Bill Scott was chatting to Dave Smart, a cup of tea in his hand. His ride in the first race had finished well down the field, but most of the tipsters in the morning papers had suggested that, if Tanglewood could beat Skinflint, the Kim Muir would be his.

'Hullo, it's Hopalong Sherlock,' Bill said as Paul approached. 'Any news?'

Paul smiled. He didn't blame Bill for being sceptical – foul play was part of racing and, if you worried about who was trying to stop you winning, you'd never get into the saddle. Sensing that he wasn't wanted, Dave Smart wandered off, leaving Bill and Paul alone.

'It's happening,' Paul said. 'We know for sure.'

'So I keep him covered up as long as possible.'

'They're going for you at the third last, the downhill fence.'

'How d'you know?'

'It doesn't matter. Stay in the centre of the course,

covered up if possible, and leave the rest to me.'

Bill shrugged. 'No problem,' he said. 'I wouldn't have hit the front by the third last anyway.'

Wishing him luck, Paul was about to return to Angie when he saw Clay sitting alone in a corner.

Never had the man looked less like a jockey. He was too big, the colour on his fleshy cheeks was too pale, the expression on his face suggested that he would rather be anywhere than riding one of the favourites at Cheltenham.

Paul was standing in front of him for a moment before Clay came out of his daydreams.

'Ah, the poker expert,' he said, aiming unsuccessfully for a jocular, patronizing tone. 'What a surprise to see you here.'

'You told me it was all over. I don't believe you,' Paul said quietly. 'If your people try to stop Tanglewood today, the world's going to know about it.'

'I told you after our little game of poker,' Clay said. 'I'm finished with all that.'

'Is your friend Alice Markwick here?' Paul asked very suddenly.

'I haven't seen her. I have better things to do than worry about who's here to see me.'

'Seems ungrateful under the circumstances.' Paul made as if to move away, then added, as an afterthought, 'I believe she had a small accident last night. You might pay her a visit – ' he smiled ' – after you've ridden your winner.'

Outside the jockeys' changing-room Paul saw Ginnie Matthews waiting near the scales for Clay to weigh out.

'Is that bloody jockey of mine in here?' she asked Paul.

'He seems to have a lot on his mind,' Paul said. He hesitated, wondering whether to tell Ginnie that he was convinced friends of her owners were out to ensure that Skinflint won, but then thought better of it. Either way, she wasn't involved.

'Paul,' she said. 'We need to talk.'

'About Clay?' Paul asked wearily.

'No, about you.' Ginnie frowned. 'I need an assistant trainer and was wondering whether you would be interested.'

Paul's first thought was of Angie. She was not exactly in love with racing and the idea of more chilly days waiting outside weighing-rooms was unlikely to appeal to her. 'I'd need to think about it,' he said.

'No hurry.' Ginnie saw Clay walking gloomily towards the scales with the saddle under his arm. 'Here we go,' she said.

'Good luck, Mrs Matthews,' Paul said, touching her lightly on the arm.

At first he didn't recognize the couple as they walked towards the entrance to the paddock – the old man seemed too old, the woman more elegant and calm than he remembered. Then, as if she sensed his presence, Zena Wentworth turned and stared at them for a moment. Her father-in-law tottered on, ignoring her.

'That's Zena Wentworth, isn't it?' Angie asked.

'Aye,' said Paul, remembering the cold knowing hand as it edged up his thigh. 'Let's get down to the racecourse.'

But it was too late. Hands sunk deep in the pockets of her mink coat, Zena walked slowly towards Paul and Angie. 'I wanted to tell you the second thing,' she said simply.

'Second thing?'

'What I was about to tell you the other day on the telephone before I was interrupted.'

'You told me enough.' Paul made to move away, but Angie caught his arm.

'No,' she said. 'It might be important.' She turned to Zena. 'Go on, Mrs Wentworth.'

'*Cherchez le père*,' said Zena. Then, as if regretting what she had said, she turned and walked quickly towards the paddock.

'What on earth was that about?' Paul asked.

'The father,' said Angie. 'She's telling us Sir Denis is involved too.'

The decision to make the hit at the third fence from home was not stupid, Paul reflected as he made his way down the course with Angie. Although, as Bill Scott had pointed out, there was the risk of Tanglewood still being covered up by other horses, there was a good chance at the end of three miles that the field would be strung out. It was a downhill fence that often caused grief as jockeys kicked on for home, so that there would be few awkward questions in the event of a crashing fall. The fact that the crowd around the fence was thinner than at the last two fences would make Tanglewood an easier target.

'Anyone you recognize?' Paul asked as they crossed the course to the inside rail where a group of photographers had gathered. Angie scanned the men as they chatted easily to one another and shook her head.

'I hope Alice Markwick was right about it being the third last,' she said quietly.

Across the course, the crowd were now hurrying away from the paddock to place bets or to take up a favoured vantage point in the stands. As the field of fifteen made its way down to parade in front of the grandstand, Paul glanced at his racecard.

Under normal conditions, it was a race of limited interest to him. Tanglewood was no more than a good handicapper but had the advantage of being ridden by one of the best amateurs around. Skinflint, the class horse of the race, was carrying two distinct drawbacks – top weight and Mr Clay Wentworth. Beyond them, there was a young Irish horse called Fiddlers Three whose best form had been over two and a half miles, a grey mare from the north called Busy Lizzie and, also in with a chance of a place, a big plain six-year-old called The Killjoy who was trained by a successful permit holder down in the West Country.

As he headed the parade, Skinflint looked about him like a horse for whom Cheltenham, with all its excitement and drama, was his natural home. Ginnie had him looking superb and, briefly, Paul felt a pang of envy for Clay, who had done so little to deserve a horse of his calibre.

Angie laid her hand on his as he leaned on his walking-stick. 'You're out there, aren't you?' she said quietly. 'Whatever happens, you've got racing in the blood.'

'Yes.' Paul thought of his brief conversation with Ginnie Matthews, and knew that he wanted to accept her offer. 'I'd rather be up there than down here.'

Like any good professional, the photographer had walked the course. Now he stood some hundred years away from the jockey and his girlfriend across the course on the stands side, and made his final plans.

Something had gone wrong last night, as he had known it would. The moment Mrs Markwick had looked at the girl, there was trouble in the air. That brisk, cruel competence had softened to something almost vulnerable. The photographer had protested when she had told him that she would guard Raven's girlfriend until the following day, but it was no good – Mrs Markwick had that look in her eyes and, as usual, she got her way.

He took the machine with him, though. There was no way that he was going to risk leaving that with her.

When he had called in the morning, there was no reply, and here was the girl, free and with her boyfriend. The photographer ran a hand tenderly over the heavy black machine that hung around his neck. It didn't matter. They couldn't stop him now.

His instructions were laughably simple.

In a darkened flat in Islington, Alice Markwick watched the field for the Kim Muir Steeplechase at Cheltenham parading before the stands. Her head was bandaged. She hated herself for last night. But she was confident. Not even Raven or his vicious little bitch of a girlfriend could stop the photographer now.

Freedom, at last.

'Good luck, Clay,' she said, and laughed.

None of the photographers at the third last fence had the look of a killer, Paul decided. Several of them he recognized as regulars at race meetings, freelances and agency men. A few of the racegoers had small cameras but nothing that answered the description of Opteeka B that Peter Zametsky had given him.

'I think we may be on the wrong side of the fence,' said Paul, glancing up the hill to the bend some hundred yards before it. 'You get a clearer view of the field as it's approaching the third last from the stand side.'

'Shall I stay here?' Angie asked quietly. 'Just in case you're wrong.'

The field were turning in front of the stand to canter down to the start. 'No, this time we stick together.'

It was as they were crossing the course that Paul saw the dark young man in a long leather coat pushing his way through the crowd on the stands side. Although he was hardly the typical Cheltenham spectator, the man had no camera. Languidly, he walked on the course, staring straight ahead of him.

A racecourse official nearby shouted, 'Horses coming!' and the leather-coated man, abandoning his dignity, scurried over to Angie's side of the course.

Paul looked across and smiled. A small-time spiv. There was nothing to worry about there.

Cazzo, he hated horses. Salvatore looked around him in the hope that no one had seen his moment of panic. A slim blonde girl glanced at him briefly, then turned away. She was just his type. Salvatore sighed – the sooner this business was over and he could return to his life of minor crime and major pleasure, the happier he would be.

Looking up the racecourse, he could see Giorgio in place at the second last fence. Doubtless Tino was covering the last. The waiting was over.

The man in the black leather coat had seemed absurd as Clay had cantered past him, leaning against Skinflint, who seemed to be pulling harder than usual today. That was one of the few points in favour of riding in races; it gave you a chance to look down at the people, mere spectators, who had come to see you.

Yes, this would be his last race, whatever happened. Briefly, he envisaged himself at some future National Hunt Festival, a solid comfortable figure in the paddock watching as some wretched little jockey was given a leg-up onto one of his horses. By then everybody would be happy – Ginnie, because Skinflint could be ridden by a professional; his father, because he was no longer obliged to come racing; and, above all, Clay himself because he was grounded, his feet on *terra firma* for the entire afternoon.

He cantered past the starter's rostrum, turned and trotted back to the first fence. 'Clear round, eh?' he said quietly, patting Skinflint in front of the fence.

'Are you going on?' Bill Scott asked him.

'We'll be up there,' Clay said, smiling palely. Normally he disliked this habit jockeys had of asking what kind of race you intended to ride – it was like a business rival casually asking for details of your development plans – but he had no worries with Scott or Tanglewood.

Briefly he wondered why Bill Scott had bothered to ask him whether Skinflint would be among the front-runners. He was the sort of jockey who did his homework and would know how Skinflint was ridden. Of course, when Clay hit the front at the top of the hill, rather than making his run later, Scott would be surprised – but then Tanglewood would be pulled from the rest of the field like a thread from a skein of wool, into the sights of Opteeka B. Clay was confident that he could outstay the rest of the field up the Cheltenham hill.

The starter stepped forward and, as the field circled around him, began to call out the names of the jockeys.

Petrin felt comfortable in his new Savile Row suit. Perhaps, when this little stunt was over, he could consider staying in Britain. Across the course, the field was lining up. No, better stick to his plan; America was better. 'They're off,' said the racecourse commentator.

'For Christ's sake, pretend to shoot some film!' Petrin nudged the overweight figure before him. With a resentful sigh, Bernard Green looked into the eyepiece. 'Who'd have thought, when I joined the Party at Cambridge, that I'd end up as a fake cameraman at a race meeting?' he muttered.

'You do it beautifully,' said Petrin, raising an expensive pair of binoculars to his eyes.

After the first mile, Clay found himself wondering whether the plan to stop Tanglewood had been necessary. Skinflint loved Cheltenham and seemed to respond to the atmosphere of a big crowd. At every fence, he outjumped the horses around him, gaining so much in the air that Clay had difficult preventing him from hitting the front.

As the field passed the stands, he was going easily

in third place behind the grey Busy Lizzie who had set a good pace, and the Irish horse Fiddlers Three. Four or five lengths behind the leading group, the rest of the field was bunched up and, as they turned into the country, Clay looked over his shoulder. There was no sign of Tanglewood.

The pace quickened down the back straight and, when Busy Lizzie made a mistake at the waterjump, Clay had no alternative but to move up on the outside of Fiddlers Three, whose jockey was already niggling at him. Behind him, the leaders of the following group were moving closer but, from the sound of the cracking whips and jockeys' curses, none of them was going as easily as Skinflint.

'Give him a breather going up the little hill before the open ditch,' Ginnie had said. 'Stay with them until the third last, then make the best of your way home.' Clay kicked Skinflint into the open ditch. The horse stood off outside the wings and landed two lengths in front of Fiddlers Three.

'Here we go,' muttered Clay. This was where he disobeyed his trainer's instructions. Bill Scott was too experienced a jockey to allow himself to be given the slip. As he set off in pursuit, he would provide a perfect unimpeded target for Clay's unofficial helper among the photographers.

Clay was five lengths clear as he gathered Skinflint for the downhill fence. He glanced at the crowd on the far side and, as if some distinct, instinctive part of his brain were tuned into the fatal laser of Opteeka

B, he sat up straight in the saddle.

'No,' he screamed.

But it was too late.

It took Paul the briefest of moments to realize two things. The first was that the man operating Opteeka B was not standing by the fence but some fifty yards back. The second was that his target wasn't Tanglewood at all.

Simultaneously with Clay's scream, Skinflint faltered, his gallop becoming an unstoppable, drunken stagger into the base of the fence. Almost balletically, the horse's hindquarters formed an arc over the fence while miraculously, and fatally, Clay stayed in the saddle, his eyes dilated with horror as the earth hurtled towards him.

There was an unmistakeable crack as horse and jockey hit the ground together.

Beside him, Angie gasped. She had looked away from Skinflint up the hill. 'Look!' she said suddenly. 'It's – ' but already she was running.

'Angie!'

The photographer glanced back and, sensing trouble, he put the heavy camera under his arm and jogged, casually at first, up the hill.

'Bastard!' Angie kicked viciously at his trailing leg and as the man sprawled on his face, sending Opteeka B flying, she fell on him. By the time he had recovered from the shock, Paul stood over them, his walking-stick raised.

'It's him,' Angie said, breathing heavily as she stood over him. 'He's the man who kidnapped me last night.'

Behind them, the field was streaming up the hill to the Cheltenham roar, but already a small crowd was gathering around Paul, Angie and the photographer.

'My camera,' the man said weakly.

'Fetch the police,' Paul said to a young man in a dark leather coat who had just run up. Briefly the man looked alarmed, then muttering 'Yeah, sure,' he walked off quickly towards the stands.

Paul looked back to the fence, where Skinflint still lay on his side. A few yards away, two ambulancemen were crouched over the inert form of Clay Wentworth.

'Why Wentworth?' he asked the man cowering on the floor.

The photographer muttered, 'Orders from the top. Give me back my camera and I'll explain everything to you.'

'Camera?' Paul glanced at Angie, who shook her head. 'What camera?'

It didn't feel like triumph, merely the satisfaction of a job done well. Tonight, when the photographer returned, she would contact Petrin for the exchange – Opteeka B for financial security and freedom. Alice looked at the silent television screen on which presenters of a children's television show were dancing about in mute inanity. Perhaps, if Clay's race had not been the last to be televised, she would have been treated to a few more shots of her business partner, prostrate on the ground where he belonged.

She imagined that he was not badly injured, simply shaken up enough to understand that no man exploited Alice Markwick and emerged a winner.

There was a price for everything.

The machine was still warm. That was odd. Josef Petrin ran a hand over the dark metal of Opteeka B which lay on the passenger seat of his hired car. It had been so simple, so painless, so casual a victory, that he felt almost tenderly towards this country in which crime was as easy as picking up an object from the ground and merging into the crowd. Bernard had squawked when Petrin had told him to take the train back to London, but that had been an easy decision. The fat Englishman belonged to the past, to the days of grim ideology and patriotic duty; he wouldn't understand that times were different now, that it was every man for himself. Doubtless, Petrin's motherland could use a device like Opteeka B, but he was going private. This time tomorrow he would be in New York. The CIA maybe? There was too much risk there. He had been told the Mafia paid well for the right product. He even had a contact, a man called Guiseppi Vercelloni.

Petrin smiled. A new suit. A new toy. A new future. It had been a useful trip.

* * *

They stood in a gloomy little group outside the Treatment Room, as the last few racegoers made their way home, their conversation desultory and weary.

'How's the horse?' Paul asked.

Ginnie shrugged. 'Tough little bugger. He'll be a bit sore in the morning but the vet says nothing's broken.'

Again, Paul saw Skinflint turning, as if in slow-motion, the look of paralysed fear on Clay's face, the crack which, he now knew, was of a human bone not a horse's.

'They say our friend is co-operating with the police,' he said. 'Alice Markwick will be receiving a call at any moment.'

'There's no evidence,' Angie said quietly. 'What can they do without the laser?'

'Apparently the whole thing is documented at Markwick Instruments. The police had received a tip-off from Lol Calloway and picked up three Italians after the last race. They didn't have the camera but seemed to know something about it.'

The moment they saw Zena standing at the doorway to the Treatment Room, it was clear that questions were unnecessary.

'He's dead,' she said flatly. 'Broken neck. Multiple head injuries. He never regained consciousness.'

Angie stepped forward and took Zena by the arm.

'It was Alice Markwick,' said Paul. 'She wanted him out of the way.'

'No.' Sir Denis Wentworth appeared at the doorway and stood, staring across the racecourse. He seemed older, a diminished and pathetic figure. 'No,' he said. 'It was me.'

'He always was Daddy's boy,' Zena said with a trace of bitterness in her voice.

Sir Denis spoke as if in a trance. 'You want to ride horses, I told him, you ride to win. Prove yourself like I proved myself. Get yourself the best horse and win the best race. Then I'll know you're man enough to take over from me.' Tears filled his eyes at last. 'Of course, he couldn't do it the straight way, he had to cheat.'

'You old fool,' Zena turned on him savagely. 'He may have been weak but he was braver than you'll ever be. And more honest.'

'He was giving that horse a good ride,' Paul said. 'If it hadn't been for the Markwick woman – '

But Sir Denis had turned and was walking with silent dignity towards the car park, as if he knew his son better than anyone and that, whatever had happened, he had been right, that he had done it the Wentworth way. They watched him as he made his way out of the racecourse without once looking back, an old man, alone.

Chapter 16

It was high summer and, although he received the occasional call from journalists raking over the ashes of what had become known as 'The Wentworth Scandal', Paul had allowed his life to slip into the routine of an assistant trainer.

Sometimes, when leading the string out on a quiet old 'chaser called Slavedriver, he found himself thinking about Alex, about Clay Wentworth and the nightmarish events of last season, but the moment would pass. He had an unspoken agreement with Ginnie Matthews that nothing from the past should distract them from planning for the forthcoming season. Once, when they were walking past the field in which Skinflint had been roughed off for the summer, Ginnie had muttered, 'If only he knew,' and Paul had smiled but said nothing.

In September, he would be required to appear in court as a witness in the case of the Crown vs Alice Markwick in which the principal charge was one of aggravated manslaughter. Although the prototype for Opteeka B had disappeared, the evidence of the photographer had been enough to build a substantial case against her. A number of further charges relating to the way she ran her business were said to be under active consideration.

Paul avoided taking breakfast with Ginnie, preferring to spend the time with Angie who had moved in with him, working as a freelance nurse in the Lambourn area.

So she was there when Paul received the letter from Sir Denis Wentworth and was leaning over his shoulder as she read it, with growing astonishment, at the breakfast table.

Dear Mr Raven

I write to you regarding the death of my son Mr Clay Wentworth.

It is now almost four months since the unfortunate events at Cheltenham and I have had much time in which to consider them. As you may be aware, I hold you in no way responsible for Clay's accident although I find it regrettable that you did not think fit to inform the police of your suspicions of Mrs Markwick.

The blame, I accept, is hers, for her financial greed, and mine, for the unreasonable expectations I had of my son. To demand that he should 'prove himself' in a way that was independent of my influence was, I now see, an

impossible burden for him to have carried. I
regret this.

I have spoken briefly to my former daughter-in-
law Zena Wentworth who believes that some
sort of compensation is due to you for the accident which ended your career. Although my
legal advisers tell me that you have no case in
law against me, I have decided to make a one-
off gesture of goodwill towards you.

As you may be aware, my son left his racehorses
to me. I have resolved to sell all of them except
for Skinflint. That horse is now legally yours.

I trust this meets with your approval. A formal
letter follows. Mrs Matthews has been informed
of my decision.

Please note that this action is taken without
prejudice and is in no sense an admission of
guilt.

Confirmation of receipt of this letter would be
appreciated.

Yours sincerely

Sir Denis Wentworth

For a moment, there was silence as Paul read the
letter again.

'His normal charming self, I see,' Angie said.

'Poor old bastard,' Paul said. 'It's probably as near
to being generous as he's ever been.'

'What will you do?' asked Angie. 'We can't afford training fees.'

'If Ginnie comes in as a partner, I can.' Paul smiled. 'You can come racing again – you know how you like that.'

Standing behind him, Angie put both arms around him and kissed his ear. 'The humane, politically correct thing to do would be to retire him.'

'All right. After he's won his third Gold Cup.'

Angie laughed. 'You're a cruel bastard, Paul Raven,' she said, allowing her hand to slip inside his shirt.

Deep in thought, Paul took the hand, kissed it and stood up. He walked slowly towards the bedroom, then turned, smiling at the door. 'How about a celebration?' he asked.

'What about your career? Your horse? What about racing?' There was a hint of mockery in Angie's voice as she walked slowly towards him.

Paul put his arm round her.

'Racing can wait,' he said.